“An electr ... ***Times***

THIS CHARMING SCOUNDREL

A devilish smile inched across his handsome face, crinkling the corners of his eyes. He was the picture of pure seduction. And he was teasing her terribly. She grabbed a handful of grass, ripping it up by its roots to hurl in his face.

He laughed. “You have always been easy to provoke, Chloe.” He stood up, towering over her. “Should prove interesting in many ways...”

Chloe blushed. She couldn’t help it.

A low chuckle reached her as he went to mount his horse. Bending over the saddle, he reached out a hand to her. Reluctantly she took it. “Use the stirrup,” he instructed her, removing his own foot from it.

Expecting him to swing her on the back of his mount as he had often done in the past, she complied. He surprised her by swinging her up and pulling her across his lap in front. His arms securely encircled her.

“John!” She struggled in his protective embrace.

“Easy, sweet. I’m just taking you home.”

Then why did his voice have a hint of seduction in it?

“Now which way was home?” His mouth teased at her ear. Hot breath skittered down the side of her neck, leaving tingles in its wake. “Guess I’ll have to take my chances and hope I find the way...eventually.”

Chloe steeled herself for a long, torturous ride.

Other *Love Spell* and *Leisure* books by Dara Joy:
REJAR
HIGH ENERGY
KNIGHT OF A TRILLION STARS

Tonight Or Never

LOVE SPELL BOOKS  NEW YORK CITY

LOVE SPELL®

September 1997

Published by

Dorchester Publishing Co., Inc.
276 Fifth Avenue
New York, NY 10001

Printed in the United States of America.

"It is not enough to conquer;
one must know how to seduce."
—Voltaire

To Joanna Cagan:
For paying attention to the minute details;
For your enthusiasm and endless support;
For having the same vision;
For always going to bat;
For your constant understanding;
and most importantly,
For your great sense of humor.
You are without a doubt
"A Legendary Editor."

Tonight Or Never

Prologue

England, 1794

If seduction had a name it would be Lord John.

At least that was the opinion of the woman with whom he was currently cavorting.

He was hot sex.

Torrid nights and musky sheets.

The man was a rake, a rogue, a libertine, and a scoundrel. A golden-haired, green-eyed, six-foot-plus package of the most interesting kind of trouble.

The woman was not alone in her opinion.

This was also the consensus of a multitude of other well-pleased and well-placed ladies of the ton; all of whom considered themselves extremely fortunate to have shared the extravagances of Viscount Sexton's bed.

The high opinion these ladies had of the strapping peer was wholly responsible for the acquisition of the nickname conferred upon him unilaterally by these women of knowledge; namely, *Lord of Sex*.

The affectionate term was testament to his good name, his startlingly good looks, and his exceptional capabilities in the art of *amour*. To add to this, the man had an overabundance of charm, a shining intellect, and an extremely wicked sense of humor.

Not that any of these other glowing qualities were on the woman's mind at the moment.

As his lordship's energetic enthusiasm propelled them both wildly across the steamy sheets of a massive Oriental lacquer bed, a single loud rap was heard on the door to her ladyship's boudoir. To say the intrusion was extremely ill-timed was the same as saying Lady Havertam's unwed niece was just a tad enceinte; it did not even begin to describe the situation.

"My lady, there is an urgent message here for the viscount!" The butler's muffled voice barely reached the couple on the bed.

Lord John hesitated.

The lady in question whispered fervently for

him to ignore it and continue on. She augmented her request with an enticing roll of her hips. The punctuation was enough of a reason for the viscount; he dropped his head to the woman's chest and vigorously recommenced where he had left off.

But the butler, being a stalwart English servant, continued to rap on the door, his voice urgently seeking the recalcitrant lord.

This time when his lordship hesitated, an outraged sound exited the woman's mouth, the pitch and level of the tone reminding John of the unfortunate squeal of a stuck pig. He gaped at her as she continued to screech at the butler to go away.

Realizing what she must sound like, the woman suddenly smiled coyly up at him.

"Do ignore him, Johnnie," she beseeched the handsome man who seemed to be viewing her askance.

While he thought it over, the small charm that dangled from a thin gold chain about his throat caught a beam of light from the candle and sparked in the darkened room.

It was an odd charm, really. . . .

A tiny gold carrot.

Many of the women of the ton had pondered the significance of the piece. His lordship was peculiarly secretive about it. The general opinion was that the Lord of Sex was having his own private joke regarding the elusive "carrot"—forever tantalizing, yet forever out of reach.

Whatever its meaning, the charm had become somewhat famous. Several ladies had joked to the viscount that the charm was his cartouche. John always smiled mysteriously at that point, saying only, "Indeed." Yet, whenever a woman touched it, he subtly guided her hand away.

Lord John tossed back his thick mane of hair. His perfect white teeth flashed a brief smile. "I do not believe he will go away, Jessymyn. Let me see what he wants—I promise I'll be right back." He winked at her, then disengaged himself to pad naked to the door.

Normally a man did not answer the door stark naked. Not in most houses, anyway.

"Johnnie!" Her ladyship's exclamation was brief and not very heartfelt; nor did it in any way deter her ladyship from enjoying the splendid sight before her. John was a stunning man. Especially unclothed.

Aware of her avid perusal, Lord Sexton grinned at her over his shoulder, revealing the infamous dimples that had caused scores of women to do unspeakable things for him.

The lady wilted back onto the covers.

Still smiling, he opened the door a few inches

and boldly stuck his hand out for the message. John fully expected the "emergency" message to be from one of his legion of women; a flowery epistle begging him to dine alfresco from a favorite balcony, or some such request.

So he was quite surprised when he read the note. Initially he smiled, a huge ear-to-ear grin. Then the smile seemed to die on his face.

The woman lying amid the tumbled sheets noted his lordship's normally dusky skin tone turning into a somewhat pale shade.

When he looked up all previous traces of good humor were gone. "I must leave at once," he told her flatly.

"What is it?" She clutched the sheet to her bobbing breasts.

"A message from my uncle." He didn't waste any time on further explanations, simply set about gathering his scattered clothes, and dressing with a speed she wouldn't have thought possible.

He was out the door before she even had time to object.

The woman blinked in confusion. *What could it be?* What would ever make the Lord of Sex leave a woman's bed? Was his uncle ill? He would have to be. On his very deathbed. Nothing less than that would drag the ardent lord away from his favorite and almost exclusive activity!

Her sights fell to the crumpled note that had dropped to the floor in his haste to depart. Gingerly, she stepped out of bed and retrieved it. But when she opened it, all it displayed were three words:

CHLOE HAS RETURNED.

So that young half-French girl, Chloe Heart, had come back from her trip to the Colonies. . . . Certainly that did not constitute an emergency! Just why was Lord Sexton so vexed? One might think he was actually in a state of panic over something.

The woman placed her fingers against her mouth, giggling. Silly thought; Lord Sexton was never perturbed over anything. Especially something so mundane as this.

Indeed, he was a man who displayed an almost arrogant courage. She herself had seen him laugh in the face of certain death at the hands of Lady Snibble's father—the best swordsman in England, or so the man claimed—when the outraged lord had caught his wayward daughter with the Lord of Sex in flagrante delicto. Now that was a situation!

This was a mere curiosity.

After all, to a man like Lord John, how much trouble could one little girl cause?

Bored with the subject, she closed her eyes and instead remembered what it felt like to have all that power and sexual passion between her legs.

Unconsciously, her lips parted.

Chapter One
Chloe Makes Her Plans

It had gone on long enough!

Chloe Heart narrowed her violet eyes as she examined the man charging across the country-side, his horse kicking up a cloud of dust as he raced toward the mansion.

It could be only John.

No one else looked that good riding a stal-lion—or anything else, for that matter. The very idea made her eyes narrow further. Oh, he was a rogue!

She continued observing him as he rode across the far pasture at a hellish pace. Freed from its queue, his gilded hair flew behind him as he bent low over the horse's neck to gain speed.

She recognized that stance—it was a trait of John's that most people overlooked. Blinded by his apparent laissez-faire attitude and stunning looks, not many saw the iron determination well hidden beneath the mantle of the devil-may-care rake.

Chloe, however, had always seen it.

Typical of John to be so unconcerned with his appearance. . . .

Despite her resolve, Chloe's expression momentarily softened. She had remembered that spun-gold hair every day for the past year and a half. It was the color of sunlit honey, and everything about him reminded her of the enticing nectar. Like his rich sense of humor with that beckoning, teasing laugh . . .

Usually making sport of you! an annoying inner voice spoke up.

Chloe chewed on her bottom lip. Yes, but he could be extraordinarily sweet. . . .

When it suits him! the voice reasonably pointed out.

Chloe pictured the way John always moved; irresistibly smooth, sure, fluid. . . .

Unpredictable and predatory! Like a targeting beast!

She squelched the annoying opinion.

Yes, John was often like honey: sweet,

smooth, rich, fluid, with a somewhat unpredictable flavor. One could only wonder if he might actually taste the same. . . .

Lord of Sex.

The play on his name that the ton found so delightfully humorous. Even at sixteen, the age he was when she had first met him, he had been sampling the pleasures of the flesh. It only got worse over the years.

From the beginning, they had formed a close and enduring bond. A lump rose in her throat. Oh, she wanted to kill him!

When she was six, she hadn't understood why women watched him so. He was simply the older boy who picked her up and swung her onto his shoulders and always made her laugh. The one who held her and dried her tears and murmured soothing little phrases to her.

The fist of her hand uncurled and she placed her palm against the windowpane, as if the simple action could bring him closer to her. *John . . .*

Rider and horse took a reckless leap over a stone border wall and continued charging forward, the horse's hooves kicking up great clods of earth. Lord John was in a hurry to get to his uncle's. In a few minutes he would arrive. After all those endless months away from him—her self-imposed exile—she would see him in the flesh once again.

Chloe closed her eyes as they filled with moisture. It had been so difficult to stay away this long! But the exile had been a very important part of the plan.

She recalled the exact look on John's masculine face when she had told him her decision to go to the Colonies with her friend, Aubrey, who was visiting an older sister in Charleston. For an instant John had seemed stunned.

"You're going *where?*"

Then he had tried to talk her out of it, but finally quit when he realized she would not be dissuaded.

"Maybe I shouldn't let you go," he had grumbled.

Chloe had laughed. "As if you have a say in what I do." *That* had made the handsome face glower.

For as long as Chloe could remember, John had fancied himself a cross between her best friend and knowledgeable guide. The realization that in fact he did not have any say whatsoever seemed to give him pause. However briefly.

Of course, she had fueled his fire when she set sail, by whispering to him that she intended to do every naughty thing she could think of during her stay in the Colonies, leaving him to wonder just what she meant. His face had gone absolutely white as the ship sailed out of the harbor. It had been immensely satisfying.

Horse and rider scaled another wall.

Surely the speed with which he came to her now indicated more than their usual friendship? Surely he would realize that things would be different between them now that she was a grown woman of nineteen?

He *must* realize how much she . . . how she always . . .

Chloe swallowed in an effort to hold at bay the reckless, emotional French side to her nature, which had a tendency to land her in trouble. She had wanted John all of her life and had waited so patiently for this day.

Didn't that deserve a reward of some kind? Of course it did!

Surely his beautiful, low voice was about to whisper her name just as she imagined in all her girlhood fantasies—

"Chlo-eee!" The front door opened with a crash and slammed shut with a force that shook the rafters. The deep male voice boomed throughout the house.

Chloe winced. Well, maybe not quite a whisper. Apparently that little mischief she had played on him when she had sailed had not set too well with him. She squared her shoulders.

Well, if that had unnerved the rogue, wait until he saw what else she had in store for him!

John was in trouble.

He didn't know it yet, but he was in deep trouble. His days of debauchery were over! For Chloe—determined little Chloe—intended to have him for her very own. Now and forever.

After she killed him.

Lord of Sex! Tales of his exploits had managed to reach her even in the Colonies. Snippets in letters from Grandmere alluding to his myriad grand passions. *Merde.* It made her ill!

Unfortunately, she had missed the rakehell too much to execute him before the noon meal.

She sighed.

It would just have to wait until later in the day.

John stood at the foot of the stairs and roared.

He was dead tired, having stopped only briefly at an inn to refresh himself with a cold bath and feed his poor horse. For some reason, there was a compelling need to get here as quickly as possible. Just to ensure that the little piddlehead was all right.

He still hadn't forgiven her for taking off like that to the Colonies. Leaving him for eighteen long months to wonder what that unpredictable ginger-pate was devising in the way of trouble!

Then again, he hadn't had to rescue her from some mischief she had gotten herself into, either.

Despite himself, a grin curved his sensual lips. Until he recalled her mysterious last words to him.

He bellowed out her name again. "*Chloe!*"

Now where was the hellcat hiding?

A smidgen of red hair poked between the upstairs banisters. It was followed by two enormous violet eyes.

"John?" She spoke his name haltingly in that sweet voice he remembered so well. No one said his name quite like Chloe. Despite all of her years in England, she still softened the *J* slightly in the French way. Something stopped in his chest. He hadn't realized how much he had missed the sprite until now.

"John!" Chloe stood up and began to race down the steps toward him, her slippered feet barely touching the rug beneath her.

The thought *She's changed* scarcely had time to register before he found himself dashing up the steps to meet her halfway. She leaped into his arms in an act of blind faith, almost sending them both crashing downward.

John threw back his head and laughed, spinning them both around. *She's not changed that much! Thank God.*

"John! John!" Chloe wrapped her arms around his neck and began quickly kissing him all over his face. John called it "Chloe's Chicken Pecks Français." It was something she had always done when they hadn't seen each other for a while, and it never failed to make him laugh.

And it didn't fail this time either. At first.

John, arms wrapped tightly around her, lifting her up to him, abruptly stopped laughing. A frown marred his smooth forehead as his hands cupped her bottom. It was fuller than he remembered and more . . . well, shapely.

He pulled his face back from her free-roaming lips. "What are you wearing under here?" His hands hefted the portion of anatomy in question, bringing her closer to him.

Chloe raised her magnificent eyes slowly to his. He wondered where she had learned that bit of coquetry.

"Nothing," she whispered to him in a throaty voice.

John's green eyes widened a fraction. He blinked once, then dropped her like a hot baguette. He studied her as if he had just turned over a rock and something "Chloe" had crawled out from underneath.

Oh, dear, she thought, dismayed. *This could be crucial. Well, he needs to stop seeing me as a child and begin regarding me as an adult woman in order for my plan to work!* It was a risk, but one she had to take in order to proceed; otherwise her long exile in the Colonies would have been for nothing.

Knowing he was watching her suspiciously from under those thick black lashes of his, Chloe threw back her shoulders, put her hands on her generously curved hips, and cocked her red head to the side. It was a calculated pose, designed to show her blossomed figure to perfection.

Let the games begin. Strength had never been a weakness to her.

John took his time observing Chloe. He was thinking that the mite had changed considerably since last he had seen her. Where had that—that *curvaceous* figure come from? Full breasts, tiny waist, rounded hips . . . She had been all youthful angles the last time he had seen her. Eyes that had once seemed too large for her heart-shaped face were now spellbinding. And her hair . . .

Where had the carrottop gone?

Instead of the orange mop-top he was accustomed to, there was the most magnificent red hair he had ever seen. Chloe was breathtaking. *Different*. An incredible beauty.

With as much experience as he had in choosing women, John knew it would be more than her looks that would take London by storm.

There was a fire in her that would be evident to every court card of the beau monde.

It wouldn't be long before word got out and the mansion was under siege. Add to that fact that Chloe was an heiress . . .

This was bound to be trouble.

And he knew for whom.

He already had a busy season planned; he didn't have time for this. John scowled. "What have you done to yourself?"

Chloe pursed her lips. This was not the reaction she had hoped for. "Whatever do you mean, John? And you can take that scowly-bear look off your face right now!"

Scowly-bear? Chloe always had a strange way of turning a phrase. He didn't think she realized that she always mixed up questionable adjectives with descriptions of the animal kingdom whenever she was angry with him. He always thought her attempts at categorizing him when she was upset most adorable. And he had a delightful way of teasing her with it.

So his lips twitched.

Momentarily.

"I have grown up, John, in case you have not noticed!" The violet eyes flashed lightning at him.

Yes. White-hot fire.

Despite himself, he grinned slowly. "Oh, I noticed," he drawled.

Mistaking his meaning, Chloe's felt her face break into a delighted smile.

"The question is—how much trouble is it going to cause me?" He stroked his chin in what was to Chloe an insufferably arrogant gesture. The smile died on her face.

Her delicate brows slanted down.

So that's where the rascal thought to go, did he? Going to play his long-suffering, I'm-responsible-for-you routine. I don't think so, Viscount.

For some reason, John had always considered himself accountable for her. Why exactly was a mystery to everyone, including Chloe. No one had ever remotely suggested the possibility to him. Mystery or no, she was not above using that inexplicable quirk of his to her advantage.

She spoke the words she knew would rattle him. "Whatever does it have to do with *you?*"

John eyed her suspiciously, green eyes narrowing slightly. "And I suppose you're not going to embroil me in one of your schemes the next time you get yourself into hot water? Which, knowing you, should be in about, oh, say, an hour and fifteen minutes?"

Chloe swallowed. Actually that was just about

the time she was thinking of springing her trap on him. It was uncanny how well he knew her.

"What's the matter, Chloe-rabbit, cat got your tongue?" His deep voice teased her.

The corners of Chloe's generous mouth turned down at the silly sobriquet, one of many he irked her with. John had a habit of tacking animals onto her name. She could never figure out the reason.

"Stop calling me Chloe-rabbit; it is just not done, John! After all, I am a woman now."

John looked up at the ceiling, then settled his mocking gaze on her. "Are you really?"

She nodded, her soft mouth curving in an enigmatic half smile.

John didn't want to believe what he was thinking. He bent toward her, bringing his face level with hers. "And tell me, just what did you do in the Colonies that has brought about this change?" The mocking lilt in his voice did nothing to disguise the mercuric glint in his eyes.

Chloe had never seen precisely that expression on John before.

She stepped back from him and almost lost her balance on the stairs. His strong arm shot out to steady her. And bring her closer to him. He did not release her elbow.

"I'm waiting."

Chloe tossed her head back, breaking free of his hold. "Don't be a snibble-toad! It is none of your concern what I have done!"

Snibble-toad hardly registered because her nonanswer was answer enough for him. His emerald gaze met hers in silence for an eternity.

Good, let him think the worst! This was an unexpected bonus for it fit in perfectly with her plans. She convinced herself that the slight sheen of moisture in his left eye was a trick of the light. Surely his feelings were not hurt in some way?

Nonsense!

Smiling softly, Chloe stood on tiptoe and patted his cheek. This close she could discern the clean scent of his hair; it always reminded her of a field of clover. "I had a wonderful example," she purposely goaded him in the softest of tones.

Against expectations, John flinched at her words and swiftly grabbed her wrist in a crushing hold, bringing her flat against him. This time she knew she saw real emotion in his eyes.

"What do you mean by that?" he hissed.

She threw her head back, bringing her lips close to his chin, so he could feel the warmth of her breath on him. "Even in the Colonies I heard about your women, John."

Her words surprised him. He hesitated briefly. "So what?"

His long lashes fanned his cheeks, the rich black color a stunning contrast to the long golden hair framing his face. Then he raised those lashes, meeting her questioning look.

"I am sure nothing I have done has ever been a shock to you, Chloe-cat." The deep male voice literally purred a sexual challenge.

Chloe flushed. It was the first time John had ever toyed with her in such a blatantly seductive manner. She wondered if he was even aware he was doing it.

She had never imagined how . . . how *potent* he could be. No, that wasn't exactly true; she had imagined it. Who would have guessed that the reality far surpassed the fantasy? Chloe wasn't sure whether she should inhale or exhale.

She settled on a better technique.

"All of these lovers," she returned in a low, intimate voice, "they must bring you great satisfaction. *N'est-ce pas*?"

He observed her in stony silence, a muscle working in his jaw.

In that moment Chloe knew she had discovered something. Something he kept well hidden. Instantly she became serious. "Why do you need all of these women, John?"

The question was a mistake. She knew it the second the words left her mouth.

John pulled away from her, moving down one step, his distance now not just physical.

Crossing his arms over his chest, he leaned against the wall. The grin that crossed his face was arrogant, rakish, and terribly annoying. "Well, I do *like* it, Chloe."

She had no doubt of that—he was a rake. Perhaps she was expecting too much from him in this regard? The man was notoriously oversexed.

"Why else would I do it?"

Why else indeed? It had been a question that had plagued her for years. This time Chloe felt the sheen of moisture in her own eyes. His seemingly careless assessment of his sordid life upset her deeply. If she did not know him as well as she did, she would have believed that was all there was to the story.

However, Chloe knew better.

With a resolve she never knew she possessed, she said very calmly, "Yes—that is my point. I believe I will like it too." Whereupon she smiled like a true Chloe-cat.

The smug look died on John's face. He abandoned his casual stance. "What are you saying?"

"I am saying, dear, imaginative rake, that I intend to be exactly . . . like . . . you." She picked up her skirt and breezed by him down the stairs. John's jaw dropped.

He still hadn't recovered when she paused to say over her shoulder, "I mean with men, of course."

Continuing down the stairs, she began counting to herself. *One. Two. Thr—"*

"You intend to *what?*"

A mischievous grin made her violet eyes sparkle as she ignored the bellow behind her and nonchalantly made her way to the central hall.

"What is all this yelling about?" Chloe's grandmother, the Countess de Fonbeaulard, rushed into the foyer from the drawing room.

John was not overly surprised to see his uncle, Maurice Chavaneau, the Marquis of Cotingham, at her side. The man had been slavishly in love with the countess for thirty years and had even left his own French estates to follow the woman to England when she had become Chloe's legal guardian.

Chloe's father had been an Englishman, like John. In his will he had stipulated that Chloe must be raised on English soil. *His* English soil, to be precise. So the countess, who loved her granddaughter far more than her beloved chateau, had left France, although she never let anyone forget the grand sacrifice she had made, nor forgiven "that Engleeeshman," Chloe's father. In retaliation, when she had moved with the six-year-old Chloe into the father's Georgian estate, she promptly renamed it *Chacun à Son Goût—Each to his own taste.*

The new name of the house reflected the countess's personal philosophy on life. She was a flamboyant, interesting woman, who maintained her enormous popularity with the males of her set. In her youth, the widow's reputation in the boudoir fell just short of John's.

Nowadays, her dazzling personality and great beauty still were admired and respected by all her contemporaries. Indeed, the marquis had been slavishly in love with her for decades. It was rumored he asked her to marry him once a week. On Fridays. At teatime.

Maurice Chavaneau, John's only living relative, was also a French marquis and preferred to be called such. John himself did not have French blood, although he could lay claim to Norse, Celtic, and Saxon blood.

The marquis was John's mother's half brother, having inherited his English title from that side of the family. And so, too, John was his only living relative. In other words, John was his heir.

It was not such a comforting thing to have one such as John as one's heir even if one was very Gallic in temperament and had a tendency to shrug off the foibles of youth. After all, John was a complete wastrel, and had never pretended or aspired to be anything else.

Still, his uncle, a kindhearted man, had great affection for the younger lord. Even if he did despair of him ever producing an heir to carry on the line.

At this point, the marquis thought even an illegitimate heir would be welcome, but John had been very careful in that regard. And apparently very knowledgeable too. No Sexton bastards had ever appeared on his lordship's doorstep.

"Ah! It is John—come to see our Chloe." Countess de Fonbeaulard smiled fondly at the handsome lord.

"Oh ho! I knew he would not stay away long!" The marquis spoke English with a thick French accent.

"Is she not beautiful, John? Almost I did not recognize her!" Maurice winked at the countess. "All the Fonbeaulard women are beautiful."

The countess tapped his arm with her fan. "Really, Maurice, you are a consummate flatterer—but I agree with you; Chloe has come into her own."

"Thank you, Grandmere," Chloe said sweetly. "You too, Maurice." Chloe joined them at the bottom of the stairs and gazed innocently up at Lord Sexton, who was still standing in the middle of the stairs, nostrils flaring.

"I think soon we shall have the coming-out party for you, my little angel."

Little angel? John gave the countess an incredulous look.

"We have already put it off far too long." Grandmere raised a scented handkerchief to her eyes, dabbing them. "It will not be long before she leaves us, Maurice. How shall I bear it?"

Grandmere was ever the dramatic one. Chloe tried not to laugh as, predictably, the marquis put his arm around her grandmother, patting her back consolingly. She knew Maurice was about to impart the Gallic wisdom that always accompanied these little nuances of life.

Right on cue the marquis shrugged his shoulders in a very French gesture. "It is the way of things, *mon amour*. We cannot go against nature."

Chloe's lips twitched with suppressed amusement. At that moment her eyes met John's. Despite his vexation at her, there was an answering glint of humor in his expression. The two of them had been watching the same scenario in various forms for most of their lives.

As usual, Grandmere recovered remarkably

fast, all traces of tears somehow vanishing immediately. The countess took the phrase *c'est la vie* as a personal motto.

"Yes, why be upset on this glorious day when we should be dining?" Turning, she took the marquis's arm. "Come along, John, we have had a place set at the table for you."

Desultorily, John ambled down the stairs. "How did you know I was coming?"

Maurice raised an eyebrow at him. "Ho ho!"

John glared at him.

The marquis wasn't fooled. Singing a silly country tune in French under his breath, he led the countess into the dining room.

A smattering of the lyrics reached John. Some nonsense about a mouse that ate a cat . . .

"Shall we go, John?" Chloe said amiably.

The viscount wasn't fooled by her act for a minute. The minx had the audacity to bat her eyelashes at him.

He took a deep breath and exhaled it. "We are not through with this, you and I."

"Oh, I should hope not! Why, I have only just begun," Chloe murmured mysteriously as she took his arm.

"Mmm. I was afraid of that."

Twice he tried to trip her as he led her into the dining room.

* * *

When they entered the dining room, the man known simply as Deiter was already seated at the table.

This was no great surprise.

Despite the strange man's unfortunate tendency to fall asleep at the oddest times, he never missed a meal.

Simply put, Deiter was family, although no one was quite sure exactly whose family. He had been with them for so long, it was naturally assumed he belonged on *someone's* side.

Deiter greeted Lord Sexton with his customary grunt. It was one of two responses the man possessed, the other being a piercing stare.

Both expressions, John had to admit, accessorized the man's constant wardrobe of black to perfection. He nodded to the squat German as he took his seat across from Chloe.

Schnapps, an exceedingly ugly pug dog—who was never far from Deiter's lap—provided the piercing stare. The one tooth the dog possessed stuck out of its mouth at an odd angle, lending a maniacal impact to the sentiment.

Between the two of them, we are sure to get the entire range of emotion. An amused dimple curved John's cheek.

John rather liked the presence of Deiter.

Not because he was fond of the man himself—one would have trouble admitting to a fondness for Deiter—it was rather because Deiter represented to John everything unique that he had come to associate with *Chacun à Son Goût*.

He had always had a special attachment to this house. It was one of the few places where he felt comfortable down to his toes. That the countess was a consummate hostess was an indisputable part of the reason.

But it was more.

There was for John a sense of happiness about this house. A sense of life and laughter that he had rarely seen elsewhere.

What was more, the countess always kept a room ready just for him. The same room. Since John was a rather impoverished viscount, having no estates of his own, the gesture she made, fueled in part by her affection for Maurice, touched him deeply. *Chacun à Son Goût* was the closest thing to a home he would ever likely know.

Luncheon was served.

Years before, the countess had brought her cook with her from France, stating seriously that one would give up the coat of arms before one gave up a good French chef. Therefore, the table at *Chacun à Son Goût* was exceptionally well laid. So why had he suddenly lost his appetite?

John gazed across the table to the young woman cheerfully scarfing down her coq au vin. Prosaically, he acknowledged the source of his problem. *Cherchez la femme.*

It wasn't Chloe's ridiculous pronouncement that she intended to imitate his manner of life that had startled him the most. Obviously she wasn't serious and had only been goading him—a thing Chloe always took great pleasure in doing. No, it was Chloe's seemingly innocuous observation that had unnerved him. *All of these lovers . . . must bring you great satisfaction.*

The truth was . . . they didn't.

Oh, he enjoyed himself, to be sure. In fact, he was very pleased with his life. But great satisfaction? Somehow that peak had always eluded him.

He had no idea why.

"John?" Chloe broke into his thoughts. He looked up at her questioningly.

"After we finish, I wonder if we might go into the garden. There is something I wish to discuss with you." She looked at him meaningfully over her wineglass.

So she was going to continue with this absurd idea of hers. He gave her a patient look. "No, Chloe."

John was being stubborn. Time for a little incentive, she reasoned. Dipping her index finger into her wine, she ran the moistened tip slowly back and forth across her full bottom lip exactly as she had seen a playactor do.

It was a shame she had no way of knowing that a droplet of red liquid had dribbled onto her chin.

Goblet raised midway to his lips, John glanced over at her and stared agog. *What on earth is she doing?*

Chloe, pleased with John's undivided attention told herself it was working. *Why, look at his face . . . he's—he's captivated!*

Propelled by her apparent success, she decided to go all-out and give him what she considered her most alluring maneuver. She unfocused her vision, donning the faraway, dreamy look of a courtesan.

Too bad it made her appear cockeyed.

John's facial expression became that of a man who had been hit sharply on the head with a cudgel.

"My lord, I insist," Chloe croaked in a gravelly voice. Violet eyes crossed.

The wine he was halfheartedly drinking caught in John's throat, choking him.

"John, are you feeling well?" The countess

leaned forward in her seat, concern on her face.

Maurice whacked his nephew on the back. "This strapping boy?" *Whack! Whack! Whack!* "But he is the picture of health!"

John grabbed his uncle's wrist to stop the hammering he was receiving. "Ex—ahem—excuse me, Countess; I thought I saw something . . . *improbable.*" He gave Chloe a penetrating look.

"Do be careful; Chef LaFaint would be terribly upset if you collapsed at his table." The countess smiled kindly at him.

John smiled back, then covertly turned to Chloe with a thunderous expression.

The garden, she mouthed stubbornly.

"Very well, Chloe." John threw his napkin down and rose. He knew that when the gingerpate had something on her mind . . . well, it was in his best interest to find out about it and nip it in the bud. There was no telling what that dangerous little brain of hers had concocted.

A lifetime of experience told him that, whatever it was, it would be the last thing he expected.

Chapter Two
John Considers It

"I want you to marry me."

John didn't know whether to laugh outright or bang his head against the brick walkway.

He settled for the former. Leaning against the tree behind the bench he was sitting on, he threw back his head and let loose a huge, guffawing laugh.

Chloe patiently waited for him to get it out of his system.

Wiping the tears of mirth from his eyes, he finally managed to croak, "You what?"

The secret to John was never to let him know she cared one way or the other. Chloe was surprised—but thankful—that no other woman had figured this out. Knowing him as well as she did—not to mention the fact that she had been an excellent spy in the past during several of Grandmere's soirees—she also knew that John never revealed himself beyond a very superficial point to the women with whom he consorted.

Chloe was never sure why he had such barriers in place; she only recognized their existence. It was said that John gave untold pleasure but never gave himself; he never became emotionally involved. Women commented that when Lord John was engaged in a liaison, he was strictly business for the task at hand.

In light of this, Chloe had always known that their special closeness had resulted only because John had never viewed her as a possible conquest. So there was a very real chance he might pull away from her now.

However, due to their past closeness, she was fairly confident she could muddle him into thinking he was safe. *Safe.* Chloe snorted. The poor unsuspecting scoundrel!

She was not the least put off by his reaction to her proposal. *Au contraire.* She was a woman with a mission.

"You heard me, John; I want you to marry me."

John shook his head—both to clear out the cobwebs and negate the horrifying image from his mind. *Married.* Him. As if he would know what to do with a wife!

What could she be thinking? He said as much. "Have you lost your mind?"

Chloe put up her hand to forestall him. "Please hear me out, John. I think once you hear what I have to say, you'll agree this is a plan that could benefit us both."

John placed one booted foot up on the edge of the bench he was sitting on and laced his hands around his knee. Bending his head forward, he purposely made his green eyes go round with feigned interest. He did nothing to disguise the mocking dimple in his cheek.

"I'm breathless with curiosity, *dearest*."

Pursing her lips at his annoying attitude, Chloe began her practiced speech. "As you know, I have always admired you—"

"I'm touched." He placed his palm over his heart.

Chloe decided right then and there she would pay him back for this at a later time. "Your life is one that I wish to emulate—you see, I believe you have the best of all possible worlds."

John rested back against the trunk. "How so, Chloe?"

"You enjoy whatever pleasures come your way, yet you are not confined by the dictates of society."

John raised a dark eyebrow. "There is a difference between—"

"I'm not finished. While it is true I am only nineteen, I am not naive."

"So you've intimated." He glowered. "Just what kind of experience have you—"

"John, please. You presume too much." Especially if he expected her to answer that! The truth was she had no experience whatsoever. It was the one thing she could not let him find out if this scheme had a hope of working.

"The point is—I like what I have discovered and I wish to pursue the—the . . . pastime."

"Pastime?"

"So to speak." She cleared her throat. "While I now have practical knowledge, I lack refinement of technique. This is where you come in."

"You have lost your mind." He stood up, towering over her. This was bordering on insult! He couldn't believe what she was asking of him. He was no one's practice drill—he was the bloody battle! "What game are you playing?"

"No game, Viscount." Chloe turned away from him. She hated having to make him believe this, but it was essential to her plan. "Grandmere is already talking of coming-out balls and such. Under the circumstances, that just won't do."

His fists clenched. "Are you saying what I think you're saying?"

Chloe bit her lip and nodded.

John ran his hand through his long hair. The slight tremor in his fingers obviously was due to shock at her disclosure and not because he was bothered by this bit of news. It was just that he had never actually thought of Chloe . . . in the arms of someone else.

But a second, more disturbing thought followed.

His palms rested gently on her shoulders. "You're not . . . ?"

"No!" She gasped, turning to face him. She hadn't meant to imply that she was! It was bad enough what she *was* implying. Grandmere would have the vapors if she ever got wind of this. The Fonbeaulard women always went to their marriage beds pure. How they behaved afterward with their husbands was another matter.

John let out a breath of relief. For some strange reason, the terrible tightening in his chest did not ease.

"Such is not at all the life I'm looking for—your life is one of great adventure and pleasure. Why should I be denied this simply because I am a woman?"

John groaned. This was worse than he thought.

Chloe pressed her case. "You know that society frowns on unwed misses seeking their pleasures. However, a married woman doing the same is ignored or even applauded by the ton. So you see why I want you to marry me . . ."

Now she had crossed the line! "Chloe, this is the most ridiculous thing you have—"

She kicked his shin.

"Chloe."

"Listen to me! Who better to ignore my indiscretions than you—*Lord of Sex?*"

His eyes narrowed ominously. "Where did you hear—"

"Who better than you to teach me the subtleties of the boudoir?"

That stopped him. *Red hair draped across silken sheets . . . His* sheets.

He squelched the disturbing image immediately. Unbelievably, a flush of bronze highlighted his cheekbones.

Chloe pressed on. "And who would I trust more to care for my estates and my well-being than you, John? You have been like a part of the family for years, as well as my dear friend."

Her sentiment touched him more than she would ever know. He realized in that moment that he had always felt closer to Chloe than any other living being. His mind on the revelation he had just had, he was caught off guard by her last statement.

"Estate? What do you mean, your estate?"

Chloe honed in on what she considered a chink in the wall, deciding to play that trump. She wanted John, and if he wanted the mansion more than her . . . well, it would just give her more time to work on him. Unfortunately, it appeared she was going to need a great deal of time for this project. Chloe never deluded herself. Rakes were a very difficult breed to reel in.

"Did you forget that *Chacun à Son Goût* belongs to me? Whosoever I wed will gain control of my property, the estate."

Noting his surprised look, she played to it by throwing her arms up in the air. "Would you let it fall to anyone? Who would care for it like you? I know you have always loved this house, John."

Her words gave him pause. Actually, he had never thought of that. *Who would take over his room?* What would happen to this wonderful house? He stared at Chloe as if he had never seen her before. And who could he trust to take care of his little Chloe? She had always been his responsibility.

He had never considered this before. Somehow, he had just assumed that everything would continue on as it had always been. Suddenly he was a man with concerns.

Chloe noticed his hesitation. She drew a bead

on him and fired. "Think of it, John. *Chacun à Son Goût*, yours."

The sensual lips firmed; the dimple, which was normally deep-set when he smiled, indented slightly. It was John's look when he was thinking about something that he was not sure sat well with him.

Chloe took a deep breath and barreled ahead. Everything that meant anything to her was standing right before her. She looked him straight in the eye. "I know what I want."

John wondered if she had any idea of what she really would be getting into with such a bargain. The moniker *Lord of Sex* was better earned then her young mind could ever imagine.

A provocative flash of emerald glittered beneath the spiky crescents of his lashes.

"You think you know me?" he drawled silkily; the long lashes swept down.

"Yes."

"Everything you've heard about me is true; I have done all those sordid things." He baited her. "And probably a great deal more."

Chloe didn't even flinch. Oh, she would curse him later in the privacy and safety of her armoire, but right now, she knew he was considering her proposition and it unnerved him. He was trying to scare her off.

It was almost decent of him, considering.

"You know, John, you are very like Don Giovanni; perhaps Mozart had you in mind when he composed it."

The corners of John's mouth curled. "Not exactly. I might engage in a dual with a husband, father, or lover, but I would never invite his ghost to dine with me. I can barely tolerate Deiter at the supper table."

"Do be serious, John."

He laughed.

Even knowing him all these years, she felt her heart flutter. Lord of Sex, indeed. That deep, full-throated sound was enough to give any woman tingles.

"Once a rogue, always a rogue, I suppose," she said under her breath. "In any case, I shan't be disappointed in my choice of tutor." She didn't know where she got the gall to point that out to him.

Silently, John continued to watch from under veiled eyes.

Nervous with his scrutiny and completely misinterpreting it, Chloe added, "Of course, I could find someone else for that part of the job, but I thought with your vast experience, you were the best man for the—*Oh!*"

John pulled her down with him onto the bench. Right across his lap.

Flames of hot anger shot out of those watchful emerald eyes. "If there's any instructing to be done, Chloe-cub, *I'll* be the one to do it." His broad palm came down across her backside.

It was more of a response than she could have hoped for. Why, John seemed almost jealous! It had been years since he'd done this.

Chloe's spirits immediately sank. What was she thinking? This was the Lord of Sex, for heaven's sake. *Jealous* was not in his vocabulary.

Yet.

Chloe wiggled around so she could sit up. "If you insist." She purposely yawned as if bored with the topic.

John's pupils contracted to pinpoints.

Chloe took that as an encouraging sign.

"There is one thing, Chloe." He spoke in a low, measured voice.

"Yes, John?" She arranged a lock of his hair behind his ear for him.

"If I consider this"—Chloe perked up on his lap—"I said *if*—then I have my own condition to make."

"Condition?"

"Yes. While my 'tutelage' is going on, I don't want you seeing other men."

The pronouncement shocked them both. However, John recovered first. He didn't care to examine why he wanted this condition, only that once it had popped out of his mouth, he liked the idea. More than liked it. He was obsessive over it.

"I don't want my guidance interfered with." He tried to smooth over the odd request. "I have an expert technique; I don't want someone else spoiling my lessons by confusing you."

Oh, really. It was all Chloe could do not to give a victory yell. It was more from him than she could have hoped. She carefully hid her elation.

Thinking fast, Chloe interjected, "I will agree to your condition if you will agree to the very same terms, John. No other women for you—while you are instructing me."

His eyelids flickered, and Chloe knew she had caught him at his own game.

"It's only fair." She smoothed out his lapels. "Improbable as it seems, I might teach *you* something. But if you don't want to, it's all right with—"

A muscle worked in his jaw. "Very well. But just until the instruction is over."

Chloe gave him a gamine grin. "Which begins after we wed."

His nostrils flared in annoyance. How had he allowed this to happen?

"Does this mean you agree to the plan?" she asked in a composed voice.

John was not ready to make such a momentous concession. He shook his finger at her. "If, Chloe-cat. *If.*"

Chloe nodded, smiling innocently up at him.

An answering dimple curved into his cheek.

I've got him, she exulted.

John strolled through the extensive gardens of *Chacun à Son Goût.*

The solitary journey always brought peace of mind to him. The beautiful, fragrant surroundings seemed to aid the thinking process. And he had much to think on.

Wed Chloe?

Him. The most notorious rake in England!

Is she insane?

She could do a lot better than him, he was positive. He kicked a pebble in his path.

Well, maybe not better, but surely as good.

He stomped his booted foot, scaring a flock of quail into flight. All right, so no one came close! He had certainly spent years acquiring and refining his expert technique.

Yes, he was the best man for the job; he could see that. He could even applaud her reasoning.

Truthfully, he had never considered marriage before. Despite pressure from his uncle to produce an heir, as well as being at the wrong end of several pistols held by irate fathers, brothers, and guardians, he had never been moved to the deed.

Despite his notorious reputation, he had never been a despoiler of innocents. On the contrary, he preferred knowledgeable bedmates, women who knew exactly what they wanted and exactly what he was prepared to give. No less and certainly no more.

He had never been a man who was hungry for money or property. John's true interests lay much deeper.

This could be tricky.

Exiting the rose garden, he turned left, heading into the maze.

Paying scant attention to the path he was taking—he could negotiate the labyrinth blindfolded—he continued to ponder Chloe's proposition.

The positive side was that she had set the parameters of the relationship, taking some of the pressure off what was to be expected. It was not as if this would be like a *real* marriage.

Something about that thought bothered him.

John ran his fingers through his thick, golden hair as he tried to view the proposition from another angle.

Of course it would be a real marriage! It just wouldn't seem like one.

And when they both were ready to . . . That is, when he had taught her all she needed to know . . .

Annoyed, he dropped that line of thinking.

Leaving the maze behind him, he headed toward the perennial gardens and the lake beyond. *Chacun à Son Goût* was breathtaking this time of year. Although, to him, the estate was incomparable every season of the year.

The idea of spending the rest of his days here with Chloe suddenly held enormous appeal. They had always gotten on famously.

For some reason, he had always been especially close to the girl. While he admired his uncle and felt very comfortable with him, it was Chloe that he always thought of when he connected to a place that dwelled deep within him called "home."

Maybe it was because he was responsible for the chit.

His lips tilted in a faint smile. Despite her mischievous streak and her tendency for headlong behavior, she had always been the sweetest of girls. He remembered one time when she was about eight—

A goose honked at her mate, breaking his concentration.

He sat down in the soft grass by the edge of

the pond beneath a weeping willow tree. A gentle breeze stirred his shoulder-length hair. Gazing across the water, he thought back on his childhood. It was not something he liked to do often.

Like him, his father had been a wastrel. Only it was not women that called to the prior viscount—it was the gaming hells. By the time John had been five years old, his father had been well on the road to ruin. When John reached the age of eight, his father was found with a bullet in his head. Presumably self-inflicted.

The strange part was that John's mother had still fancied herself in love with the ne'er do well, even after he had left them practically impoverished. The estate was gone, his inheritance gone; they barely had a roof over their heads. That roof was a small crofter's cottage.

His mother did what she could to protect her young son. Sometimes it was not enough. She died a few years later, leaving John alone.

It was believed she expired from a congestion of the lungs, but John knew better. In the young viscount's mind, it was his mother's love that had made her vulnerable; it was his father's weakness that had ruined them.

It was not the best of examples of the joys of matrimony to an impressionable mind. Nor was it a testimony to the noble aspects of love. Over the difficult years that followed—years that John never spoke to anyone about—the sensitive boy had learned how to protect himself. In body, mind, and heart.

By the time his uncle found him at the age of sixteen, he was half-starved and wild. Still, somehow, throughout it all, he had retained his unique sense of humor and his brash attitude.

Maurice was convinced it was John's bravado that had saved him from worse horrors. But the trait also shielded him from having to face his emotions.

As he matured, the devil-may-care attitude continued to cloak him; a thick, impenetrable shield.

That year, he had met Chloe.

She was six years old. A tiny girl with laughing violet eyes and carroty hair. And no parents. Her beguiling ways, winsome personality, and mischievous streak immediately captivated the young viscount. Chloe became the focus of his concern. He watched over her, protected her, cherished her.

From that moment on, John made himself responsible for her.

He believed he was the only one who could understand what could happen to her, so he was the only one who could shield her. Not once did it ever dawn on him that Chloe was never in any danger. He saw his own situation in her, and the young viscount guarded her zealously.

It was only to Chloe that his true vulnerability was revealed.

John threw a rock across the water, watching it skip across the surface. Remembrances of his past always brought on a melancholy mood. Why had he even ventured there? It had no place in his life today, no bearing on his current situation.

What should he do about Chloe's proposal? Marry her to secure her estates? The idea, which had at first seemed ludicrous, now held a certain appeal. Especially in the quiet of this garden, next to the pond.

Stretching out on the soft grass, he rested his head on the pillow made by his folded arms. The light wind riffled his hair, cooling the back of his neck. The sound of the lapping water soothed him, and he felt himself relax, becoming drowsy.

What should he do about Chloe's proposal?

It was not gardens or estates he thought of as he drifted off to sleep. In that state between waking and dreaming, the lapping water became waves of red hair floating toward him. In his mind's eye, he saw himself reach out simply to touch a tendril of hair before it floated away, and instead found himself wrapping the strand securely around his fist.

There was no way in hell he was going to let it slip by him.

John was lying prone on the grass, fast asleep. The classically handsome face turned toward her was almost completely hidden by his loose hair. Black breeches molded muscular buttocks and powerful thighs.

He looked too beautiful by half.

Chloe shook her head. John could fall asleep anywhere. She supposed it would be a necessary trait for a rake to possess.

She sat next to him on the lawn. Watching him. There was a silly little grin curving those sensual lips, and he seemed inordinately pleased with himself. The arm his head was resting on had a clenched fist.

I wonder what he's grabbing. She could just imagine the sordid exploits the rogue was dreaming about! Chloe sighed. It was going to be difficult to reform him.

But not impossible.

She knew just what she had to do in order to achieve her objective. Chloe was going to give him enough tether in the rope she offered to him so that he might hang himself. Metaphorically speaking.

How can such a wicked man look so innocent when he sleeps? She rolled her eyes at the preposterous picture he made. An innocent Lord of Sex. *Ha!* Trying not to laugh outright, she leaned forward to gently smooth back a strand of hair from his face.

John was worth reforming.

There was something extremely likable about him; everyone who met him saw that at once. Still, Chloe had always believed there was more to John than simply his easygoing, likable, rapscallion self.

Indeed, throughout her life he had given her glimpses of so much more.

The truth with John lay buried deep within: a heart of gold imprisoned by the walls he had erected. Chloe hoped with all her being that she was the key to unlock it.

Undeniably, from the moment they met, he was hers. Oh, not in body, to be sure, but definitely in spirit. It was something she had always sensed: they belonged to each other.

They always had.

And they always would.

It was up to her to make the dunderhead see it. Then admit to it.

There was the rub.

How does one bring a six-foot-two-inch rogue to heel? Well, she was about to find out and write the book. She took a deep breath. *I can do this. . . . I know I can.* It was Chloe's once-in-a-lifetime chance and she was going to reach for it. Snapping off a blade of grass, she bent over him and lightly ran the tip across his lips. John's green eyes opened a fraction. As she suspected, he was very sensitive to physical stimuli.

"Mmm, hello, sweet," he whispered sleepily.

Trusting as a babe, she thought with a snort. At least until he regained full wakefulness. "Had a hard night, did you?" she goaded him.

He rolled over onto his back. Several buttons on his white shirt were undone; Chloe got a very nice glimpse of taut, golden skin and a flash of a gold chain before it slid under his shirt.

Lacing his hands behind his head, he gazed up at her, eyes sparkling with humor. "I rode like hell to get here and you know it."

"Yes, I suppose. . . ." She glided the blade of grass across her lips in a seemingly unconscious action. His gaze fell instantly to her mouth.

Chloe knew the exact moment he realized it was the same blade that had just run across his own lips. His eyes darkened. She was thrilled. It was a very good sign. In fact, he seemed to have made a decision of some kind.

"Come lie down here with me." He spoke quietly as he held his hand out to her.

Chloe swallowed. She had wanted a reaction,

but not this strong of a reaction. "Wh-what for?"

John raised an eyebrow. "So we can discuss the English economy. What do you think 'what for'?"

"I—you—you can't be serious!"

"You were the one who said you wanted to improve your technique. Well, I'm in an 'improving' state of . . . mind." He patted the grass beside him.

The reprobate! That was not what she had said! She bit her lip. It *was* what she had said. . . .

However, it was not what she had meant! "That was not the entire package. If you recall, I proposed an agreement with you regarding marriage."

John had already decided to accept her proposal. Not that he was ready to tell her yet. He wanted to see if . . . There it was. Chloe's bow mouth pouted. It always did when she was forced to wait for an answer she might not like.

John smiled to himself, then observed something *different* about the facial expression. How was it that he had never noticed how lush and full her lips were? He stared at her mouth, captivated. Once the image of that enticing mouth was brought to his attention, he couldn't seem to let go of the sight. What would those soft, full lips feel like beneath his own?

Chloe's lips.

Opening for him, inviting him inside . . .

The unbidden image almost caused him to groan out loud. Fortunately, he was able to stop himself in time.

John blinked; he had never even thought of Chloe in that way before. Be that as it may, now that he had imagined it, he intended to investigate. Fully. The very idea suddenly made him hot. Red hot.

He would have to pounce, of course.

The situation called for nothing less. So John rubbed his chin as if still mulling her words over.

Chloe watched him, alert as a hawk.

Almost time, he told himself, *but not yet . . .*

Sensing John was close to telling her his answer, Chloe held her breath and leaned forward.

"I agree, then, Chloe; I'll marry you." *Now!*

Chloe released the breath she was holding, only to choke on it when his hands quickly came up to clasp her shoulders and tug her down on top of him.

"John!" She squirmed in his hold.

"First I want to have a taste of what I'll be getting." Strong arms encircled her, bringing her close. He dipped his head toward her.

Chloe gasped and tried to pull herself back. What had gotten into him? He had seemed so docile a minute ago. . . . Yes, like a sleepy-eyed tiger! she admitted ruefully. There was no way she could allow this! As far as it went, she must remain off-limits to him until after the ceremony.

For one thing, he was far too experienced for her even to think she could control him; she would never be able to stop him from taking her. For another, if he found out how inexperienced she was, he would be off to London in two shakes of a rake's tail.

As his lips descended she instantly put her hand up in front of her face to stop the contact.

"Whaf ar you doin?" he mumbled against her fingers, voice muffled.

"No, we cannot." She spoke succinctly so he would understand her.

His arms tightened around her waist. He turned his mouth slightly so he could speak. "What do you mean, we can't? Of course we can. You said yourself you—"

Chloe shook her head. "It is a—a tradition with the Fonbeaulard women. We never anticipate the marriage bed." That part was true, as far as she knew. It seemed like a good excuse, too.

"Tradition?" He looked as if he had never heard the word. "What do I care for some ridiculous tradition? Don't be silly, Chloe, let's—"

"No. I mean it, John. Not until after the wedding."

So that's what a frustrated rakehell looks like, she marveled. *Must be a new look for him.*

John was irritated—more than he cared to admit. What did she mean, *no*? "I don't understand this. You've already—"

Chloe swallowed. *Courage.* "That's different. You are to be my husband. According to the tradition, we have to wait." *There. That sounds perfectly reasonable.*

He observed her intently. "Hmm."

Was he getting suspicious? Chloe decided she needed to change his line of thinking.

"I mean, if you were anyone else, why then, it would be fine." She peeked up at him from under her lashes.

He seemed somewhat flabbergasted.

"Are you—are you saying you would be with someone else but not with me?" he choked out.

"Yes, of course. In fact, our agreement doesn't have to go into effect until we are actually wed, so . . ." She let the thought trail off meaningfully.

He just stared at her, dumbfounded.

This was a gamble, but one she had to take. "We could both be free, so to speak, until then. That is, if you wish it." She nodded enthusiastically to nettle him further.

It proved effective when that muscle in his jaw began working.

Please don't do it, John. Chloe waited for his answer on pins and needles. *Why doesn't he say something?*

"As far as I am concerned," he finally bit out through clenched teeth, "the agreement is in effect. We'll wait. *Both* of us."

It was all she could do not to hug him. Instead, she feigned a nonchalant attitude, shrugging. "Whatever you wish."

Her capitulation mollified him somewhat, even if he still seemed a bit disgruntled. "Does this mean we cannot even kiss till then?"

"Better not," she intoned. "I can never seem to stop myself with just a kiss, John," she confided to him.

The jade eyes narrowed.

Chapter Three

Maurice Bags a Viscount

"John and I are to be wed."

Stunned silence filled the room.

Chloe had decided to announce the momentous change that was about to take place in her life as soon as they were all gathered together in the drawing room after the evening meal. The "rope" had been looped about the rake's neck, and she surmised this was a good time to give it a yank.

John glared at her.

Well, what did he expect? She returned his look with a catlike smile. *Sorry, John, no reprieve for you.*

Grandmere had just finished commenting on the conditions in France, saying that nothing had been the same since the Parisian mobs had pulled that red bonnet over the ears of Louis. At Chloe's announcement, she sat back in her chair, her hand coming to her throat in a gesture of shock.

Apparently the Terror could not hold a candle to this bit of news.

Deiter grunted and Schnapps showed a tooth.

Maurice was the first to recover. Eyes gleaming with an unnamed satisfaction, he gave his nephew a knowing look. "Ho ho!" John shifted in his seat, refusing to meet his uncle's eye. He seemed to take an unprecedented interest in the pastoral scene depicted on the wallpaper to his left.

Maurice began to hum the same tune he had earlier regarding the mouse and the cat.

"*Mon Dieu,* is this true, John?" Grandmere finally found her voice.

John leaned forward in his seat, elbows resting on his spread knees, hands linked together between. He'd best try to explain this. And he would . . . as soon as he figured it out for himself. How had Chloe managed it? He had been wondering that all afternoon.

"Well, you see, Countess—"

"You haven't!" Grandmere turned pale. "But you have only been back a few hours, John. *Mon Dieu,* tell me you haven't debauched her!"

The countess looked back and forth between the two of them. John seemed ill at ease, while Chloe looked like . . . like a mouse who had just swallowed a cat.

"In my village, men who take such liberties are tied to the side of a barn for four weeks." Deiter always had an anecdote involving the mysterious village in Germany where he supposedly grew up. The tales never seemed to make much sense, but Chloe thought they were deliciously lurid.

That was, when he managed to finish one without falling asleep.

"We are not talking of barns, Deiter; we are talking of our little Chloe being ruined!" The countess whipped out her lavender-scented lace handkerchief and began dabbing at her eyes. The handkerchief afforded her the shield she needed so she could flash a secret smile to Maurice.

Maurice covertly winked back at her.

John frowned. "No. If you just listen to me—"

"I think it is very romantic." Maurice shrugged in a typically Gallic manner. "It is spring, is it not? The season for *amour*."

John tried again. "This has nothing to do with—"

" . . . Such men are left without food or water," Deiter continued inexorably, his black eyes taking on a strange glint. They always glowed when he was getting to the fiendish part of the tale. "Soon they begin to howl at the moon—"

John rolled his eyes. "For God's sake, man, will you let me finish what—"

Seated on Deiter's lap, Schnapps began baying right on cue, lending atmosphere to his master's words.

John threw his hands up in the air. He turned to Chloe, who had started the whole mess.

She was sitting in her Chippendale chair, looking as innocent as a lamb. Except for those violet eyes. They were flashing with deviltry and something akin to satisfaction.

"Feel free to aid me at any time, Chloe," he said dryly.

"Oh no, I think you're doing spendidly, my lord." She gave him a gleeful grin.

Damn, but she is enjoying this. John rubbed the side of his forehead. Somehow he knew this was only the beginning.

He faced the countess again. "Chloe has asked me—"

"Chloe has asked you?" the countess echoed incredulously.

"You see, she feels . . . she feels . . ." John wasn't sure how to proceed.

"I feel, John?" Chloe prompted.

He leveled a menacing look at her. He couldn't just tell them about Chloe's proposal and their strange bargain.

Maurice frowned. "Are you saying you have not seduced her, my boy? *Mon Dieu!* How disappointing are the youth of today!"

"They begin to foam at the mouth. . . ." Dieter pierced John with his eyes, locking him in his sights. Schnapps growled low.

That was it. John stood and shouted to the room at large, instantly rendering everyone silent again. "*We are to be wed and there is the end to it*!"

It was all he intended to offer for an explanation. Let them piece it together in whatever fashion they wished.

Once again it was the marquis who recovered first. "Ah yes, we understand, John; you do not have to explain to us."

He narrowed his eyes. "What do you mean by that?"

Maurice only shook his finger at his nephew and began to hum the same tune again.

John faced Chloe. "What does he mean by that?"

Chloe shrugged her shoulders. John noted she had a very suspicious look on her face.

"When is the wedding to be?" Grandmere asked prosaically while returning her hankie to her pocket.

John noted that her eyes were suspiciously dry. It did not pass by the viscount that his uncle and the countess seemed to accept this match all too eagerly. In a moment of honesty, he admitted to himself that they were accepting for his sake, not Chloe's. It was painfully obvious that the chit could have anyone she wanted. Why she chose him—the most notorious rake in England—must be a puzzle to them all.

Yet they had accepted it.

Such acceptance spoke highly of the nature of the bond between the marquis and the countess. Added to the fact that the countess had always adored John and treated him like family. John's brow furrowed.

But as so often happened when John came upon a facet of emotional revelation, he immediately sought to squelch the troublesome concept.

Shield firmly back in place, he walked over to the Sheraton sideboard and idly poured himself a glass of Hock.

As he brought the drink to his lips, he happened to gaze into the wall mirror facing him. Chloe sat in profile to his view. The firelight reflected off her delicate features, gilding her red hair with highlights. Something about the scene struck him, and he found himself staring at her in the mirror while she was unaware of his perusal.

Who was this self-assured woman?

Oh, she was still his little Chloe, but she was something more now. . . .

Maurice interrupted his reflections. "Well, my boy, we have not heard from you; when is the wedding to be?"

John hesitated. The season was starting and he supposed it could wait until after that. It wasn't as if he were in any hurry to get married.

His gaze lifted to the mirror again. A spark from the fire illuminated Chloe's bountiful décolletage. The rake's sights riveted there. Chloe was beautifully formed, he realized. His hand would just cup . . .

"As soon as we are able," he found himself saying.

Chloe looked over at him in surprise. She had expected to have to battle him on this issue.

Realizing what he had said, he quickly amended, "That is, after the season, of course."

Chloe pursed her lips. *The reprobate!* If he thought she was going to let him harry off to London for months to do God knew what, well, he had better think that one over again. *Your days of being out and about are over, John. Over.*

She readied herself for a contest of wills but, surprisingly, Maurice came to her rescue.

He shuddered theatrically. "How well I remember the agony of waiting in my youth." Maurice was ever the Frenchman. And to a Frenchman what could be worse than the horror of delayed desire?

The countess raised her eyebrow. She couldn't recall the marquis in his younger years ever waiting . . . for anything. He had always been a most impetuous and daring lover. She wondered what the old fox was up to.

It was no secret that he had despaired of John ever marrying. Many times Maurice had mourned the fact that there would be no heir to their family, since he and John were all that was left of the Chavaneau line. Technically, John was not a Chavaneau, as Maurice's father had married John's grandmother, an English widow who had a little girl. That little girl was John's mother. Maurice was born of their union.

So while Maurice and John shared the same blood, it was not French blood. A fact Maurice had a tendency to ignore. Even though the marquis had English blood as well—indeed, he had inherited his marquis title from his English side—he was French through and through. Consequently, John had become a Chavaneau.

The countess also knew that Maurice viewed Chloe as if she were his own granddaughter. It had long been a hope of his that the two children would wed, uniting the families that had always had tremendous affection for each other. In view of Chloe's announcement, Maurice must be dancing on air.

So why was he so contained? She watched him closely.

"The men of my generation have never believed in putting off such things . . . too much time and the woman may change her mind. . . ." Maurice let his words drift off to indicate that any man would be foolish to take such a risk.

A smile played about the corners of the countess's lips. Now she knew exactly what the sly boots was about—he was concerned it was *John* who might change his mind. After all, the rake had never been predisposed to marriage before. The marquis wanted his nephew secured as soon as possible. Knowing Lord Sexton as well as she did, she couldn't blame Maurice. John was a lovely boy, but he *was* a scoundrel.

John, however, was too wily for his uncle's machinations. He had claimed he would marry Chloe and he intended to—at his own pace.

"Who said anything about waiting?" His low voice held more than a hint of suggestion.

"John!" The countess gasped in false outrage.

"You promised!" Chloe blurted out before she could stop herself.

All eyes focused on Chloe at this disclosure.

The jade ones looked plainly furious; the others were simply shocked.

Chloe supposed that a Lord of Sex who promised to wait was more than anyone would dare to imagine.

After a telling pause, everyone began speaking at once.

"*He* did?" That was Grandmere.

"I don't believe it!" Maurice wasn't sure to be angry or elated. On the one hand, it was Chloe they were speaking of; on the other, there was a certain standard to maintain when one was young and active.

"Tie him to the barn!" Deiter didn't really have an opinion, but he was always up for a little blood. That was, when he was up.

John closed his eyes, pinched the bridge of his nose with two fingers, and shook his head. Could this get worse?

"Sir Percival Cecil-Basil!" the butler announced in a deep tone right before a flamboyant, bedecked man came bouncing into the room, all cheery smiles and frilly lace.

John groaned. *It just got worse.*

"Hi-ho, everyone!" The heavy scent of eau de cologne preceded the droll voice.

"Sir Percy!" everyone called out in delight. Everyone, that was, except John.

"I have just seen Lady Hinchey and she remarked that you had taken yourself off to the country in some haste, Sexton. Naturally I had to come see for myself that nothing was amiss." He raised his lorgnette and peered at John, presumably looking for wear and tear.

"Lady Hinchey's?" Chloe narrowed her eyes. So that was where the rogue had been! She could just imagine what had tired him out. Chloe took a deep breath to still her jealousy, refusing to look at him.

Which was a shame, because if she had she would have noticed that Lord Sexton seemed slightly uncomfortable with the disclosure, although his overall demeanor was, as usual, unapologetic.

"You needn't have bothered, Percy," John intoned wryly, and he meant it in more ways than one.

"Yes, I see why you have left London in such a hurry—our Heart has returned!" He bent over Chloe, taking her hand to kiss it. She flushed becomingly, which somehow managed to irritate John.

"Do take a seat, Sir Percy. Would you like some refreshment?"

"Thank you, Countess, I believe I shall. It was a tiring journey." He waved his beringed hand in the air, seating himself with aplomb. "But I was overcome with worry for John, you see."

"He's fortunate to have such a friend as you. You will be staying for a visit, I hope?" The countess handed him a cup of warm chocolate.

"John and I look out for each other; we've always been the best of friends." He took a sip of the delectable drink, closing his eyes in appreciation. "I can stay for a while, yes."

John's nostrils flared. He sat fuming silently.

Years ago, out of the blue, the man had proclaimed himself John's best friend and that had been that. It had instantly become an accepted reality throughout the ton.

Why the man fancied himself his friend, John could never quite figure out, but wherever John went, Percy was soon to follow.

It was irritating in the extreme.

What was more, the man seemed to have an uncanny ability to know his whereabouts and dealings. He knew with whom he had slept and when, what scandals he had caused, what revelry he was pursuing.

It had been going on for years; John had long since given up trying to make sense of it.

It wouldn't be half so bad if Percy didn't get on his nerves so much!

The man was a self-proclaimed connoisseur of everything. Fashion, the arts, music, cuisine; if it was mentioned, he was the authority. His manner was always balanced on the edge of extreme boredom and provocative innuendo. Latin phrases dripped from his tongue at every opportunity.

He was flamboyant, gossipy, and, well, silly. In short, he was a bird of startling plumage even amongst the flock of peacocks known as the upper crust. In recent years, he seemed to become almost obsessed with fashion and appearances, delving into pursuits deemed frivolous even by John's standards.

Yet both the countess and Chloe adored Sir Percival Cecil-Basil.

All of the ton adored him. He was welcomed into the best homes and he made it his business to know what was going on *in* those homes. By his decree, his close friends called him Sir Percy or just Percy as the name Cecil-Basil was a tongue twister best reserved, in his words, "for the uninformed and the lesser classes."

"So, when are you coming to town, Countess? We miss you dreadfully." Percy was ever the flatterer. In this case, he was sincere, though.

The countess smiled. "Not for some time, it

appears. But we have some exciting news to tell, and you shall be the first to hear it, dear Percy!"

Ah, the two magical ingredients of interest to the fop: gossip and being the first one to hear it. John smirked as he watched Percy lean forward eagerly in his chair.

"Do tell, sweet lady. I am all ears."

John closed his eyes and leaned back in his seat. This was going to be a trying night; he could tell.

"Chloe and John are to be wed!" The countess beamed.

"Oh, that." Percy sat back.

"You don't seemed surprised," Maurice said, surprised.

"Why should I be?"

John opened one eye. "Why aren't you?"

"*Res ipsa loquitur.*" John cringed at the Latin phrase. "The thing speaks for itself, my dear man."

"Really." John raised an eyebrow. It seemed the anticipated event of his own wedding was news only to himself!

"Quite so. Congratulations, dear, sweet Chloe, although maybe I ought to give you my sympathies." Pale blue eyes gleaming, he smiled into his cup, irking Lord Sexton. "When is the blessed event to take place? I shall be the groomsman, naturally."

John didn't know which vexed him more, the idea that Percy wasn't surprised by his upcoming nuptials or the fact that he had just named himself his groomsman!

"I'm sure whenever it is, you shall be the first to know," John said sarcastically. "Kindly inform me, would you?"

His irony apparently went over Sir Percy's powdered head.

"Will do, good fellow," he replied seriously.

Chloe stifled a chuckle as John's cheekbones deepened in color—a sure sign he was put out.

Maurice placed his cup and saucer on a nearby table. "We haven't seen you about for a while, Sir Percy; where have you been keeping yourself?"

Percy threw his hands up in the air. It was the moment he had been waiting for—carte blanche to gossip. "Oh, I have been here and there and everywhere! It has been an *annus mirabilis*, a wonderful year. In fact, I have just returned from Lord Blankford's. He claims to have heard the most interesting pianist on a recent trip to Vienna—it was at Baron von Swieten's; remember him John?"

John opened his mouth to reply, but as usual Percy did not wait for him to answer.

"He claims the fellow will go someplace, although he said he was quite grim in appearance. I daresay Blankford claims the man had a head shaped like a bullet. . . ." He trailed off to gaze keenly at Deiter, who was sleeping in his chair.

Everyone's sights followed his gaze. *Perhaps bullet-shaped heads indicated a latent musical talent?* 'Twas an interesting theory.

The German man let loose a huge snore.

John's lips twitched.

Chloe looked up and their eyes met, each pair brimming with laughter.

"What was the man's name?" Maurice inquired.

"He is a disciple of Haydn . . . let me see. . . ." Percy tapped his chin. "I believe it was Beethaurel. Yes, that was it! Ludwig van Beethaurel."

"Ludwig?" Chloe crinkled her nose. "I should hate to be called Ludwig."

John leaned over and playfully tickled her arm.

"What other news do you have, Sir Percy?" Grandmere was obviously hoping for some information about the goings-on in her homeland.

"I'm afraid the stories circulating about France, madam, are not very encouraging. The Terror continues and more go to their deaths every day. Last I have heard, the Countess Zambeau was the latest victim. They say she put rouge on her face on her way to the guillotine." He shook his head sadly. "Who could ever find fault with a woman that so valued fashion?"

"Zu-Zu?" The countess's eyes filled with tears. "Not Zu-Zu." She sniffed into her handkerchief.

Chloe was stunned at Grandmere's behavior. The woman had been an impossible thorn in her grandmother's side for years. "You have always called her a bitch, Grandmere!"

The countess dabbed at her eyes. "Yes, but she was a *glorious* bitch."

"De mortuis nil nisi bonum. Of the dead say nothing but good," Percy added solemnly.

Maurice exhaled heavily. "Has the Black Rose made any appearances lately?"

The Black Rose had made his first showing in France almost two months ago. The man had already had something of a reputation before that time in various skirmishes and endeavors, although his identity remained a secret.

In the past few months, he had miraculously and single-handedly rescued many an aristocrat's neck from the guillotine while still managing to remain one step ahead of the French authorities. The rumor was that he never appeared as the same person twice, donning expert disguises to cover his tracks. It was assumed he was an expatriated aristocrat himself, although no one knew for sure.

"I haven't heard," Percy answered Maurice. "However, I have written a poem about him—would you like to hear it?"

John winced. Percy was terrible at poetry.

The man stood in the center of the room as if he were about to recite Shakespeare. And in his mind he was.

"They seek him high, they seek him low;
The proletariat wonder where he could go;
Near or far, where can anyone suppose . . .
Is that blasted, evasive Rose!"

Everyone in the room applauded energetically at the amusing rhyme. John rolled his eyes.

"I'm so sorry about Zu-Zu, Countess." Percy placed a consoling hand on her arm.

"What do these monsters want?" Grandmere threw down her hankie. "What do they hope to gain by this madness?"

"Liberty, equality, fraternity," John intoned the motto of the revolutionists.

"And I suppose you agree with them, John?" the countess challenged him.

"I do . . . in theory. Not in their practice, though."

It was no surprise to Chloe that John felt this

way. His entire life had been one of rebellion against convention and morality.

Sir Percy gazed at John thoughtfully. "How like Don Giavanni you are, Sexton . . . laughing in the face of authority and flaunting society's mores." He picked up his lorgnette and peered at him through it. "I say, you make for a stunning study, my man."

"Especially since he seems to have no real convictions," Chloe added provokingly.

John's well-shaped lips lifted. "I work hard at that, Chloe-kit."

A line marred her forehead as she thought about his statement.

"Wonderful wit!" Percy gleefully chortled. "The man's one conviction is to have *no* convictions!"

Maurice snorted. "What am I to do with you, John?" He wagged his finger at his nephew.

Chloe was pondering the same.

A flock of thrush flew out of the glade.

Captivated as she was by the sight, Chloe's hand skipped across the page as she attempted to capture the scene on her sketchpad.

Hours ago, she had set out on her mare, Nettie, in search of a suitable site.

She had come upon this secluded spot rather

quickly. Percy's revelation last night had disturbed her. Chloe needed to think, and sketching often helped her to sort her thoughts out.

The sorting and drawing had been going on for some time.

It wasn't so much that she needed to think as that she needed *not* to think. Of John and Lady Hinchey.

He hadn't been unfaithful to her. There had never been any kind of understanding or commitment between them of that nature.

Yet it still pained her deeply. She was taking a terrible risk here, she knew. She was about to place all of her trust in him. A known and admitted rake—who was she kidding? The most notorious rake in England. What was she going to do if he didn't . . .

Her horse nudged her shoulder, interrupting her troubled thoughts.

"Not now, Nettie; I'm busy," she mumbled distractedly to her mare over her shoulder.

The vibration of a deep answering voice skittered down her neck, causing her to jump. "Nettie wandered back to the stable hours ago."

She scrambled around and looked up from her seat on the ground. The subject of her turmoil sat complacently before her on his stallion. "You startled me!"

"Did I?"

He looked far too innocent. "What are you doing here?" she asked suspiciously.

"I'm counting the leaves on the trees. "He exhaled gustily. "Obviously I'm looking for you. Did it ever occur to you that it might worry . . . people . . . if your horse returned without you?"

Chloe suddenly felt much better. "People" translated into *him*. John never liked to admit how much he worried over her. Even if everyone else knew it.

"Don't be silly; she always returns by herself. You know Nettie cannot go more than an hour without her feed. Why, she always escapes back at the first opportunity."

True. The mere hint of something to eat sent the lackadaisical horse into a galloping frenzy. It was the only time John could recall seeing the mare move faster than a snail's pace.

His answer was a noncommittal "Hmm."

Chloe went back to sketching, hoping he would take the hint and leave.

He didn't. She heard him dismount behind her.

Joining her on the grass, he lay on his side next to where she sat with her sketchpad in her lap. He was silent for several minutes. Chloe continued to draw.

Finally he spoke. "Why did you come out here?"

She glanced at him; his head was resting on the perch of his bent hand. Chloe sighed. He was too clever by half. And she was not about to answer him.

She put down her drawing. A gentle breeze lifted a strand of her hair that had come loose from her chignon. The long tendril whispered past John's cheek.

Chloe viewed their surroundings. "It's so beautiful out here."

But John wasn't paying any attention to the land. He caught the strand of red hair and wrapped it around his finger. Examining the fine texture, he marveled at its silken feel before murmuring, "Yes, it is."

Chloe swallowed and purposefully watched the horizon. "This will all soon be yours, John."

There was a long pause.

"Will it?" he asked quietly.

She still refused to look at him. "Nonetheless, I expect you to consult with me, should—should you seek to change anything, Lord Sexton."

"Chloe."

She turned slowly and looked down at him. For an instant she could have sworn there was a flash of pain in his eyes. The expression was gone so quickly she convinced herself she was mistaken.

"Yes?" she acknowledged him haltingly.

His other hand came up to stroke the curve of her cheek. "I have made you a bargain, as you have me. We have never broken our words to one another, have we?"

She shook her head no.

The stroke became a caress.

"Then you need not worry; I will always consult with you."

He was telling her he would stick to their bargain. "You—you promise, John?"

"Yes," he whispered.

The hand that was caressing her cheek moved to the back of her neck, smoothly bringing her down to him. His beautiful green eyes darkened. Chloe almost fell into them. Almost. She pulled herself back in the nick of time.

It took a moment for her head to clear. *He is dangerous*.

"You snork-slug! You promised something else as well," she admonished him.

A dimple curved his cheek. "What was that, Chloe-monkey?"

Chloe stood up, briskly brushing her skirts off. "You said you would wait," she reminded him pointedly.

"Am I not?"

"What?"

A devilish smile inched across his handsome

face, crinkling the corners of his eyes. He was the picture of pure seduction. "Waiting." He spoke the word as if it were something else entirely.

And he was teasing her terribly. She grabbed a handful of grass, ripping it up by its roots to hurl in his face.

He laughed. "You have always been easy to provoke, Chloe." He stood up, towering over her. "Should prove interesting in so many ways . . ."

Chloe blushed.

She couldn't help it.

A low chuckle reached her as he went to mount his horse. Bending over the saddle, he reached out a hand to her. Reluctantly, she took it.

"Use the stirrup," he instructed her, removing his own foot from it.

Expecting him to swing her on the back of his mount as he had often done in the past, she complied. He surprised her by swinging her up and pulling her across his lap in front. His arms securely encircled her.

"John!" She struggled in his protective embrace.

"Easy, sweet. I'm just taking you home."

Then why did his voice still have that hint of seduction in it? *Were his teeth nibbling on her earlobe*? Chloe froze in his lap.

It was at that point she realized he was going to have to marry her right away. For it wouldn't be long before he either saw through her ruse to her inexperience or the rogue seduced her.

"Now which way was home?" His mouth teased at her ear. Hot breath skittered down the side of her neck, leaving tingles in its wake. "Guess I'll have to take my chances and hope I find the way . . . eventually."

Chloe steeled herself for a long, torturous ride.

By the time they arrived back at the house—the trip taking much longer than it should have—Chloe was convinced she was right.

How to accomplish the deed swiftly was the problem.

Once again, it was Maurice who came to her rescue.

Apparently the marquis decided to take himself on a viscount hunt. That very day, he announced to John that he had procured a special license for them; they could be wed immediately. In fact, he told them the countess was already making the arrangements.

Lord John had been bagged.

Chapter Four
The Absurdity Begins

The marriage was to take place just before noon today on the estate.

At least, that was according to Sir Percy, who had diligently informed John late last evening of the time, place, and date of his own wedding.

John had no doubt whatsoever that the information was accurate, considering its impeccable source.

He fumed silently as he gazed out his bedroom window to the grounds below. The thought that this would soon no longer be his bedroom briefly crossed his mind.

His would be the master suite, with all the responsibility such accommodations entailed.

His nostrils flared.

It was not that he objected to wedding Chloe. In truth, now that he had gotten used to the idea, it sat rather well with him. What perturbed him was the speed with which everyone was moving to make sure it became a reality.

Yesterday, when he had ridden up to the house with Chloe, Maurice had been waiting for them. His uncle had taken one look at the way he had been cuddling Chloe on his lap, and delivered an ultimatum in the form of a very pointed stare.

The silent message he sent was clear: *Get your name on her before you cause a scandal.*

Ordinarily, his uncle had a tendency to overlook infamy. In this case, however, he was drawing the line.

Right across John's . . . foot.

At the time, John had acknowledged the challenge with a quirk of his eyebrow. He made especially sure to lower Chloe to the steps extremely slowly.

That was when Maurice had informed his nephew of the special license. Saying nothing, John had simply turned his horse toward the stables. It was a calculated stance, neither assenting nor dissenting.

Despite being irked that his uncle sought to take matters into his own hands, John recognized the simple truth. Regardless of what anyone believed, he was going to marry Chloe. If it made his uncle feel better to conclude he was controlling the situation, then so what? The fact of the matter was that John never did anything unless it was his own *desire*.

Wedding Chloe had become a desire.

Desire led to certain other thoughts. His imagination began to work on the evening's possibilities. . . .

On the drive below him, a coach and four suddenly careened around the bend on two wheels, narrowly missing a servant girl.

John swore under his breath. It was the fifth time today they had almost lost a member of the staff to the traffic.

Somehow, word of his marriage had gotten out.

He could just imagine what was being bandied about. *Did you hear? The infamous Lord of Sex is getting married! What delicious thing could have precipitated such an unlikely event?*

Yes, that was what they were saying.

The proof was in the pudding.

Since early this morning, coaches, hacks, landaus, phaetons, gigs, barouches, and curricles had been making a demented dash for *Chacun à Son Goût*. The ton was descending in all its mad glory.

The unannounced arrival of "the upper ten thousand" had sent the household into a frenzy of activity.

Excuses for their unannounced, uninvited, unwelcome appearances—which he had overheard before making himself scarce—had been laughable:

We were in the area and we thought we'd stop in for a quick visit.

Our coachman lost his way; might we impose on you for a few days?

Heard you were ill, Countess, and came immediately. . . .

The ridiculous pretenses went on and on.

In the midst of all this, the countess had declared a Fonbeaulard custom and taken herself off to the conservatory garden, claiming she had to make an herbal posy for her granddaughter's wedding. Some nonsense about the herbs ensuring a virile groom.

As if he needed that.

Poor Chloe had been pressed into service and was valiantly trying to find rooms for everyone while fielding impertinent questions about their intimate relationship. Some had even extended their condolences.

Good-naturedly, John had offered to rescue her by stealing her off to Gretna Green so they could "go over the anvil."

Chloe had quipped that the Lord of Sex had only himself to blame for the furor the news caused—if his reputation hadn't been so noteworthy, none of this would have occurred. Therefore, she admonished with a shake of her finger and a reluctant grin, he'd best own up to the notoriety.

She had the right of it there, he supposed.

Besides, she had looked rather adorable rushing around the house, blowing the hair off her forehead, muttering under her breath in French. His sensuous lips twitched. It wouldn't be long before the hoyden took herself off to the back of her armoire to vent steam.

He couldn't count the number of times in the past he had gone searching for her, only to pass by the commodious piece of furniture, and hear French invectives issuing forth from behind the wooden panel.

Apparently the Fonbeaulard women did not air their dissatisfactions to the outside world.

They preferred to vent spleen on mahogany. Naturally, one would overlook a piece of furniture that had a disgruntled voice spewing from inside it! He chuckled. Chloe could be so enchanting—

A different voice reached him from the corridor outside his room. It was the noncommittal grunt of Deiter. This was not so enchanting.

". . . Do not tell me you intend to appear at the wedding dressed entirely in black!"

That disdainful voice plagued his nightmares; it belonged to Sir Percy.

"It is just not done, my man!"

"It is acceptable," Deiter grumbled.

A shriek of dismay issued forth.

John winced. He could almost hear Percy clutch the wall for support.

"Nothing is so unacceptable as something that is simply acceptable!" A *tsk-tsk* followed. "Where is your sense of style? 'T won't do!"

John rolled his eyes. He almost felt sympathy for Deiter; Percy had fixed his fashion sights on him.

"What is wrong with clothes I wear?" The fierce voice held a snarl, the Germanic accent heavier than usual. Schnapps echoed the snarl. In German. *Voof!*

Percy was undaunted by the ranks. "Well! Don't take my opinion! Who am I? I only happen to have the ear of the king."

A skeptical snort followed this declaration. "Your king suffers from bouts of madness."

There was a pause. John supposed one couldn't argue with that. ". . . Very well, let us ask Lord Sexton's opinion on the matter. . . ."

John's eyes widened. *Bother it!*

The voices got closer.

Oh, no, you don't. John scanned the room for a means of escape. He had no intention of being waylaid by the two of them.

Fortunately, he was an expert at escaping bedrooms. Half the husbands of the ton knew that.

Under the bed? No, too obvious.

In the wardrobe? Could be risky.

Behind the curtains? Lacked finesse.

The balcony. Unlatching the doors, he dashed outside on the ledge, reclosing them just as the door to his room swung open. Sir Percy never knocked, considering it his God-given right to enter at will.

"John!" Footsteps traversed the room.

Lord Sexton flattened himself against the outside wall. "I say, I could have sworn I saw him come in here earlier."

More footsteps.

"Well, doesn't matter . . . look here, Deiter; this is what I mean."

John heard the sound of his wardrobe being opened. He grinned, showing a flash of white teeth. *Just as I surmised—too risky.*

Percy began rummaging through the contents. "Perfect! Try this on."

On guard, John carefully peered around the

corner through the glass doors. The sight that confronted him made him grind his teeth. *That's my favorite waistcoat, damn it!*

Deiter reluctantly tried on the gold satin garment. The shoulders swam on him and the waist wouldn't button.

"Here; allow me." Percy went to stand in front of the German. Taking both sides of the waistcoat in his hands, he gave a sharp tug, quickly buttoning the bottom button before Deiter could exhale.

Even out on the balcony, John heard the sharp ripping sound.

It appeared the back stitches had liberated themselves from the tyranny of the seams.

John's palm slammed silently against the brick masonry.

"Now see what we have here . . ." Percy, overlooking the rents in the back of the garment, turned Deiter toward the carved mirror on the wall.

Deiter stared at himself in the mirror, giving a circumspect grunt.

"Do you not see the difference?" Percy circled his hand in the air with a flourish. "Notice how the color brings out the highlights in your hair."

Highlights? John shook his head to clear it. *What flummery!* The man's hair was pitch black.

Deiter lifted a bushy brow as he inspected his image.

"And see how the tone gives you a forceful presence? Gold is, as everyone knows, the monetary standard that upholds nations!"

John's eyes crossed. *Give me strength.*

Stranger still, as Deiter continued to examine his reflection, the somber man began to actually preen.

Percy patted his shoulders. "*Ars gratia artis,*" he intoned solemnly. "Art for art's sake."

John had to stifle his laughter.

The two of them left shortly after the lofty proclamation. With his waistcoat.

The odd part of it was that John could have sworn that he saw a hint of a secret smile on Percy's face right before he closed the door.

He also could have sworn the man looked straight toward the balcony when he did it.

John stood in front of the armoire in Chloe's room.

Muffled words were wafting through the wood.

". . . *cherchez* Chloe! What do they think—I have nothing to do on my wedding day but see to their comforts? Is it my fault they are bored? So they come here! *Faute de mieux!* For want of something better! Are we an hors d'oeuvre for their insatiable curiosity? *Non!*"

The corner of John's sensual mouth curved into a deep groove. Just as he had suspected, Chloe was in a fine lather.

He opened the cabinet door and rested against the jamb. Arms folded over his chest, he waited.

A few seconds later Chloe's head poked through the clothes, red hair mussed.

"How did you know I was in here?" she asked seriously.

He quirked his brow. "Lucky guess," he intoned dryly.

Chloe was still cross from the unexpected arrival of so many demanding guests, several of whom she had never seen before. She did not have time for this! She needed to concentrate on what she was going to do about tonight.

Her wedding night.

How was she going to get around her virgin state? There was no hope that John wouldn't notice. The man had a tendency to pay attention to minute details, especially when those details had to do with women! There wasn't a chance he would overlook the small . . . inconvenience.

A line furrowed the center of her smooth forehead. She had to come up with a plan and quickly!

Her heart hammered in her chest as she

gazed up at him. John was put together like a work of art . . . what would it be like to touch him as she had always wanted to?

She squelched the image immediately; she didn't have time now to fantasize, either.

Anyway, her fantasies were about to become a reality. She needed a plan!

"What do you want?"

As if he read her libidinous thoughts, he rejoined silkily, "Go and find your grandmother, sweet."

"What for?"

"Tell her not to put too many herbs in the bouquet . . . we won't be needing them." The captivating green eyes sparkled with blatant implication. All sexual.

Chloe had never seen *that* suggestion on John's face.

Oh, well. Add it to the growing list of intriguing expressions he had been sending her way lately.

All things considered, she supposed she had asked for it. More than asked for it.

She had fought for it.

Her palms got moist. She rubbed them on the front of her gown. She needed a plan! Inhaling deeply, she gathered her frayed nerves. It was just a first night—nothing to be alarmed about.

The one positive aspect of her intended's vast experience was that he would make it as enjoyable for her as he could.

In that regard, she had complete confidence in John. His capabilities were legendary.

The other little matter, though, needed some tending.

How do I stop him from discovering it?

Getting him inebriated was out of the question. John had an amazing capacity to hold his drink, and something told her he would not be persuaded to overimbibe today.

Finding Grandmere might not be such a bad idea; perhaps she could lure her into divulging some boudoir secrets that would allow Chloe to come up with a workable plan.

She would have to be extremely careful; Grandmere must not suspect her real reason for seeking such advice. The countess might not readily accept that her granddaughter was trying to hide from her new husband the fact that she was untouched. Chloe had no intentions of explaining the strange business.

Course of action settled, she elected to hide her present nervousness with brashness. She placed her hands on her hips. "You might help with the guests, John, instead of standing there like a stallion on loan to stud!"

His jaw dropped. He couldn't believe his ears. "*Chloe.*"

Chloe squirmed out from under a pile of clothes and pushed past the dumbstruck viscount. "I'm very busy, John; I don't have time for this." She neglected to clarify exactly what "this" was.

"The ceremony is in two hours." She pointed a stern finger at him as she headed out the door. "I expect you to be ready and . . . and . . . prepared."

With those cryptic words, she disappeared from view.

John watched her leave with a knowing glint in his eyes. He idly wondered if she had any idea how *prepared* a stallion he could be.

Chloe found her grandmother in the conservatory.

It was a truly beautiful room and Chloe's favorite. No matter the weather outside, plants and flowers bloomed profusely inside the glass walls of this airy space.

Her grandmother was something of an amateur perfumer, having been intrigued from an early age by the stimulating and enticing powers assigned to the efflorescence of plants. The lands around her ancestral estate flourished with these plantings, and the family had sponsored their own perfumery for ages.

Here in England, she grew many aromatic varieties; roses, true myrtle, jasmine, and, of course, French lavender.

The countess also took great pleasure in concocting fragrant oils for the skin and bath. Scores of the little odd-shaped bottles lined the stone floor of the room.

Chloe was especially fond of a scent Grandmere had made just for her, containing jasmine, tuberose, and lilac oil, with a hint of exotic spice. Apparently John was fond of it too, for he had commented on it on more than one occasion.

"Grandmere, I need to speak with you."

The countess looked up from the lovely herbal posy she was fashioning for her granddaughter. "What is it, *ma petite?*"

Chloe bit her lip. How to start? "Well . . . it's about . . . you see . . . tonight."

Grandmere put down the bouquet, smiling gently at her. "You are worried about the wedding night, my angel?"

Chloe started to shake her head no; the countess's arm coming around her shoulders stopped her.

"There is nothing to fear. You will be just fine. I am positive John will know exactly what to do."

She winked at her granddaughter. "Even if he is not French."

"But—"

"Do you think I would entrust you to just anyone? *Non,* you will see; John has always taken care of his Chloe and he will tonight—listen to your Grandmere. Of this I am certain."

"I'm not sure what—"

"He will lead you; follow his direction."

She intended to. This was very nice but it was not helping her with her problem. "How shall I . . . handle him, Grandmere? Everyone knows he goes his own way."

"Ah. It is an age-old problem, this." The countess nodded sagely. "The woman must be in control, of course."

Now we are getting somewhere. Grandmere was extremely knowledgeable in the ways of men. "And how do I do that?" she asked candidly.

"You must give him everything," the countess stated with the conviction of the femme fatale.

"*Everything*?" That sounded dangerous.

"Everything." The older woman grinned slowly. "But . . ."

"But what?" Chloe leaned in to get this priceless bit of advice.

"You must let him *think* you are holding something back."

She considered the wisdom in this. "What good would that do?"

"It will drive him crazy! He will keep wondering what it is you are *not* giving him; and if he is a real man, he will always come back to claim what he believes should be his."

"Even though it does not exist?"

"*Mais oui.* The man seeks to conquer the woman—to make her his. By letting him think he hasn't fully done so, you are engaging him in a contest of wills. Men adore challenges—it keeps them lively."

Chloe wasn't convinced. Furthermore, John seemed lively enough as it was. "Are you sure about this?"

"*Oui!* Very sure."

Hmmm. "Is—is this what you do with Maurice?"

"Yes! For years, every time he asks me to marry him, I refuse. *C'est ça,* he is in the palm of my hand." The countess gestured with her fingers.

Chloe cocked her head to the side as she contemplated the prudence of such an approach. "It could be risky."

"Anything worthwhile is risky."

"I suppose . . ."

"Don't worry too much, dear; they never seem

to catch on. Men often have to be hit over the head simply to see what is in front of them. Such is their nature."

Chloe blinked as the solution became crystal clear. *Of course!* Why hadn't she seen it earlier? It was brilliant. John would never know!

"Oh, Grandmere, thank you so much!" She hugged her grandmother to her, then ran excitedly from the room.

The countess smiled fondly after the girl before returning to the posy.

Well hidden and seated behind a dense array of plants, Maurice Chavaneau raised his brows.

He had been hiding from the guests in the conservatory.

The soothing lap of the water fountain combined with the lush surroundings had lulled him to sleep long before the countess had even entered the room.

Their conversation had awakened him.

A slow grin spread its way across his still-handsome face.

Ho-ho!

John had to fight his way to the front of the room. The small chapel on the grounds was filled to overflowing. One man had rudely elbowed him in the side, saying, "Too bad, old chap! We were here first! Go back and find your own place."

John had pierced the man with a deadly look. "Yes, but *I'm* getting married here . . . old chap."

The man had turned beet red. "Sorry," he mumbled.

John forged ahead. This was impossible! Perhaps one good thing to come of it would be that Percy wouldn't be able to—*Blast!*

There he was. Right at the front.

Along with Maurice and the countess and—

He misstepped.

Deiter was wearing John's gold waistcoat with a purple sash. Even Schnapps had a little silver hat tied to his ugly head. The small dog glared at the guests, his one tooth showing.

It was the only time John could recall being in total agreement with the sour-faced pup.

His sights scanned the rest of the area at the front of the chapel. There she was. His bride.

Something in his chest kicked. She looked beautiful.

Dressed in a simple gown of white batiste, she was the most exquisite thing he had ever seen. A floral headdress of tiny yellow rosebuds wreathed her head.

He came abreast of her and took her small

hands in his. "You look lovely, sweet." His finger lightly trailed her soft cheek. "Much too faultless for the likes of me."

Chloe smiled up at him, all the happiness she felt shining in her eyes. "On the contrary, John, it is you who are the picture of elegance."

And he was, from his gray jacket and knee breeches ending in leather top boots to his silver waistcoat and white silk shirt. She had never seen him so handsome. A thin black ribbon tied his golden hair to the back of his neck in a queue.

It seemed he wanted to say something else to her, but at that moment the parson ushered them to their places. Just as John signaled the man to begin, Percy quipped in a loud voice, "*Morituri te salutamus!* We who are about to die salute you!"

Everyone burst out laughing. Even Chloe had to suppress a snicker.

John looked over his shoulder at his groomsman, shooting him a fulminating glare.

The service began. Every now and then John gazed down at Chloe out of the corner of his eye. For some reason he wanted to remember the way she looked when she spoke her vows, becoming his wife.

My wife.

That something in his chest kicked again. He valiantly suppressed it.

The ceremony was over before he knew it; he was instructed he may kiss his bride. He bent down and, cognizant of the avid onlookers, chose simply to brush his lips across her forehead.

Chloe gave him a puzzled look. He squeezed her hand, discreetly shaking his head. When he kissed her for the first time he did not want an audience. She seemed to get his silent message, for she lightly squeezed his hand back.

Then they were walking down the aisle to hearty congratulations and some very off-color remarks.

The countess was sniffling, and Deiter appeared almost nonthreatening.

"It is romantic, is it not?" Maurice sighed.

"Sink me!" Percy exclaimed. "It's just occurred to me that heart, as in Miss Chloe *Heart*, has just wed sex, as in *Sexton!* What do you make of that? How apropos!"

Maurice chuckled.

"One can only wonder what will come of it." Sir Percy planted the question that would soon be in everyone's mind.

Heart and "Sex." What *would* come of it?

The frenzied wagering began before the guests had even left the chapel.

* * *

The meal following the wedding, often referred to as the *déjeuner,* or breakfast, despite the midday hour, commenced. The hall was full to overflowing, and Chloe marveled that the staff had been able to prepare such a lavish feast for so many in such a short time. She made a mental note to mention to John that they should reward their service with something special.

She watched her husband seated next her from beneath her lashes. Chloe could hardly believe it was a fait accompli. Lord John was finally hers.

Well, not hers completely, but soon enough.

Her cheeks deepened in color. How on earth was she to pretend she wanted lessons from him?

Best not to dwell on that just yet. She was going to need every ounce of courage she possessed to proceed with her plan. One last hurdle to get over today . . .

Sir Percival Cecil-Basil clinked the side of his crystal glass with a spoon, garnering everyone's attention. "A toast to the newlyweds!"

"Hear! Hear!" chorused the assemblage.

John pasted a stoic expression on his face. He had a feeling he knew what was coming.

"To the Lord of Sex"—several guffaws erupted in the room—"and his sweet bride; may they find happiness in the simple joy life has given them, a shared commitment." Percy captured John in his penetrating stare.

Surprised, John searched the man obliquely. How much did he know? With Percy one could never be sure.

Percy saluted them with his glass before bringing it to his lips, the other diners following suit.

"Thank you, Percy," John responded diplomatically. "That was very noble of you."

Percy waved John's words away. "No need to thank me, good fellow!" A shrewd grin spread over his lips. "The thing speaks for itself."

"Really," John intoned softly.

"Quite." Percy's attention was captured by Lady Moresby.

As the meal progressed a curious phenomenon seemed to descend upon John. The strangest thing happened. A sheen of sweat broke out across his brow. His palms became moist. A feeling of queasiness rose up from within him.

In fact, the more the knowledge came home to him that Chloe was now his *wife*, the stronger these symptoms became.

This was Chloe. His Chloe. He had never even kissed her before! At least not on the mouth—in that way.

What if he disappointed her?

Impossible.

He would never disappoint her.

But . . . what if she didn't like the way he . . . the things he . . . Could he do that with her?

This was Chloe. It mattered. . . .

He was going to be sick.

His hand trembled slightly as he snatched a goblet of wine off the table and downed it in one swallow. He needed time—time to get used to this.

John settled in for the longest, most prolonged meal of his life.

By midafternoon Chloe began giving her husband curious looks. It was customary for the bride and groom to have a "going away." While they hadn't had time to arrange one—indeed, with all the visitors it was more like a "coming in"—it was expected that the couple would take themselves *off* at the earliest opportunity.

At the very least they would retire to their chamber to celebrate their nuptials in private.

In disbelief, she watched her husband consume yet another piece of Portuguese cake. His fourth. He didn't seem at all inclined to leave the party. It was beginning to get embarrassing. Already she could see several people whispering to each other.

Whatever was the matter with him?

"John," she whispered to him.

"Mmm, yes, Chloe?" He snagged a passing footman, motioning the man to fill his plate with another serving of berry pie.

"Don't you think we should . . ." She wasn't sure how to finish.

He turned to her, jade eyes rounded. "What?" He swallowed. "What shouldn't we do? I mean, should we?" He closed his eyes and inwardly groaned. He sounded like a callow youth, for God's sake!

He took a deep breath. "Yes, Chloe, of course." Chloe smiled at him in a way she never had. His stomach flipped. "That is . . . after I have some of this interesting-looking"—*What is that stuff?*—"stuff," he finished lamely.

Chloe slumped in her chair.

She had never seen John eat so much. Perhaps he thought he needed strength to—She wouldn't even think it.

By the time they had finally wound their way upstairs it was almost evening.

At the top of the stairs, John suddenly announced his desire for an early evening bath and took off in the direction of his old rooms.

Chloe entered the master suite and sagged onto the enormous four-poster Elizabethan bed. Earlier in the day, she had prepared the room for the plan. Her sights took in the pitcher and basin strategically placed on the stand next to the bed.

Everything was in place.

All she had to do was wait for her errant husband to return.

John was behaving a bit peculiarly. She shrugged her shoulders and headed for the dressing room. Grandmere had given her an especially pretty nightrail for her wedding night.

Pity she had no intention of wearing it for very long.

Chapter Five
Chloe Gets More than Bargained For

He puked his guts up.

Half sprawled across the floor, clutching a chamber pot, John rested his damp forehead against the side of the bed. Closing his eyes, he waited to see if this latest bout of nausea was the last or if his stomach was going to do another roll and flip on him.

Taking deep, even breaths, he attempted to regain his usual state of well-being. What was the matter with him?

Ordinarily he'd point to the food as his source of discomfort, but Chef LaFaint was an extremely fastidious cook, and the feeling in the pit of his belly had come on before he had eaten. In fact, it had begun at the beginning of the meal. Right after Percy's toast.

Yes, the initial complaint had begun simultaneously with the words *shared commitment* and the realization that Chloe was, in fact, his wife.

From then on, the odd malady seemed to gather strength.

He took another deep breath. This very minute, Chloe was waiting for him down the hall in their bedroom. Waiting for him to perform.

For the first time in his life, John was apprehensive about the act of sex.

He rolled his shoulders to loosen some tension. It wasn't that he didn't want to. . . . And it wasn't that he couldn't. It was that—John banged his forehead against the edge of the mattress—this meant something to him, damn it!

Chloe was the only person to whom he had ever revealed himself. He trusted her; he took care of her. What would happen after they . . . ? Would the advent of a physical relationship affect their intimacy?

John snorted. That had to be the most bizarre question a man had ever asked himself! *Leave it to Chloe to put the thought in my mind.*

He rubbed his temples with two fingers. This was insanity. He was going to take his bath, put on his robe, and go to his wife. They would enjoy each other immensely, and *nothing* was going to change.

That decided, he stood up, making a resolute stride to his bureau. Grabbing his brush and tin of tooth powder, he yanked open the tin with a determined pull. Powder flew all over him. He closed his eyes and counted to ten.

In typical male fashion, he dabbed the moistened brush into the powder gathered in the well of his collarbone and commenced brushing his teeth.

That accomplished, he rinsed his mouth out with rose water and headed for the tub set before the fire. This was his second bath of the day. The servants had given him the oddest looks when he requested more hot water.

Well, now that they had done all that work, it was only right that he use it. He sank down into the water.

Grabbing a bar of soap, he began washing himself, his plan of action formulating. As soon as he finished his bath, he would go to her.

Right away. Immediately.

Perhaps he should rewash his hair first?

Yes, as long as he was in the bath, he might as well. He dunked his head under the water and began to scrub his head vigorously. That he had just washed his hair a few hours ago did not seem to register in his fogged brain.

It was an exceedingly long and thorough washing.

If the House of Lords could have been privy to the scene, they might have had a rousing debate regarding what Viscount Sexton actually thought he was cleansing.

Mission accomplished, John thought it might not be a bad idea to let the hot water relax some of his muscles, which suddenly seemed a little stiff and could surely do with a soak.

Stretching his tall frame out as best he could in the cramped confines, he leaned back and closed his eyes. The gold chain with its small charm nestled into place.

The draining aftereffects of his recent bout of sickness combined with the soothing warm water surrounding him caused him unwittingly to drop off to sleep.

When next he opened his eyes, the water was ice cold and the clock on the mantel said it was two hours later. At least his hair was dry.

He couldn't put it off any longer.

He was going to have to go to Chloe.

And he was going to have to tell her that they needed some more time. He wanted them to get used to the idea of being married to each other before they had intimate relations.

Mind made up, he donned his dark green brocade robe and made his way down the hall.

It never once occurred to him how strangely he was behaving, how at odds with his persona. He was one of the most notorious rakes in England; yet of the scores of women he had slept with, of the countless liaisons he had had, it was only the woman he had chosen to marry that he was hesitant to be intimate with.

All John knew was that he did not want to test Chloe's friendship. She was the one person in his life he had always protected. *Lose Chloe?* Nausea churned up his throat.

It was too much of a risk.

Where was he?

Chloe paced the length of the room in the frothy lace night rail, her long hair trailing down her back.

She had been walking back and forth for hours, her anxiety increasing with every step. Why hadn't he come? What was he doing? She wrung her hands with worry and indecision.

Perhaps she should go to his room to see what was keeping him. She bit her lip, thinking it over. Everything was prepared here, in this room. What if she went to check on him and he decided to . . . to *do* it right then? What would she say? *Excuse me, John, could you stop right there and move this down the hall?* She couldn't very well—

The door opened and closed softly.

Chloe held her breath and turned.

John stood by the entrance of the room, an enigmatic expression on his face.

He was wearing a green robe, and by the look of him, she supposed nothing else. His hair hung loose about his shoulders; firelight gilded the gleaming, silken mass. The slight vee in the front of the robe revealed a glimpse of taut golden skin and the flash of a gold chain beneath the garment.

Chloe's heart skipped a beat. She had never seen him look more handsome. Or more desirable.

They stared at each other for what seemed an eternity.

A spark of wood popped in the fireplace, breaking the spell they were under. They both spoke at once.

"I need to—"

"Do you—"

They both stopped.

Chloe laced her fingers together in an attempt to stop their shaking. "What, John?" she asked breathlessly.

He rubbed the back of his neck under the fall of his hair.

For an instant Chloe wondered what it would feel like if it were her hand doing the rubbing. She wanted to feel his hair just like that, let the strands slide through her fingers slowly. She wanted to kiss him in tiny nibbles around his hairline at the back of his neck. She wanted to bury her face in that clean hair that always had the scent of clover.

". . . so you see, it's just that I feel, that is . . ."

Chloe blinked. What was John saying? She had been so caught up in her fantasy that she had missed his last words.

"The thing is, Chloe, I think we should proceed with this slowly. You have to admit this all happened rather quickly and we haven't had time to . . ."

Oh, my God; John is having second thoughts! This wouldn't do at all! What if he decided it was a mistake to agree to the bargain and wanted an annulment? *Mon Dieu,* everything would have been for nothing!

Chloe panicked. She couldn't lose John, not after all of this! The course of her next action became crystal clear. There could be no waiting.

It was tonight or never!

Before she could stop herself, she launched herself at the unsuspecting viscount. Caught by surprise, John had no choice but to catch her as she wrapped her legs around his waist and grabbed his face between her small, determined hands.

For the first time in her life, Chloe pressed her lips against John's and kissed him for all she was worth.

John's mouth parted slightly in shock; his dazzling green eyes blinked in astonishment.

At first nothing happened.

Then it happened.

Like a volcano erupting, molten heat spread through his system, fired down through his arms, up his legs, straight to his groin. The overpowering sensation almost rocked him off his feet.

Of their own accord, his arms came around her like a vise and, without conscious thought, he kissed her back with every ounce of passion he possessed.

Which was a considerable amount.

Pressed against him, Chloe moaned against his fiery onslaught. The adversary appeared to be engaged. She tried to prepare herself for the sensual battle that was sure to follow.

He was hot, wild, and intense. The real John, she acknowledged to herself, exulting in her victory. His burning kisses made her almost mindless.

He tasted of everything she had imagined and so much more. The full impact of the Viscount Sexton was more than she bargained for!

Despite his earlier ruminations and firm decision about waiting, John could not seem to stop himself. The instant his mouth claimed hers, he knew this was going to be different. He felt it, tasted it, breathed it down to the core of his being.

Somewhere in the back of his mind, he realized he was behaving in a way completely foreign to his usual nature. He was not the conquering-hero type—he was more the artful seducer. Sophisticated, with a genuine flair for finesse.

However, it was not the voice of the accomplished rake that rasped hoarsely, *"I can't wait to make you mine"* in the little shell ear next to his marauding lips.

Nor was it the voice of a shy, naive girl who shivered and uttered back, "Yes, yes . . ." while breathlessly capturing his mouth again with her own.

Chloe's enthusiasm—more than a match for his own raging hunger—propelled John across the room toward the bed.

In fact, John was so overcome by the experience of having Chloe in his arms that he didn't even realize how unpolished her kisses were. He only knew that her artless response was sending him over the edge, interpreting her bearing as being caused by her own overwhelming excitement, which apparently matched his own.

In the course of all this, the tip of her sweet tongue began to tease at his mouth. John actually trembled. *Oh, Chloe . . .*

She tasted of the single most compelling thing that would ever appease his longing.

He groaned, drawing her inside his mouth even as he drew her down onto the bed.

From that moment on the viscount was lost to rational thought.

Which was a very good thing—considering what was about to happen to him.

While John was recklessly kissing her and unbuttoning the placket of her night rail with the expert touch garnered from his countless experiences in doing such tasks with ladies' garments, Chloe valiantly tried to maintain her sensibility.

In the wake of such a gale, it was not an easy task.

True, she had wanted John in such a state, had even dreamed of it on many an occasion, but somehow the reality was far different. For one thing, she never realized how . . . how . . . uncontrolled he could become; for another, she never thought he would immediately make her the same.

She took a deep breath in an attempt to find her resolve. It was of the utmost importance that she did not lose herself here; she must—had to—remain in control or all would be lost.

His scorching lips burned a trail down the side of her throat. Against her will, a small sound of pleasure escaped her lips. The utterance seemed to incite him further.

Perhaps if she ignited him still further, he would hurry even more.

Yes. That would be best. It was her only hope. She needed to make him as wild as she could while still maintaining her own restraint.

Her gaze went reassuringly to the nightstand beside the bed, where the porcelain pitcher had been strategically placed. It waited patiently, a sword of Damacles for the unsuspecting viscount.

Chloe bit her lip. She hoped Grandmere would forgive her; it was one of her favorite pieces.

Her concerns were interrupted as John's white teeth captured her earlobe with a sexy little tug. The action caused tingles to skirt down her neck and shoulder.

This was proving much more difficult than she had imagined! What if he swept her away with his lovemaking? Chloe closed her eyes and swallowed.

That she could not allow. Not this first time.

Thinking to speed him up, Chloe thrashed beneath him, untying the knot on the sash of his robe. It soon came undone and she tugged the garment off his shoulders, tossing it onto the floor next to the bed.

When her hands encountered the bare expanse of his backside, Chloe realized she was right. John hadn't worn anything underneath.

Curiosity getting the better of her, she tried to peer over his shoulder to get a glimpse of the treasures she had uncovered. She had never seen a naked man before, and rumor had it that John was exceptionally well endowed *everywhere.*

Unfortunately, she didn't get the chance, for, with her bold act, the man gave a low growl of desire deep in his throat, then immediately yanked her night rail right over her head, coming down upon her full-length.

The touch of all that Sexton skin was enough to give her pause. The touch of the flat of his hands skimming down her body was enough to leave her breathless.

This is John. Touching her. Loving her.

She gasped out his name on a wave of longing.

"Chloe . . . Chloe . . ." he panted brokenly, his hot breath fanning her.

His powerful thighs wedged tight between her own, and she felt something hard and scorching pressing against her lower belly. The tips of his fingers scored her back, and she knew she would not be able to take much more without surrendering herself completely to the sensual web he seemed determined to weave about her.

Irrationally, his considerate lovemaking was irritating her. As if she needed any more incentive!

She was actually shaking with her desire and cursed the fact that she couldn't let herself enjoy it more. God knew after what the scoundrel had put her through, she deserved a little enjoyment!

But that would have to come later.

Rogues—she sighed—must be dealt with very delicately, lest they champ at the bit. She purposely rubbed against him, giving what she deemed an appropriate sound for the circumstances.

John paused for a second to give her a puzzled look, his disheveled golden hair falling across his forehead in an altogether enticing picture.

Hmm. Perhaps I did sound a tad like a yipping pup. She quickly lowered the tone and tried again.

It worked. He answered her with his own gravelly moan, his mouth instantly covering her own.

Despite her feelings for John, her desire, and her resolve, when John began to probe her feminine core gently with the tip of his erection, Chloe had a moment of fear. Sheer determination held it at bay. Barely.

He must go through with this now, she kept telling herself, trying not to give in to her terror. Now. *Now!*

"Now!" she blurted out loud.

In her inexperience, Chloe had no way of knowing that John was simply testing the waters and was actually planning on a much lengthier bout of loveplay. Hearing her fevered outcry, however, served to excite that notion right out of his head.

"Yes," he rasped, "yes, sweet, now . . ."

He reared back in preparation for his thrust forward.

Chloe's hand went around the handle of the pitcher.

He spoke her name, pupils dilated with passion. *And stroked.*

Three things happened at once. Chloe screamed; John froze, stunned; A vase crashed over his head.

Chloe watched him expectantly. The lovely green eyes focused intently on her just before they began to slowly cross.

"You—" was all he got out before he fell on top of her, unconscious.

Zounds, he is heavy!

Pushing him with all her might, she managed to roll the rake half-off her, allowing her to scramble out from beneath him.

Clutching the bedpost for support, she took two deep breaths to calm her fraying nerves. There wouldn't be much time . . . the first thing she had to do was clean herself up, then see to the shards of pottery.

She quickly went about her task, gulping down the faint wave of dizziness that assailed her when she spotted the blood on her thighs. That done, she checked the bed for any signs of the doomed pitcher.

Satisfied she had found all the pieces, Chloe began to sift through John's hair, making sure to fluff it up as best she could. Hopefully he wouldn't notice the nugget that had sprung up on the back of his head.

By the time he woke up, she would be sleeping beside him as if everything were normal. John would think he had fallen asleep after they had finished and have no clear memory of what had transpired just before he was whacked with the vase. Everything would be exactly the way . . .

Chloe sat on the edge of the bed, her hand on her forehead. Perhaps she should have thought this one out a little more. What if he remembered? Nonsense. A few kisses, a few cuddles, and he would—

Two lethal emerald eyes pierced her in their sights.

Chloe gasped. How could he be awake already? He wasn't supposed to be awake yet!

She had seen that look on John once before; she had been ten years old and had put itching powder in every pair of breeches he owned. *Damnation,* he had been in a lather over that one.

Once he had caught her—climbing right up a tree after her to do it—she hadn't been able to sit for two days.

By the look of him, he was more furious with her now.

A strong hand reached across the bed to grab her wrist.

Chloe screamed and bolted off the bed.

Naked, hair streaming behind her, she raced through the bedchamber into the sitting room, straight for the door.

Throwing the heavy oak door open, she bolted

out, fleeing as fast as she could down the east wing.

"Chloeee!" John roared down the hall.

It was not one of those times when one stopped to think over the situation. *Mon Dieu,* the man sounded like a raging bull! She would talk to him after he calmed down.

Which, by the sound of his bellow, would be in about three or four months.

Chloe never expected John to come after her. Her first clue that he was not far behind was the slapping of his bare feet on the parquet floor as he resolutely chased her.

Her second clue was the screech of the upstairs maid, who happened to round the corner at the same time with a stack of linens. She was confronted with the new master of the house running buck naked down the hall, bellowing his wife's name.

Rooted to the spot, the poor maid dropped her load of linens, covering her eyes with her fingers as she caterwauled at the top of her lungs about the heathen ways of rogues.

The moment his lordship had barreled past, sensibilities notwithstanding, said fingers separated, allowing the woman a substantial peek at the muscular backside. She sighed at the fabulous sight.

Realizing no one could hear her righteous outrage, she shrugged. Picking up her pile of linens, she continued on down the hall.

At the maid's screech, Chloe winced. Thank goodness Grandmere had kept this wing relatively free of guests! She skidded into a corner, looking for an avenue of escape.

She should have remembered that John had an annoying habit of seeing a matter through. Chloe rubbed her backside in remembrance, ducking into a curtained alcove.

Sights trained on his quarry, John completely ignored the blathering maid. He was too furious to be distracted. *Now where is that little termagant?*

His sights went knowingly to the alcove. The curtain in front was quivering slightly. *Mmm-hmm.*

He was about to barge his way through the drapery when two violet eyes peeped out to check the area. They widened considerably when realization struck that he was standing right there.

At the same time, John heard voices coming up the far stairwell. It was probably some late-night guests returning to their chambers. And the lord and his lady were standing in the hall without a stitch of clothing on! He winced as he imagined the rumor mill *that* would produce.

He quickly came through the curtain, covering Chloe's mouth with his hand as he backed her into the far corner against the wall.

"Not a sound," he hissed in her ear.

She stared at him over the edge of his hand, eyes enormous. The voices outside got closer.

John leaned into her; his warm, dry skin blanketing her. She felt all of him, the muscles and strength of him, as he held her in place. There was no question that he was seething.

Anger fairly radiated from him—anger and something else she didn't recognize.

"I could take you here—right now—against this wall." His deep voice was a mere undertone. "Did you know that, Chloe?"

She stiffened. The words were not meant to charm; they were meant to give her pause.

She shook her head, her hair brushing his chest.

"But then, there are a lot of things you don't know." He spoke very low against the curve of her throat. His free hand slid down her back to cup her derriere, bringing her in close contact with him.

He was hard and swollen as he pressed their lower bodies together. His manhood throbbed as it skimmed her lower stomach.

Despite her apprehension, the curious part of

Chloe wondered what he looked like. He felt very large and she still hadn't seen . . .

He removed his hand from her mouth, seizing her lips in a punishing kiss. She was not used to John kissing her. *The Lord of Sex*. Her knees buckled.

His powerful arms held her.

"Why did you lead me to believe you were not a virgin, Chloe-cat?" He spoke quietly, his lips a hairbreadth from her own.

The voices were almost upon them now.

Chloe swallowed. She had hoped his anger was due to her coshing him on the head, not that other thing. She was not having very much luck tonight!

"You know about that too?" she said in a squeak, disappointed.

His voice rumbled in her ear, the furious murmurs not at all hidden by the sibilant tones he was forced to use to prevent their discovery. "Do you not listen to those rumors you told me of—that I have been with almost half the women in England?" He exhaled warm breath against her ear. "Of course I knew."

Chloe wasn't sure she heard him correctly. There was an odd note in his voice. She looked up, trying to see him in the darkened alcove, but could not make out his features.

"Answer me, Chloe."

The flat, self-possessed tone alarmed her. However, she noticed that his tender touch was strangely at odds with his vocal demeanor.

Chloe decided it would be best to tell him the real reason. This reason wasn't the entire truth, but he didn't need to know all of that yet. "B-because you wouldn't have agreed to the plan!"

"Plan?" Chloe heard the shock in his voice. "Don't tell me you still have that mad notion to—"

"Was I right?" She quickly interrupted him; she had no intentions of answering *that* question.

He hesitated.

So she was right. "See? I couldn't very well tell you, John; you would have gotten the wrong idea." Her double meaning was lost on him. Which was just as well. She sighed. This was not easy for her.

The voices faded down the hallway.

"Even so, if you had simply told me tonight, beforehand, I would have been more . . . careful with you." Surprisingly, his lips pressed her forehead.

Tears filled her eyes. His action, meant to comfort, was a blow to her heart. His affectionate concern was as it had always been—that of a family friend. The kiss he placed on her brow was not the passionate act of a husband or lover.

A tear spilled over the corner of her eye, down her cheek. In the darkened alcove, it splashed on John's hand.

He felt instant remorse. Chloe rarely cried; he must have hurt her terribly when he took her. "Chloe-cat, I'm so sorry." He encircled her in his arms, hugging her to him.

His kind action in conjunction with his total misinterpretation of her behavior made her cry all the more. She buried her face into his chest, trying to stem her tears, but failing.

John wrapped her tighter in his embrace. "Please, sweet, don't . . ."

"Just gi-give me a minute, John." Chloe hiccuped.

He smiled faintly, rubbing his chin on the top of her head. "The tip of your nose is cold."

"It is?" She sniffed.

"Yes, monkey. You must be getting cold—let me take you back to bed." He lifted her in his arms.

When he exited the curtained alcove, the wall sconces cast a dim light on the woman in his arms. She gazed up at him, violet eyes still moist from her recent tears. Her soft lips were slightly puffy from his kisses, her cheeks lightly flushed from the events of the evening.

John stared down at her and that *something* happened to him again.

He wasn't sure what it was, but he recognized the sensation. It was the same damn thing that had happened to him in their bedroom when she had first kissed him.

Their eyes met. Everything around them seemed to fade.

"Let me taste you, Chloe," he whispered.

She raised her mouth for his taking.

John covered her lips. A small sound of pleasure rolled in his throat.

John deepened the kiss, sweeping inside her mouth, drawing on her lips even as he claimed her taste.

This was definitely the kiss of a husband! Chloe thought.

She pulled back, staring deeply into his eyes. With her newfound woman's knowledge, she realized he wanted her. *Really* wanted her.

He began walking determinedly back to the bedroom.

During the entire trip, he never once broke eye contact with her.

Chloe wasn't sure who was more surprised.

He kicked the door shut.

From his demeanor, Chloe half expected him to lean her up and take her against the wall the way he had suggested earlier.

Truth was, John considered it and rejected it. He didn't want her that way. At least not tonight.

He headed straight to the bed. Lord Sexton knew exactly what he wanted.

No elaborate positions.

No impressive techniques.

Just her. Wrapped around him tight.

He laid her gently on the bed, carefully fanning her red hair across the pillows. It was exactly as he had envisioned. His heart pounded in his chest. *She was so damn beautiful.*

Several thick candles illuminated the room and the bed. His raking glance took in everything about her. He had not really had a chance to observe her at his leisure before. Now he afforded himself the pleasure.

He had seen other women, narrower of waist, perhaps, and longer of limb, but none had ever come close to comparing in his eyes.

Chloe had always been perfect to him.

Now more so.

Placing one knee up on the bed, he leaned over her and wrapped a tendril of the red hair around his wrist over and over. With her securely fastened, he came over her.

For some reason, Chloe was more nervous than she was the first time. This time John was going to make love to her. Completely. She could see the resolution on his face.

Even though she wanted him, what they had done before had been very painful. While he had been examining her, she had been investigating him as well, and it seemed to her that he was very . . . *large.* So it was bound to hurt again.

She wasn't sure she was ready for that on top of everything else she had experienced this evening.

Some of her apprehension must have shown, for his hand cradled her cheek. His thumb brushed across her full lips.

Thick black lashes shielded his eyes as he watched his own stroking actions and the play of her full bottom lip under his thumb.

A small tremor shook him, but Chloe felt it.

He raised his eyes to her; they were kindling with emerald fire. His voice was very raw and very determined.

"I'm going to give you so much pleasure. . . ."

Chapter Six
The Players Engage

He was caught in a sensual spell.

When he came over her, the thin chain around his neck dangled in front of her face.

Chloe glanced at the small charm, then gasped in shock. It was a carrot. *Her carrot*. "You—you kept it!"

John arrested his motion, seemingly surprised by her discovery. Either he didn't think she would remember or he had been wearing the charm for so long that he hadn't thought to remove it.

He didn't answer her. Cheekbones turning a dull bronze, he looked away, a muscle working in his jaw. He appeared self-conscious. As if someone had found out something about him he didn't want known.

The charm! She remembered the day he had given it to her. It was her thirteenth birthday. There were many reasons why she had never forgotten that day.

Every year since she was six, John had given her a little golden charm to add to the bracelet she wore. Each charm had a special significance known only to the two of them, for the charms represented his pet names for her. There was a kitten for "Chloe-cat." A bear cub for "Chloe-cub." A parakeet for "Chloe-keet." A monkey for "Chloe-monkey." A bunny for "Chloe-rabbit." And a baby elephant for "Chloe-phant."

That year he had given her the carrot.

The carrot charm alluded to her hair color; John loved to tease her by calling her "Carrot-top" or "Chloe-carrot," or just plain "Carrot." He knew it really got under her skin, so naturally he used the carrot nicknames the most.

Later that day she had climbed a tree to spy on John and the Lady Mirot, who were ensconced on a bench in a secluded part of the garden. Chloe had noticed them giving peculiar looks to each other during luncheon and she wanted to see what it was all about.

She soon found out.

Lord Sexton and the lady in question were locked in an amorous embrace, John's hands reaching down the woman's bodice.

A deep, horrible pain had sliced into her heart and she felt as if she couldn't breathe. Up until that point, she had assumed that John was hers alone; she knew nothing of his ways with women.

It was the first time in her young life that she was confronted with inconstancy, and she had felt betrayed.

Too young to understand, she had climbed down the tree to face him in her rage. Chloe had never been shy about letting her opinions be known.

When he spotted her out of the corner of his eye, hanging from a branch preparing to jump down, he was both furious at her invading his privacy and concerned for her safety. He released the woman from his hold, yelling out Chloe's name in angry offense.

Chloe released the branch, falling to the ground. He immediately ran to her to see if she was unharmed, but she quickly backed away from him in disgust. Her action affected him deeply; Chloe had never turned from him before. To cover his own uncertainty, he lashed out at her.

"I am a man—what did you expect?" But he wouldn't look her in the eye.

Tears rolled down her face. "I hate you!"

John was visibly distressed. He reached toward her with a supplicating hand. "This has nothing to do with us, Carrot."

That had hurt the most. She had taken the charm and yanked it off her bracelet, tossing it to his feet on the grass. Then she had turned and fled. He had repeatedly called her name but she wouldn't answer him. It was months before she spoke to him again. By that time she knew all about his proclivities, and their relationship was never the way it had been before. They were still close, in some ways closer, but a barrier had been crossed, a new level reached.

He never called her Carrot again.

Yet he kept the ornament.

Chloe's hand captured the tiny charm. Once again tears filled her eyes, although for a different reason this time. *John had kept the carrot*. He apparently wore it around his neck always. The chivalrous deed spoke volumes to her.

She felt John's hand cover hers.

Instead of moving her hand away as he always did with the women who touched the piece, John laced his fingers around hers, capturing the gold carrot *and* her hand securely within his grasp.

The simple, tender action affected Chloe deeply. Her arm curled around his neck into his silky hair.

Closing her eyes, she raised her lips and kissed him affectionately.

John sighed into her mouth.

It was then that Chloe realized he had been holding his breath, awaiting her reaction. She gave herself a mental shake. *For all his experience, how much did he really know about a woman's heart?*

In response, she embraced him to her, her hands clasping his strong shoulders.

He entered her. Marginally.

Chloe could feel the tremors flowing through that part of him as he hesitated just barely inside her.

"I don't want to hurt you, sweet," he choked out, a wealth of hidden meaning in his heartfelt utterance.

"You won't, John. Not ever again."

And he wouldn't. Not in any way that mattered. There was not a doubt in Chloe's mind that she had done the right thing.

For both of them.

With her revelation, her apprehension melted away. John seemed to sense the change in her; he placed a soft kiss on the swell of her breast.

A puff of air escaped Chloe's parted lips at the

touch of his mouth on so intimate a place.

He raised his face and caught her surprise, the corners of his sensuous mouth curving slightly at the innocent sound of pleasure.

"Has no one kissed you here, Chloe?" His silken lips drifted across the satiny skin of her breast, taking small nibbles as he went.

"N-no." She inhaled a shaky breath.

"Or here?" The tip of his tongue flicked teasingly across the peak. The stimulating action caused the small pink nub to harden and protrude.

"No." She gasped, amazed at the response of her own body. Like a flower blooming just for him, the bud seemed to reach for his mouth.

"Then I don't suppose you've ever felt this either." He captured the delicate bud between his lips and drew it into his mouth.

Chloe moaned at the exquisite sensation. A line of fire snaked from the point where he touched her to the very core of her being. "*John . . .*"

"Mmm . . ." His agile tongue flicked the nubbin in his mouth as he continued to suckle her. Chloe had never in her life felt anything as pleasing as this. She deemed it only right to let John know her opinion.

"This is quite fascinating; I rather think this is a very good thing to do, John."

He blinked. *This was definitely Chloe speaking.* No other woman he knew would take the time out of reality to reflect on the aspects of the situation. He chuckled. Telling him her viewpoint about the facets of lovemaking as if it were a regular debate topic brought up for discussion and not a physical act!

Amused, he continued to draw on her, catching the sweet tip between his white teeth to tug softly. Her honey moistened the head of his manhood.'

He pressed into her slightly.

Chloe shivered. He was coming inside her, joining them together. As one. She inhaled shakily. *Yes, yes . . .*

It was his eyes she watched—they were hazy, clouded with his passion. She couldn't seem to stop staring at those bottomless green eyes.

When she shivered, an intense corresponding response reverberated through John. He lifted himself over her, while still keeping them joined. He knew she watched him—he looked right in her eyes.

And bore down.

Even though her moisture eased his way somewhat, she was still narrow and very tight. Virgin tight. He was not able simply to slide into her; the passage needed widening, especially to accommodate someone his size.

Despite her resolve not to, Chloe cried out. She closed her eyes, turning her face away from him, the ramming pressure seeming too potent, too unyielding to bear.

"Look at me."

She drew in a tremulous wisp of air, not daring to move or breathe.

"Look at me, my lady."

Her eyes flew open. She stared at him, questioning.

Never breaking eye contact with her, he lowered his mouth to hers and drove into her. Chloe moaned against his mouth as he breached her completely, truly joining them.

John captured her exclamation, swallowing it inside him. A rough roll of satisfaction purred in his throat. Not once in his entire life had anything ever felt like this.

"Chloe." He spoke softly, shaken as much as she.

How long they stayed like that—quiescent, joined together—neither knew. After a time, Chloe felt John nuzzle the sensitive area of her throat below her ear.

"Wrap your legs around me"

Chloe did as he asked, delighted to discover that the sensation intensified. "Like this?"

"Yes . . . a little higher—near my waist." His

tongue swirled around the perimeter of her ear, the tip teasing the canal.

"Oh! That's—"

"*Mmm-hmm*. We're just beginning, sweet." Carefully he began to move in her, small, shallow thrusts designed to please her without giving discomfort.

"I . . . I . . ." She attempted to let him know her opinion on this as well.

"Shh. Just experience it, Chloe." He stroked a little deeper.

A tiny sound escaped her lips.

"I know," he murmured huskily, his own breath racing.

Cognizant of her untried state, he valiantly attempted to control his motions by regulating the depth and strength of his thrusts. It was not an easy thing to do; every time he sank into her he almost lost all restraint.

Her pure, virginal responses to his lovemaking, however, reminded him to tread cautiously.

Forehead dotted with moisture, he maintained his steady, sure rhythm.

Chloe wiggled beneath him, not knowing what she wanted exactly, but realizing it was something *more*.

John groaned. If she kept moving like that, there was no way he could hold back. "Chloe, you—"

"I never realized you would be so hard, John."

"Oh, God." *Restraint be damned!*

"Did I say something wro—"

His mouth fused over hers and he thrust into her with a man's power. Over and over.

At first Chloe was stunned, but soon she was matching him move for move. "Wha-what comes next?" she asked, panting.

Her question, occurring at the most awkward time, well-nigh might have unmanned a lesser gent. The Lord of Sex grinned as he took her mouth again.

"This." He drove into her, rotating his hips in a side-to-side motion as he captured the rosy peak of her breast in his mouth and suckled hard.

Chloe cried out, this time in acute pleasure, as wave upon wave of joyous satisfaction tumbled through her. Clinging to him in her completion, she wrapped her arms around him, bringing him into her as tightly as she could.

John, breathing raggedly, felt his own release coming. It churned up from deep inside him, finding its way home in Chloe.

It was powerful and untamed, and erupted from him like pressure kept too long contained. He too hugged her to him in a firm embrace, whispering her name again and again as he flowed into her.

Several minutes later John still lay inside her, his face burrowed into her flower-scented neck as he tried to regain his composure.

What had happened to him? It was her first time, but he felt like the one taken.

For once, there had been nothing missing.

Nothing at all.

Furthermore, he was surprised to see he was nibbling the curve of her neck where it met her shoulder like a man reluctant to leave the dinner table.

Like a man preparing for a second helping.

He had to force himself to roll off of her. She was tender and, he knew for a fact, sore. Until she got used to him he would have to be very careful with her. After all, this had been her first time.

There had been anger at what she had done; but, oddly, there was relief as well. She had been untouched. He could not deny the feeling of elation that accompanied his discovery.

Her first time. A fragment of disturbing memory came to the surface. Sitting back against the headboard, he draped his arm over his bent knee, his thoughts going in a surprising direction.

Chloe turned the bedside lamp down, then lay on her side by her husband. Moonlight illuminated his handsome profile, and he seemed to be deep in thought. She still hadn't regained her composure after the incredible experience he had given her. If she dwelled on it, she would want to begin anew, and she wasn't sure she was ready for that.

A tiny furrow grooved the center of his normally smooth forehead. Chloe wondered what he was thinking about that had put so contemplative an expression on his face.

His voice broke through the sudden stillness in the room. He spoke in a monotone, as if his emotions had disengaged themselves from what he was about to say.

"I was twelve years old . . . big for my age . . . A vicar's wife told me to come inside, that she would give me something to eat." He paused significantly.

"I was starving, you see. *Afterward,* she gave me a piece of moldy bread and sour broth. I ran into her stable and cried."

Chloe watched him silently, stunned by what she was hearing. John never revealed to anyone what had happened to him those years he was forced to fend for himself.

Now she had a fairly good idea what must have transpired. At sixteen, he had been extraordinarily handsome; at twenty-nine, he was breathtaking. Even at so young an age as twelve, his good looks must have been apparent. How he had survived became apparent as well. It explained a lot to her.

Her spirits sank a little. *This is going to take time.* More time than she had thought. She hadn't known that about him.

Chloe saw the young viscount as he must have been—scared, alone, hungry; her heart cried out for him. *John.*

As if he heard her silent call, he turned to her.

"So you see, Chloe, first times are very important. We never seem to forget them."

She reached over to touch his forearm. "Then that's good, because you have given me a beautiful memory that I shall always treasure."

He smiled faintly at her. "Have I?"

"Oh, yes. I hope your memories of our first time together are the same."

"Yes . . ." His eyes held a lambent shine. "An incredible memory, *Carrot.*" He teased her with the reference. She blushed prettily.

"Let it supplant that other memory, Lord Sexton." She notched her chin in the air. Her tone challenged him to do just that.

He laughed. "Consider it done, madam." His hand cupped the side of her head, his fingers lacing through her hair. "For that I thank you, Lady Sexton." His lips brushed her mouth.

Lady Sexton. The name had a very nice "ring" to it. Feeling the weight of the gorgeous emerald he had given her, Chloe smiled at her accidental double entendre.

Chloe's arms twined around his strong neck as she leaned into the kiss, giving it depth. Should she live to be a hundred, she doubted she would take his kisses for granted. They were simply too special. Evocative and alluring, they seemed to satisfy while beckoning for more.

It was an expertise Chloe doubted could be learned.

This is John.

No wonder the women of the ton found him so irresistible. One taste and she was craving more. Delectable . . . so very luscious.

While she cataloged his attributes, the edge of her little finger skimmed along his earlobe.

She blinked.

His lobe was so incredibly soft—like downy velvet. *What a fabulous discovery!* She immediately began to nibble at his ear.

"Chloe, stop! We need to be—"

"No, really, John, I need to check something here."

He chuckled, but when she stopped nibbling to tease his ear with the tip of her tongue, he put a stop to her play by pulling back.

"I'm serious; I don't want to injure you. We need to rest. *You* need to rest."

"If you insist." She sighed mournfully.

"I do." He kissed the top of her head. "I want you well rested for what I have in mind for tomorrow."

"If you insist," she repeated in a dull voice, exhaling a gust of air. "We wouldn't want to have you overdo it your first day," she said grouchily.

Smiling, he tugged playfully on her earlobe. "No, we wouldn't want that."

"Very well." She sighed dramatically, snuggling in to go to sleep. "But I expect a better showing tomorrow."

"Oh, you shall have it," he drawled sexily.

"Promises, promises . . ."

"Mmm." His broad palm cupped the back of her head as he gathered her closer in his embrace.

"Although you do make a very nice pillow." She yawned.

Already she sounded sleepy; he was glad he had called a halt. Well, not all of him was glad. He shifted his position slightly, trying to relieve a burdensome pressure.

It wasn't very long before gentle puffs of air drifted across his chest. She was fast asleep. He looked down at her lying in his arms. Sweet,

sweet Chloe. How had he ever deserved this?

When he had discovered she hadn't been with another man, he had felt something close to gratitude well up in him. He had no right having such feelings. Not with his past.

This was more complex than he first thought.

He examined the dainty profile that he could probably draw in the dark. It had been etched into his psyche when he was sixteen. That very day—the day he met her—he began worrying about her.

And he was still doing it!

Briefly, he wondered if, once you took it up, it became a lifetime position: Chloe's Official Worrier. He snorted.

Tonight she had been more than any man could ever hope for—responsive, giving, warm, and . . . trusting.

It was the trusting part that bothered him.

Why did she trust him so? He had told her time and again she must never trust any man in this area. Of course he didn't mean *him*—he'd never deceive her; he couldn't.

Still, she should have more sense.

Gingerly, he felt the bump on the back of his head, his eyes narrowing. Then again, when he gave her that advice, he never thought he'd be in a position to—

Just what did you think?

That was precisely the dilemma. He had never stopped to think about the future, hers or his.

Now the future was here; they were wed and there were certain terms he would be expected to abide by. The terms of their agreement. He was to share his sexual knowledge with her so she could lead the same life he did.

So she could seek out other men to . . . !

A masculine, territorial, possessive, heretofore unheard voice within him seethed.

Why should I allow that?

Well, he *had* given her his word.

So what if he did? An astute man could always find an alternative interpretation to an agreement.

Could he get away with it? Chloe was extremely sharp. He exhaled deeply, closing his eyes. *Exactly what kind of a bargain have I made here?*

The kind that spells trouble, he acknowledged prosaically.

Feminine lips teased his collarbone.

"Chloe . . ." he murmured sleepily, eyes still closed.

"How did you know it was me?" she teased him.

He smiled, opening his eyes. "Lucky guess."

"You scapegrace." She nipped him sharply on the nose.

He laughed heartily, white teeth flashing. "No, I'd know those lips anywhere."

Chloe fell for the bait. "Really? How?" She rubbed his nose with her own.

"Nibble nibble, pause to examine the situation, nibble nibble . . ."

"You are shameless!" She pinched a vulnerable spot between his arm and chest.

Two dimples curved his cheeks. "Besides, who else would sleep all night with her arms around my neck and her pinkie cuddling my earlobe?" He snickered at the Chloe oddity.

She blushed. "It is so soft, John; it feels just like velvet."

The lids of his eyes instantly lowered. "It does, does it? Would you like to feel something else just as soft?"

John's voice had changed from amused to seductive in the blink of an eye. *Very good.*

Matching his tone, she peeked up at him through her lashes. "What would that be?"

"This." His hand covered hers. Entwining their fingers together, he lifted their hands from his chest and placed them on her breast.

Under the command of his, their two hands stroked the soft underside.

"Like satin, sweet," he said on a breath.

Chloe stared at him, watching his pupils dilate to the tactile sensation he created for both of them. She had always known he was a sensuous man.

"And this . . ." He skimmed their entwined hands down her torso to barely sweep at the curls at her juncture.

His knuckles skimmed her cleft. Chloe sucked in her breath.

"And *this*." He brought her closer to him so their hands brushed the tip of his erection.

While still gripping her, John maneuvered his thumb and forefinger around her forefinger, straightening it out to point. Holding her this way, he moved his hand in a circular motion so that the pad of her finger caressed the tip of him.

He was downy velvet there too. So soft, yet so hard.

"You feel so exquisite," she whispered, awed by his magnificence.

"Men are not exquisite, Chloe-keet." He pressed a kiss on the corner of her mouth.

"You are." She turned her head, capturing his mouth.

He ardently returned her kiss.

Taking her hand, he trailed it down the length of his staff, allowing her finger to make the long slide on the underside of him. An appreciative purr reverberated in his throat.

Since he liked it so much, Chloe decided to take over the motion, running her finger up and down the thick shaft and around the blunt tip.

"Yes, oh yes," he affirmed in a hint of voice. He suckled on her lower lip, drawing it delicately into his mouth.

Releasing her hand, he trailed his own forefinger down the curve of her belly, running the pad around and around the rim of her navel, and then down again into her nether curls.

Mirroring her action, he inserted his finger in her dewy softness, circling and stroking up and down the damp cleft. Concurrently, his agile tongue delved deeply into her mouth, stroking and sliding in a matching rhythm.

The sensations he created were overpowering. Chloe stopped her own motions for a second, overcome by what he was doing to her. Perhaps this needed an opinion?

"Don't stop, my beautiful wife. Not now."

My beautiful wife. With that encouragement, Chloe grasped his member in her hand and massaged its entire length. Impossibly, he seemed to grow even larger and firmer within her grip.

Chloe marveled at what she had done; there was a feeling of genuine accomplishment. *Just look at the size of it!* His manhood jerked in her palm, reminding her that it wanted more.

She gave more.

Rolling the head around the center of her palm, she sheathed him with her other hand, massaging gently. An exclamation of sheer bliss followed the tremor that shook him.

A matching tingle skipped through her from the place where he was playing so skillfully.

His lips captured the peak of her breast to suckle.

Chloe shuddered at the augmented sensation. John was very, very good at this.

"I want to come inside you, Lady Sexton."

His enticing suggestion, uttered in a drawling half whisper, added to her arousal.

Chloe nodded, nuzzling her cheek across the edge of his sensual mouth.

He clasped her knee and lifted it over his hip as they lay on their sides. The position brought them in perfect alignment.

"Bring me to you," he coaxed, his hot breath fanning her lips.

She looked at him and knew what he wanted. Grasping him firmly, she brought the head of his manhood to her woman's portal.

John watched her. "Now guide me home, love."

Chloe moved forward and down on him, bringing him slowly inside. Inch by inch he sank into her, filling her to the hilt. They both moaned.

When she could go no farther, he placed his hands on her hips and drove into her that little bit more.

Chloe could not hold back her opinion on this. "Ohhh."

"Are you all right?" He stilled, speaking raggedly in her ear. "No discomfort?"

"N-no, just incredible pleasure."

"Ah . . ."

Her small hands cupped his face. "Let's stay like this forever."

He drew in a sharp breath. *Have mercy.* Where did she ever learn to ignite a man like that? "Chloe . . . when you say something like that, I—"

He didn't finish, just melded his mouth to hers. Chloe moaned at the rich, fiery dampness of him.

"When you're ready . . . move. Do whatever feels comfortable." His tongue teased at the small dimples at the corners of her mouth.

Cautiously, she began moving against him. They both felt every nuance of the motion; they both relished the sensitive experience.

Soon her novice motions picked up speed and ingenuity. She changed the pace. She writhed; she slid; she moved in an altogether sinuous way.

John maintained his stationary position, his mouth playing with her throat, her ear, her collarbone—once even biting her shoulder when she ground against him hard.

The Lord of Sex let her find her own way, patiently allowing her to take *him*.

After a time, his palms came down to cup her derriere. His hands began to guide her on him in a different way. Bringing her up tight and close, he rotated her upon his shaft with an expertise seldom seen.

She moved but could not control the style of motion. He stayed immobile, but controlled the strength and depth of her thrusts.

It was an incredibly erotic experience for them both.

In this way—with his strong, knowledgeable hands guiding her energetic movements—he brought them both to a shattering, masterful culmination.

It was not an end, however.

Chloe soon learned that John was only beginning. She barely had time to catch her breath before he began anew, showing her yet another variation of the same technique.

Throughout the day and long into the night he made good on his promise. In fact, his performance was outstanding. She wasted no time in telling him so.

The viscount's rich, deep laughter resonated in the bedchamber. "I'm glad you approve, madam."

He winked at her rakishly.

And continued to thrust.

Chapter Seven
Zambeau Ensconces

A pounding on the bedroom door awoke them.

"Don't answer it." John burrowed back into the curve of her shoulder.

"I must; it sounds urgent, John." Chloe wiggled away from his warm embrace, reaching for her dressing gown.

"Bother it!" A few additional expletives from the center of the bed followed her to the door.

She couldn't really blame him: he was just preparing to . . . Well, he said he was going to show her how he best liked to cuddle.

Chloe grinned as she made her way to the door. She adored this other side of John. This sexual side of him.

The pounding grew more intense, almost

frantic. It was a good thing John had locked the door or else Chloe was sure whoever was on the other side would have burst in.

She chuckled, because when she had questioned John as to why he was locking it, he had crossed his arms over his chest and given her a dry look. "I know this household only too well."

He did at that.

"I'm coming! I'm coming!" Chloe hollered out as she tied the sash of her robe.

She unbolted the door and opened it a few inches to peer out.

Grandmere was there, looking positively frantic. Chloe had never seen her grandmother appear so upset. "Grandmere! What is it? Is something wrong? Tell me!"

"Oh, it is terrible, my dear, terrible!" The countess stood in the hall, wringing her hands. "Something awful has happened!"

Oh no! Chloe put her hand to her chest. "What is it; you must tell me."

"*Non*! I will speak to John—he is the master of the house now; it is for him to deal with. Only him."

"But John is—" *Naked.*

Chloe heard her husband pad smoothly across the floor. A strong arm circled her waist and she was drawn back into his warmth behind her.

Mon Deiu, he hasn't even bothered to put any clothes on!

His tousled blond head peered around the door frame. "What is it, Countess?" he asked calmly.

Grandmere began wringing her hands again. "Something terrible has happened, John."

Her husband became instantly serious. "What is it?" He paled suddenly. "It's not my uncle, is it?"

"Good heavens, no; it is worse than that!"

"Oh, not Schnapps!" Chloe wailed loudly.

John glanced down at the top of her head incredulously. She actually had an affection for the ugly little dog.

"No, no, my angel . . . worse, much worse."

John frowned in puzzlement. Not his uncle, the countess was obviously fine, Schnapps lived and growled, and one was never quite sure whether Deiter was alive or dead. So what could be worse? He asked as much.

Grandmere drew herself up with the importance of the horrendous news she was about to impart. "Zu-Zu has arrived."

Chloe and John both stared at her blankly.

"Do you not understand what I am saying?" Grandmere threw her hands up. "The Countess Zambeau is here! On your very doorstep!"

John just gazed at Grandmere. "So?" he said at last.

"Oh ho! You will see what 'so'! You must come at once. I have given her a suite in the south wing; already she has gone through three maids! And she has only been here half an hour."

"Are you saying this—this woman is staying *here*?" John asked, appalled.

"*Oui*. Come quickly!"

"I will not." He pulled Chloe closer to him. "I am busy with my wife."

The countess blew out a breath of exasperation. "You must deal with her! If you do not, she will have your house in an uproar."

John was not particularly perturbed.

The countess shook her finger at him. "My dear, young viscount, she will take it upon herself to run the household for you, then demand you thank her for the privilege." The countess waved her hand impatiently in the air. "I have seen her do it before. Say *au revoir* to the *Chacun à Son Goût* as you know it and *bonjour* to the Zambeau Chateau!"

John's nostrils flared. "Who *is* this woman?"

Chloe turned in his arms to look up at him. "You remember her, John; she's the one Grandmere was crying over when she presumably went to the guillotine."

"Ah, yes—the 'glorious bitch.' What is she doing here?"

Chloe turned back to her grandmother. "Yes—how did she escape the guillotine, Grandmere?"

"We don't know yet; I suppose she will inform us in minute detail of her harrowing adventure. In the meantime, John, you must come down and deal with her."

Chloe nodded in agreement. "Yes, John, you must go."

"What am *I* to do with her?" he thundered.

Grandmere started down the hallway. " 'Tis simple, John, just smile at her. Zu-Zu adores men who smile."

"What do you mean by that?" he asked the countess suspiciously. When the countess didn't answer, he turned to his wife. "What does she mean by that?" he asked Chloe.

She shrugged her shoulders.

"Remember—just smile. The Countess Zambeau will take it from there," Grandmere predicted from down the hallway.

"Hmm," was all he said.

When she rounded the corner, the Countess de Fonbeaulard smiled broadly.

The two of them had looked so adorable standing together in the doorway like that. John seemed very protective of his new bride. And much more committed than one would have believed. As Sir Percy said, *Res ipsa loquitur.* The thing speaks for itself. The task was to get John to listen.

Not to worry, Grandmere had a plan.

First she had to deal with that bitch, Zu-Zu.

What would she have done without the dear Zambeau to make life interesting? Thank God she had escaped the execution!

Spice was a very important ingredient in one's life.

Especially if one could use it to flavor a new marriage.

"It was right before my eyes! Looming enormous, it was raised to its full potential!"

Everyone in the room gasped.

Everyone, that was, except John, who groused under his breath something best not vocalized out loud.

Chloe, sitting next to him on the settee, elbowed him smartly in the side. Dutifully, he gave a feigned gasp.

The Countess Zambeau preened, taking the gasps as her due.

Grandmere was the first to find her voice. "The man who saved you?" she verified, somewhat shocked at the description.

"*Non!*" Zu-Zu frowned. "I am speaking of the guillotine."

"Ohhhh . . ." everyone said, slightly disappointed at the turn of the tale.

"So how were you rescued, Countess?" Chloe inquired.

"Yes, do tell us, Zu-Zu!" Percy leaned forward in his chair, avidly awaiting the story. Considering it was fodder for his endless prattle, John wasn't overly surprised.

"*Bien*, there I was in the Place de Greve; I was being pulled from the cart by a soldier when I looked up to see a vision of unyielding determination and unrelenting precision."

"The guillotine," Grandmere affirmed.

"*Non*! The man who saved me." Zu-Zu leveled a catlike look at her lifelong friend and competitor. "He was quite something, Simone; it is too bad you could not have seen him."

Grandmere rolled her eyes. "*Oui*, next time I will place myself before the guillotine so I may have a glance at this specimen!"

John snorted.

"Was it the Black Rose?" Percy practically drooled at the thought.

"Of course it was the Black Rose! Who else would save me, the Countess Zambeau!"

A lesser savior would never have done. The

woman was impossible. *No wonder the peasants are revolting.* Utterly bored, John closed his eyes and rested his head on the back of the settee.

"What did he look like?" Chloe wanted to know.

John opened one eye. "Why do you want to know?" There was just a hint of suspicion in his voice.

Chloe was overjoyed. She replied innocently, "Everyone wants to know, John; he's the talk of the ton."

"Oh, he's marvelous!" Zu-Zu sighed dramatically.

"Really?" Chloe waited for more while she observed John out of the corner of her eye. The viscount was starting to sulk, which was a very encouraging sign.

"I hear he always appears in disguise, Countess; how could you tell what he really looked like?" Percy had a perplexed expression on his face, as if the intricacies of disguising one's appearance were too taxing for him.

"Well, he appeared that way for the others, but with me he was simply himself! We became very intimate during the long journey here."

"All the way across the channel," John said sardonically while smiling at the countess. Accompanied by his lazy, masculine smile, the sarcasm went right over her head.

"So what does he actually look like?" Chloe repeated her question.

"He's very handsome! Tall, with the hair of brown and dark eyes. Most compelling and quite accomplished in the boudoir."

"Really?" Chloe remarked speculatively.

Not liking the contemplative look on her face one bit, John enclosed her hand firmly with his own. "You already have someone in that department, Chloe-keet. The position has been filled."

"Only for now, John," she whispered back, purposely goading him.

The jade eyes narrowed.

Zu-Zu fluttered her fan in the air. "You should have seen that beautiful red hair of his in the moonlight; it was—"

"You just said his hair was brown, Zu-Zu," Grandmere smugly reminded her.

Zu-Zu faltered for a moment. "Did I? Well, I meant red-brown, of course."

"Of course." It was obvious that Zu-Zu had never actually seen the true man. Whether she had consorted with him was another story. The Countess Zambeau was a stunning woman, and despite the fact that she was overbearing in the extreme, her exploits in the boudoir were a well-known fact.

"How did he get you away from the soldiers, Zu-Zu? Surely there were plenty of guards?" Maurice, who had been silent up to this point, chimed in.

"A whole battalion! You should have witnessed his bravery, Maurice; he was incredible! Rarely have I seen such swordsmanship! I could have watched him all afternoon."

"If it weren't for the guillotine looming over your head, so to speak," John put in dryly.

"John!" Chloe admonished him.

Zu-Zu wagged a finger at him. "He is being naughty and this I like." She smiled at him in an altogether coy way.

Out of habit, John winked lazily at her.

Chloe looked back and forth between the two of them.

The Countess Zambeau had been eyeing her husband since she met him an hour ago. At first Chloe hadn't put any assignation to the glances; after all, most women ogled John—besides his uncanny good looks, he had a certain steamy aura that seemed to call forth to females on a subconscious level.

On second inspection, however, she realized that the Zambeau was highly interested and planning a conquest.

Not with my husband! Irritated that John had

winked at the woman, Chloe turned her back on him.

The action did not go unnoticed by John, who was at a loss to understand why Chloe was suddenly upset with him. The wink he had given the countess was not even a glimmer in his thoughts. What was in his thoughts was getting his wife back to their bedchamber as soon as possible.

He couldn't recall ever wanting a woman so much. Since that first taste of her, she had been driving him mad! He had been in a state of semiarousal since they had come down to the sitting room.

Uncomfortable, he shifted his position on the settee.

His emerald eyes fixed their sights on her pouting lower lip. The exact feel of that luscious, soft lip on certain parts of his body came to mind, hitting three of his five senses at once.

He shifted his position again.

"An amazing story, Zu-Zu. Everyone in London town is talking about him, you know." Percy paused to take a sip of his tea.

"Speaking of which, where is every one?" John gazed around the room, noting for the first time the absence of the upper ten thousand from his house.

Percy gaped at him. "Did you not hear the

racket yesterday when they cleared out, John?"

An embarrassing silence filled the void.

"No; don't suppose you would have." That the viscount was summarily engaged with his new bride to the point that he had not even perceived the sound of scores of conveyances being loaded and the mass exit of a great many people said much for the alluring charm of Lady Sexton.

Percy covered his faux pas smoothly by returning to the subject of the Black Rose. "They say he is completely daring, laughing in the face of the proletariat as he sweeps the aristocracy from under their noses. Naturally, we must take these stories *cum grano salis*, with a grain of salt."

"I say he was utterly charming, darling." Zu-Zu was certainly biased about the man who had saved her life. "I owe him everything. Everything!"

And probably gave it to him, John thought, weary of the woman's habit of overdramatizing every sentence she spoke.

"I have written a poem about him; would you like to hear it, Zu-Zu?" Percy practically chortled.

"Yes, I would love to!" Zu-Zu reached for a bonbon on the table next to her.

"Oh, please do, Sir Percy!" Chloe clapped her hands.

Damn and blast! John gritted his teeth. *Not the poem.*

With a flourish, Percy stood up, positioning himself in the center of the room so not an eye could wander away from his performance without his knowledge.

He cleared his throat noisily. Three times.

> *"They seek him high, they seek him low;*
> *The proletariat wonder where he could go;*
> *Near or far, where can anyone suppose . . .*
> *Is that blasted, evasive Rose!"*

Everyone applauded vigorously at the delightful ditty.

Everyone, that was, except John, who sat stone faced.

"Thank you, thank you!" Percy beamed, blowing kisses to the room at large.

John groaned. *Spare me.*

He leaned over to speak quietly to Chloe. "Let's go back upstairs, sweet. This is boring me and I can think of better things for us to do."

Chloe swerved her head, almost bumping his nose. "Everyone else is enjoying it, John; perhaps you should continue winking at the Countess Zambeau—then you shan't be so bored." She faced away from him.

"What are you talking about?" He spoke low so the others wouldn't hear.

Chloe focused forward, speaking from out of the side of her mouth. "If you wish her attentions, then that is your choice, Lord Sexton; I will consider the agreement between us over."

Chloe held her breath, waiting to see what he would do. She didn't have to wait long.

"You will do nothing of the kind, madam!" he all but roared.

Everyone turned to stare at him.

He instantly lowered his voice. "The agreement is definitely in effect—remember that, Lady Sexton."

Chloe exhaled. "If you insist." She toyed with him, not able to stop herself. It was so pleasant after all these years to see John squirm.

"I do, indeed."

Chloe shrugged as if the matter were of no concern to her one way or the other.

Those patrician nostrils of his flared.

It was more than she could have hoped for at this juncture. John was coming along very nicely. He was nowhere near the finish line, but he was making excellent progress.

And for that he deserved a little reward.

She took hold of his chin with her thumb and forefinger and brought him closer to her, placing a soft kiss on his mouth.

He viewed her suspiciously. "What was that for?"

"To seal the continuation of the agreement."

"Oh, I see." His eyes twinkled. "You'll have to do it again, Chloe-cat . . . I don't think that one took."

Smiling at his ploy, she brushed his mouth again. He surprised her by quickly wiggling his tongue on her lips as they swept his mouth. She giggled.

"What are you two wicked people doing over there?" Zu-Zu interrupted their pleasant play.

"We're waiting to hear more of your story, Zu-Zu." John smiled at the galling woman, showing her his teeth.

"There is more, but, my darlings, I am afraid it is not pleasant."

John said in an aside to Chloe, "Some of this was pleasant? What have I missed?"

"Shh! I think she has some important news."

"It is a black day for France." Zu-Zu lowered her fan; a single tear fell from her eye.

"What is it?" Maurice was alarmed.

"The Cyndreacs. They were taken." Her voice was for once without its bouncy inflection.

Grandmere and Chloe both shouted at this bit of news.

The exclamations were followed by a large snore from Deiter.

"Not the Cyndreacs!" Chloe was appalled.

"*Mon Dieu,* it cannot be—all of France will weep this day!" Grandmere sniffed.

"Not all of France," Maurice said pointedly.

John's brow furrowed. The Cyndreacs were notorious throughout France. There were seven brothers, all of them counts and all of them unwed. Each and every one of the young men had reputations for chasing muslin. Their wild reputations had garnered them the sobriquet of the Seven Deadly Cyns. He had met them himself briefly on several occasions at soirees he had attended.

"All of them?" the countess asked sadly.

"Not all—I believe one escaped, but of this, I am not sure."

"Which one?" Chloe had known the Cyndreacs her whole life—this news was sorely distressing to her.

"Who could tell?" Zu-Zu waved her hand in the air. "They all look alike with that black hair and those Cyndreac eyes." The brothers were stunningly handsome; each had inherited the famous golden Cyndreac eyes.

"Do you know these men well, Countess?" Percy asked Grandmere while dabbing at his eyes with his hanky. Percy did not know the Cyndreacs, but, presumably, he did not want to feel left out of the emotion of the moment.

"Yes, quite well," she replied softly. "Their chateau was adjoining my own in France. This is very disheartening. Were they alive when you left, Zu-Zu?"

"*Oui,* but not for long. I heard a guard say they were scheduled for execution." She shook her head. "Half the women of France will be prostrate with grief, myself included. Already they were lining up outside the prison, tossing roses through the gates, wailing their hearts out."

Grandmere's shoulders sagged. "Their beauty of spirit and zest for life will be missed."

"*O tempora! o mores!*" Percy intoned solemnly. "Oh the times! oh the customs!"

"At least one escaped," Chloe said quietly, wondering which one had been so lucky.

"*Dum spiro spero,*" Deiter spoke, surprising everyone, since he had been sleeping the whole time and had never spoken in Latin before.

Percy viewed him through his lorgnette. "Very true, my good man. Where there is life, there is hope."

Well said, but Deiter was snoring again.

John muttered under his breath as he made his way back to the house.

Just as he had found the perfect time to make

his excuses and drag his wife back to their rooms, Percy had cornered him with the request that he join him for a walk about the grounds so he might discuss with him a matter of "an intensely personal and urgent nature."

Put in such a way, the request was impossible for John to refuse. No matter how much he wanted to be alone with Chloe, he was obligated to accompany Percy.

They walked to the far pond. It was an extremely long, tedious journey for John, who ached to be with his new bride.

Percy prattled on about this and that until John was forced to ask, "So what is this urgent matter you wish to discuss with me?"

Sir Cecil-Basil removed his handkerchief from his pocket to dab at the perspiration dotting his brow. Clearing his throat, he focused on the water lapping across the surface of the pond, seemingly too embarrassed to look John in the eye.

It was a few moments before he could gather his composure to speak. When he finally did, he voiced in a near-croaking whisper, "What do you think of Spanish fly?"

John blinked, stunned at the question. "I beg your pardon?"

Percy cleared his throat again. "I say, what do you think of Spanish fly?"

Of all the inquiries, John never expected this! "Well, I . . ." What was he supposed to say? "Some prefer absinthe, I hear."

"Absinthe? What has absinthe to do with it?" Percy made a face. "Hideous-looking stuff—made with wormwood, I hear. Now what about the Spanish fly, John?"

"Are you thinking of trying it?"

"You won't say anything?"

"Of course not, but—"

Percy exhaled a sigh of relief. "I knew I could trust you, John. So what do you think?"

"It's your choice, of course, but I prefer the natural approach."

"Yes, but it is so boring of late." He waved the handkerchief; a whiff of cologne irritated John's nose, causing it to twitch.

"It doesn't have to be; there are many things one can do to liven up the—"

"I've tried them all; I need something fresh, something stimulating."

"It's a risk, Percy; there's no telling what its permanent effects might be."

Percy sighed. "I know. In addition, my reputation in such matters is sterling; I hate to jeopardize it."

Sterling reputation? With women? John gave the fop an incredulous look. Percy was definitely a legend in his own mind. "There's no accounting for ladies' tastes." His dry response was lost somewhere among the multitudinous layers of lace the man wore.

"The thing is, Sexton, do you think it too bold?"

"What does the lady in question say?"

"Lady in question?" Percy seemed perplexed. "What lady in question?"

"The one you plan to use this with." John stopped, viewing Percy in shock. "It is a lady, isn't it?"

"I should say not!"

John's eyes widened. He stepped back. Two steps.

"I plan to experiment with it on myself. Why would I ask a lady to try it?"

John didn't know what to say to that. Percy was odder than he thought.

"I think it goes quite naturally with my complexion. Furthermore, I believe it will be the coming rage. Always like to be on the forefront, you know."

Goes with his complexion? Lord Sexton shook his head to clear it. "What exactly are you talking about, Percy?"

"I told you, Spanish fly—the dark green color; seen it on a few fashions; I believe it's the coming thing."

John saw red. *Carmine* red. "You called me out here to discuss a—a shade of—of color! That was the intensely personal and urgent matter?" Not waiting for a response, he thundered, "Do you realize that I left my new bride to come out here with you?"

"Calm down, John; when you think it over, you'll realize that fashion is always a matter of extreme urgency."

Several choice expletives followed *that* remark.

John turned on his booted heel and stomped back to the house.

Sir Percy watched his exit with extreme interest.

Although his mouth was shaped in a moue at Lord Sexton's abrupt departure, an enigmatic smile hinted at the corners of his lips.

Still in a lather, John went in search of Chloe as soon as he stepped inside the house.

She was nowhere to be found.

He came across the countess in the conservatory. She was repotting some herbal plants, elbow-deep in dirt and apparently loving it. Normally the aristocracy did not put their hands in dirt, but the Countess de Fonbeaulard was an exception. In every way.

Like her granddaughter.

"Have you seen Chloe, Countess?"

"Yes, John, she went back to her room to rest." The countess smiled as she patted the dirt around the base of a plant. "You've worn the poor dear out."

Another man might have appeared slightly embarrassed by such an observation. Not John.

He flashed her a look of pure satisfaction.

The countess grinned, shaking a finger at him. "Now be gentle with her; she is not used to your ways."

"I am always gentle with her," he said as he was leaving. "It is my one weakness in life."

Not so, my young Lord Sexton; it is your best strength.

The countess acknowledged the superior quality to herself, placing her flowerpot on a shelf.

A movement from behind the ferns startled her. The marquis revealed himself, coming toward her.

"Maurice! I did not see you there!"

"*Non*, you did not," he said enigmatically.

"How long have you been there?"

Maurice could tell she was thinking about something else. Something that had occurred several days ago in the same place—a rather revealing conversation.

"Oh, not too long," he replied noncommittally.

She seemed to relax.

He took her around, placing a kiss on her shoulder. "He is like his uncle, no?"

The countess laughed, leaning into him. "Exactly."

"I was never as wild as him, though." He nuzzled her throat.

"Oh! You have selective memory, Maurice."

"True." He took her face between his hands. "I can only seem to remember the part of my life that includes you, *mon amour*."

He could still take her breath away. "Maurice . . ."

His lips claimed her.

No one could be more romantic than a Frenchman.

Especially if he had an agenda.

Chloe lay on top of the covers, sound asleep. A gentle breeze from an open window ruffled both the strands of her free-flowing hair and the white muslin undershift she had left on. She looked like some fairy-tale princess awaiting the kiss of her prince.

Well, he was no prince, but he was definitely willing to kiss.

Removing his clothes, John got into bed with her.

Leaning over her, he examined her features as she slept. The enormous violet eyes, closed now, covered in a gentle sweep of lashes; the small, pert nose; the determined chin with its feminine cleft; and those full, soft lips.

Since that day she had asked him to marry her, he hadn't been able to stop thinking of those lips. They were slowly driving him insane.

Now that he knew how they actually felt against him, on him, and under him, he really couldn't get them out of his mind.

There was *something* about the way Chloe's lips felt that was different from all of the others. The instant her lips touched him, he became racked with desire tremors. His whole body seemed to heat all at once with a . . . a *pleasure chill.*

It was almost as if he was beginning to actually crave her!

So far, he couldn't seem to get enough.

Maybe he never would. Maybe he was addicted to a Carrot.

He cast aside the fanciful thought, noticing how innocent and vulnerable she appeared lying across the bed in her white shift. He bent closer toward her, his hair brushing across her chest.

"Cold," she murmured in her sleep.

"Chloe." He spoke softly so as not to startle her. She was like a gentle lamb, lying there. . . .

Her hand suddenly came up and fastened onto his hair in a death clench.

As if it were a personal coverlet for her, she yanked the silken mass toward her in her sleep while turning on her side. Pulling him right along with her.

Pain was the word that came to John's mind.

"Good God! Chloe, let go!"

She didn't seem to hear him.

John reached over, trying to pry her tenacious grip from his hair. It took a while, but he finally freed himself. Minus several golden strands, which trailed from her fingers like a battle trophy.

Rubbing his scalp, he stretched out on his back next to her.

Some lamb. She had almost scalped him! He rubbed the side of his head again, this time continuing around the back of his head to feel the condition of the bump there. It had gone down quite a bit and wasn't nearly so sore any—

Whap!

The back of Chloe's hand was flung right into his eye.

He remained perfectly still until the agony subsided.

At which point he methodically lifted the small wrist with his thumb and forefinger; placing her hand down on the mattress between them.

Then he let loose. He was aching in so many places, he lost track of the count; the one below his waist was by far the worst. All of them, however, were caused by his turtledove.

"Dammit!" Already he could feel his eye swelling.

Instead of waking up, the hellcat turned cozily on her side away from him and snuggled back into his warmth. John's nostrils flared.

We're going to nap? Fine, if that was what she wanted; but he was not going to give her the chance to mutilate him again.

He turned on his side, moving in as close to her as he could get. Wrapping his legs around her, he tightly embraced her with his arms as well until he had the darling cocooned.

There. That should keep him safe.

Using her shoulder as a chin rest, he soon fell asleep.

He awoke to her thrashing. "John, let me loose! I can't move!"

"That is the idea," he drawled, half-asleep.

"What do you mean?" She squirmed about.

He released his hold, yawning.

Chloe flipped over, facing him. "Why did you—

What happened to your eye?" She gasped. "It's all black and blue."

He stared at her stonily.

Her fingers tentatively felt around his cheekbone, examining the area. The tender concern on her face was evident. "How did you do this?"

"You . . ." He paused, noting her genuine distress over the injury. Gallantly, he replied, "I walked into a door."

"You should be more careful, John!" She bit her lip as she cupped her palm over the sore spot. "You have to pay attention to what you're doing."

If he paid any more attention, he would have been coldcocked.

He gave her a crooked smile. "I have a good excuse; I was thinking of you, sweet."

She paused in her action to view him. "You were?"

"Mmm hmm." He took her hand from his face to kiss the center of her palm. His hot tongue swept a circle.

Chloe felt his swirling actions down to her toes. "Wh-what were you thinking?" She raised her mouth in invitation.

"I was remembering what you tasted like." His mouth claimed hers in a heated press. Once more he brought her tight within his embrace. This time she squirmed in pleasure.

"Remembering what you felt like . . ." His hands skimmed down her body, molding her to him.

"And you didn't see the door?" She kissed him before he could answer.

He cupped her buttocks, rubbing her right against his member. The thin cotton did nothing to disguise how erect he was.

"I didn't even feel it, Chloe-cat."

She purred at that report.

John lifted the shift over her head and tossed it over his shoulder. Under the circumstances, he thought he would be forgiven his embellishment of the tale. Especially since his motives were purely altruistic.

Or as altruistic as a rake's motives were likely to get.

Chapter Eight
A Curious Coincidence

They never made it down to dinner that evening.

The countess had thoughtfully sent up a cold collation to their suite.

Chloe smiled when she spotted the sprig of rosemary her grandmother had placed on the tray. Rosemary was a symbol of friendship, love, and faithfulness. Traditionally it was used in weddings, but it also gave one support to see things through.

Her grandmother was sending her a secret message to stay the course, for the prize was well worth the effort.

So, Grandmere knew. And she stood behind her granddaughter's choice. In that moment, Chloe had never loved her grandmother more.

Noticing her pensive expression, John lifted her chin with his finger. "What is it?"

"Nothing." Smiling tremulously at him, she stood on tiptoe to give him a quick peck on the lips. His arm came around her waist and he deepened the kiss. They had just made love for hours, yet he still indulged in the experience of her.

Reluctantly Chloe broke away. "I should like to bathe before we dine, John. Would you mind waiting?"

"Not at all. In fact, I'll tell them to bring up some extra water; we're bound to need more," he said with a comical leer.

True. The man never seemed to stop making love to her. Not that she was complaining. Although Chloe had no way of judging the meaning behind his energetic behavior, all in all she deemed it an encouraging sign. Besides which, he made her knees weak. One steaming flash of those emerald eyes from under those spiky, black lashes of his and she was ready to be dished out like a side of mutton. Never in her life had she experienced such pleasure!

Already John had more than demonstrated his special expertise.

It was not so much what he did—indeed, they were only beginning to explore that realm—it was *how* he went about it. There was something altogether sensual about John. He had the ability to immerse himself completely in the feeling of the moment.

Remembering the way he had touched her, and moved within her, she already wanted him again. She loved the way he *felt* inside her; strong yet gentle, in control yet willing to be piloted.

He was right—they were going to need more water.

Chloe nodded her head in agreement with his statement. "Why don't you just tell them to bring up a trough of hot water?" she stated seriously.

John threw back his head and roared with laughter. "It crossed my mind."

As soon as the tub was filled, Chloe gratefully sank down into the steaming water. Muscles she didn't even know she had were aching—but it was a good ache.

"Ahh, this feels wonderful." She rested back against the rim.

"Would you like me to help you?"

"Help me what?"

"Bathe." He watched her with a heavy-lidded expression indicative of a man who had discovered a treasure that suddenly belonged to him.

Chloe wasn't sure she trusted that look.

"Really, John, how could you help me bathe?"

Her wary response amused him. "Like this . . ."

He picked up the bar of scented soap she had left by the tub. Bringing it to his face, he took a deep inhalation of the flowery, light scent. It matched the perfume she wore, and he particularly loved that scent.

Whenever he caught the aroma of that fragrance now, it brought back to mind what it had felt like to be inside of her that first time. What it felt like every time . . .

"Are you just going to stand there smelling my soap all night, or are you going to show me what you meant?" she quipped from the tub.

He raised an eyebrow at her. "Patience, Chloe. I'm getting to it."

Kneeling next to her, he wet the soap, working up a good lather between his palms. Chloe closed her eyes as she waited for him to proceed. He was taking his own sweet time to—

His large, soapy hands began washing her shoulders and chest, paying careful attention to her breasts. Chloe could feel his tapered fingers lightly skimming around her aureole while he soaped and rinsed.

"Ahhh . . ."

"Like that, do you?"

Eyes still closed, she asked, "How can you tell?"

Two fingers slid across her breast, catching the pebble hard nub in a scissors grip. He tweaked.

Chloe sat straight up in the water. "John!"

He chuckled. "Easy, sweet; I'm not nearly finished."

That was what she was afraid of.

Continuing his job of cleansing, he smoothed his soapy hands down to her waist and around the curve of her hips. Stopping to relather, he washed each leg from the top of her thigh to her toes.

"You have beautiful legs, Chloe." His voice had gone husky of a sudden. Seductive.

"I do?" She held one dainty foot up in the air to see what it was he found so fascinating. Seemed like an ordinary leg to her. She shrugged. Whatever it was that had beguiled him had made his voice drop a register. At times, men were quite peculiar.

"Your legs are much nicer, John." She examined the muscular line of his legs from his thigh to his calves. They looked very strong. "I wager you could ride all day without tiring."

He pinched the bridge of his nose. Two laugh lines curved his cheeks as he grinned, shaking his head. "Chloe-monkey, you are definitely unique."

"Why is that?" She looked at him, perplexed.

"Never mind." He kissed the tip of her nose.

"Oh." Her violet eyes rounded as both the double meaning behind her innocent remark and his soapy hand at the juncture of her thighs came to her at once.

A deep dimple indented his face. "Mmm-hmm." His finger wiggled playfully between her nether lips.

Chloe was mortified. "John, don't!"

"I'm just washing you, sweet." He gave her an innocent look that failed to pass muster.

She grabbed his wrist. "No, you are not. You're playing and I won't have it!"

"Won't have what?" he asked suggestively, continuing to tease her with his hand.

She pursed her lips. "Very well, but just remember—I intend to return the favor, and I will be washing you next—so be careful what you do, for it will be returned to you tenfold."

He grinned outright. "Is that supposed to be a threat?"

Chloe threw a wet rag at him, which he neatly fielded.

Dropping his voice to an intimate tone, he leaned closer to her. "Let me give you a clue.

When you want to threaten someone, 'tis necessary to use something they would not welcome *wholeheartedly*." He roared with laughter at the surprised pout on her face.

"That is it! I am finished bathing." She stood up in the water, dripping wet. John's gaze traveled the length of her, a spark of desire lighting them.

"Let me wipe you off."

Before she could refuse, he wrapped her in a linen sheet, his hands guiding the material to the especially damp spots.

"Enough of that!" She pulled away from him, reaching for a bucket of hot water. "Your turn."

He backed up. "You aren't going to toss that on me, are you, sweet?"

"Of course not. It is for the tub." She smiled benignly at him.

Cautiously, while keeping a watch on her, he stepped into the tub. Fitting his tall frame in the cramped confines, he sat. "Now, what about that—"

Splash!

He waited until the water sluiced off his face. *Then* he reached for her.

Chloe was laughing and squealing at the same time. "No! Don't you dare!"

"I forgot to wash your hair . . . now come here,

my lady." He yanked her into the tub with him, pulling her across his lap.

"John, don't get me wet again!"

His white teeth flashed in a roguish grin. "Surely you don't mean that, Carrot."

Chloe blushed as red as her hair. "*Mon Dieu!* You are really too terrible!"

He blinked guilelessly. "Me? Terrible? Surely not!" The linen sheet covering her was yanked from her body and tossed over his shoulder to land on the carpet behind him.

"Now I am angry! I want to get something to eat and—"

Splash!

She waited for the water to sluice off her face. Tendrils of dripping hair streamed down her back.

"For that, you will pay!" She quickly grabbed the bar of scented soap and attacked him with it. Wielding it like a small weapon, she proceeded to lather him everywhere at once, leaving trails of bubbles in her wake.

John was laughing too hard to stop her. Even if he did smell like a bouquet of spring flowers.

She even laid siege to his head, soaping until his hair stood on end.

"There! Now you will think twice before—" She stopped to survey her creation. John had a soap cap, a soap beard, and soap breasts. Chloe's hand covered her mouth.

He batted his eyelashes at her.

She broke out in peals of laughter.

John chuckled with her. Capturing her chin with a soapy finger, he brought her mouth to his for a moist kiss. At the same time, his other hand massaged the back of her head.

Or so it seemed.

When he released her, he leaned back to view his own handiwork. Chloe sported a foam *chapeau.* "Would you like a feather for your new hat, dearest?"

She stuck her pink tongue out at him.

His strong fingers wove through her wet hair, pulling her close to him. "I dare you to do that again," he whispered against her mouth.

She did.

He captured the pink tongue with his teeth.

"Weleeze me!"

"Uuug uug."

Neither could speak clearly; however, both understood the other.

"Yohn!"

He snickered. *"One conditin."*

"Wha?"

"You finiss wassin me."

"All wight." She readily agreed.

He let go of her and rested back against the rim of the tub, spreading his arms. "I'm all yours, Lady Sexton."

She threw him a look that said *You'll be sorry.*

Taking the soap once more in hand, she preceded to lather up his chest, making wide, circular sweeping motions. She continued down his torso to the plane of his flat stomach.

Something brushed the edge of her hand.

Chloe looked down. Instead of cooling him off as she had intended, the brisk, no-nonsense motions appeared to be stimulating him. The head of his manhood broke the surface of the water, bobbing like a great underworld creature coming up for air.

Her mouth dropped open. " 'Tis a sea serpent!" She gasped in false terror.

John roared in laughter.

"I shall have to harpoon it!"

All laughter was cut off midchuckle. He sat bolt upright. "Don't even think it."

Chloe gave him a sly look as she rinsed off her hair. "Then I suppose I'm finished washing you?"

"I would say so, madam."

Chloe quickly stepped out of the tub and began drying off. Lord Sexton was very playful; however, Lady Sexton was very hungry.

John dunked his head under the water to cleanse it of soap. When he came up for air, he shook his head, flinging the water off, reminding Chloe of a pup after a bath.

She smiled softly. For all his sophistication, John had a lot of charmingly boyish traits.

They decided to eat their meal sitting on the carpet before the fireplace, even though no fire burned. It was a warm night for the time of year, and John had opened the French doors to the balcony, letting a gentle breeze into the room.

Both of them were wrapped in linen sheeting. Chloe had twisted a sheet around her hair like a turban. John teased her about being a sultan and he, the love slave.

Chloe snorted. "Do not attempt to pretend to be a woman's slave, Lord Sexton; it is simply not believable."

"Really," he intoned enigmatically.

She quickly yanked the turban off; he had a glint in his eye and there was no telling where that lively imagination was headed.

The spring breeze, redolent of fresh, blooming flowers, wafted about them as they ate.

John fed her little bits of cold roast beef, a potato-vegetable salad, and Spanish olives, sharing the same plate with her. For dessert, he tempted her with morsels of gingerbread and a spicy punch to wash it down.

By the time they finished eating, their hair was dry. It was late into the night; all the candles she had lit earlier had burned down to a soft glow.

John stood, offering her a hand up.

When she stood before him, he reached toward her and slowly removed the linen sheet she had wrapped around herself. He dropped it to the floor along with his own.

Thereupon, he swiftly picked her up in his arms and carried her, not to the bed as she had expected, but out onto the balcony.

"John!" Chloe protested, wriggling in his arms. They were stark naked!

He ignored her thrashing, carrying her over to the edge. "Look, Chloe; it's a full moon."

"Someone will see us! We can't—"

"No, they won't; it's late and this balcony overlooks the private gardens below. We are perfectly fine. Isn't it beautiful?"

Still unsure of being on a balcony, any balcony, without her clothes on, Chloe reluctantly viewed the scene before her.

Nightfall had brought with it a serene, lush splendor painted in shades of black and white, its tranquillity broken only by the occasional hooting of a white owl in a nearby tree.

Moonlight filtered down from above, silvering the gardens beneath them. In the distance, the light shimmered across the pond in ripples, silhouetting the pine trees in the forest beyond.

There was an enchantment to the night.

The air around them, sweet-smelling, seemed to beckon, as it mingled with the garden plantings bursting into bloom this early spring. The complete serenity made her ache inside with a feeling of gratitude that she was alive on this night, in this man's arms.

The flawless scene was a dreamscape come to life.

"*Chacun à Son Goût.*" She whispered the name of the beloved estate, awed by its magnificence. The ancestral estate of the Heart family that she had entrusted, along with herself, to John.

"My Garden of Eden," he said, bending his head to kiss her passionately. "You've given me a treasure, Chloe." He wasn't just speaking of the estate and they both knew it.

She put her arm around his neck, bringing him back down to her. "It was mine to give."

Moved, John moaned deep in his throat as his mouth took her. Always when he kissed her it happened—

That *something* kicked in his chest.

He felt like a man starving for air, while tasting euphoria at the same time. It was an enigma to him—he wanted her more and more. Each time he kissed her, he *had* to kiss her again. Each time he entered . . .

The precise recall of intimacy caused John to elicit his desire; a gravelly, purring declaration of pure sexuality.

Chloe responded to his sensual murmur; it was a part of John that spoke to her, a side of him she intuitively knew she alone could reach. Not just reach. *Intensify and ignite.*

Together they were magic.

Chloe was beginning to suspect that John recognized that fact as well.

Carefully he set her on the ledge of the balcony. The smooth stone wall was cool and about two feet wide. Light wind lifted her hair with a caress of breeze, sending the red tendrils up into the night.

John knelt before her, watching, as the same wind ruffled his own golden hair, now silvered from the moonlight. He seemed mesmerized by the sight of her.

Chloe had no way of knowing her beauty humbled him. Her entire essence seemed revealed to him as she sat upon that ledge, the stars crowning her. He was spellbound and could do naught but watch her haloed against the night.

His large hands held either side of her waist.

Eventually he rested his cheek against her knee. "Chloe," he finally whispered.

Chloe's fingertips brushed the silken hair along the side of his face. *Wake up, John,* she willed the handsome man before her. *Please, wake up.*

He raised his face to meet her gaze, emerald eyes heavy-lidded with physical passion. It was not what she had hoped for . . . but it was on the right pathway.

She had known John almost her whole life. Knew his thoughts, his moods, and now his yearnings. Chloe knew what he wanted from her.

Strange, but she did not feel shy at all about this.

Whatever John's feelings, Chloe knew he accepted her for who she was. She had always been comfortable with him.

She lifted his chin with the curve of her hand. "You wish to taste me, Lord Sexton?"

The green eyes flared with raw hunger. "Yes," he said. "Oh, yes."

His hands fell to her knees, separating them gently. Without hesitation, he began to make love to the delicate inner skin of her thighs, his mouth tender and careful as he introduced her to this new form of loving.

Chloe watched his golden head between her legs.

Satin lips glided along her limbs, laving in the softest of caresses. Taking his time, he nibbled lightly up and down her thighs, coming close to but not reaching his supreme destination, as if that particular portion were a favorite dessert he was saving for the ultimate treat.

He rubbed his face along her yielding softness, whispering something unintelligible, only to place a small kiss very close to the juncture of her thighs.

Then he laid his head upon her, hugging her to him.

Chloe cupped the side of his face.

He closed his eyes, leaning into her hand. Kissing her palm. "Bring me to you. Like you did that first time."

She did as he asked. She brought him forward to her as he knelt between her legs. Until she felt his warm breath against her.

She trembled.

He kissed her there. A reverent placement of lips and mouth upon her woman's mound.

Chloe closed her eyes, her head falling back at the exquisite sensation of him at such an intimate place, his breath hot, his lips hot.

John murmured something against her,

something that sounded erotic and sensual. *Something that was desire.*

He cradled her derriere in his grasp, bringing her closer to him; he wanted to capture this special experience and make it theirs alone.

A silky masculine tongue slid along her cleft.

Chloe cried out at the feel of him.

He brought her even closer to him and slipped inside her. And paused. And flicked. And paused. And licked.

Chloe clutched his broad shoulders, not believing the sensations he was capable of giving her.

He stroked his tongue inside, withdrawing to flick a hidden part of her that was hard and throbbing. Her fingers sank into his thick hair, clutching the silken mass in her grip.

He suckled her nether lips, stroking and caressing. Lost in what he was doing, he clutched her tight against his face, drowning in her scent, her texture, her taste. So immersed was he that he never consciously heard her mewling cries, her uninhibited moans of pleasure.

He simply loved her with his mouth.

And it was then that Chloe truly knew why he had been labeled the Lord of Sex. John had surrendered himself completely to the physical. Every ounce of feeling that the man possessed was channeled into his sexual actions. He was raw intensity.

He began licking her—long, even strokes. She called out to him with the passion he was arousing in her. It only increased the beat of his private dance. John grazed and swirled and flicked; she couldn't catch her breath. She sobbed out loud.

He scraped his teeth against her; she screamed his name.

He only responded to her with his tongue. Holding her firmly against his lips, he plunged into her. When he felt her quiver around him, *he* groaned aloud.

The vibration of his exclamation further added to her intense sensation. A tumult of waves flooded her, sending her cascading over the top like a waterfall.

"Sweet, sweet," he rasped, burying his face in her liquid essence.

The aftermath still shook her, and he seemed determined to milk every tremor he could out of her.

Chloe threw her head back. Bonelessly, her hands rested on his head; she could not seem to move them. She opened her eyes to the moon in the sky above. White fingers of clouds stretched across the ink sky like wispy, beckoning tendrils.

So perfect, she thought. *So very perfect.*

She would remember this night for as long as she lived. It was forever etched into her mind; a light-and-dark painting of her soul.

John's actions slowly dwindled down to an occasional lick of his tongue; he snuggled his face against her mound lovingly, his arms embracing her around the waist as he held her close. He didn't want to release her. Ever.

John had never experienced anything like what had just happened to him.

He wasn't sure what exactly *had* happened to him, but he knew it was significant. As soon as the tip of his tongue captured the first droplet of her dew, he was lost beyond reason. A hot chill raced through his body. Again, he had been like a starving man discovering a banquet laid out before him.

What was happening to him?

Whatever it was, it was getting worse—or better, depending on one's perspective. As before, the more he had, the more he wanted.

It was starting to worry him.

Although there was no need to worry. She was here with him and she was his wife, so there was no cause to . . .

Then why did he feel uneasy?

Since the first evening of their marriage he had worried over the possibility of losing her friendship with the advent of intimacy; this apprehension had not subsided. The concern was still there, only now the focus had shifted considerably. His concerns had taken on a new tone and direction.

His desire for her was overcoming him.

What was more, he had known from the moment he had first kissed her—Nay. At least he could be honest with himself. He had *always* known that he would never share her with anyone.

Then why had he let her believe that he would?

A voice inside whispered, *So you could marry her.*

The disturbing thought echoed in his mind.

It was true. He had married her under false pretenses. He had wanted her solely for himself. How was he ever going to tell her that?

She might not like the idea very much—especially since she had bargained with him for her freedom.

To hell with that idea!

Lady Sexton belonged to Lord Sexton, and no one was going to lay a finger on her except him!

She would just have to get used to—

What about him?

Was he going to give up his mode of living as

well? A strange revelation occurred to him. He didn't care about his other women.

Not a whit.

Not compared to what he had with—

He looked up at her suddenly, his face awash with wonder. He didn't care about his past life! This was the life he wanted! The life at *Chacun à Son Goût*.

"What is it?" Chloe smoothed her hand across the side of his face.

"I . . ." He didn't know what to say. What *could* he say? That he suddenly decided to forgo the terms of their agreement and keep her to himself? How would she respond to that? What possible reason could he give? She would be furious and rightly so. He had misled her.

And he didn't even understand the entire situation himself. Truthfully, at the moment, he was more than confused. Besides which, that foreboding feeling was back, warning him to retreat.

There was no need to panic just yet, he reasoned.

They were still each honoring their pact, and there was plenty of time for him to work this out. He took a deep breath. "Nothing." He drew her to him, burying his face in her midriff. "Nothing to be concerned about, my Carrot."

Chloe hugged him back, not fooled for a minute. She knew him too well. *Something* had occurred to Lord Sexton. Just what it was, she would have to wait to find out.

John stood between her legs, bringing her closer to him. With his arm wrapped firmly around her waist, he brought her leg up and around his lean hip as his lips sought out her throat.

Chloe wrapped her arm around his strong neck, wanting him closer. His member rubbed along her cleft, sliding back and forth without entering her in a motion designed to torment and please at the same time.

"Come inside, John, please," she whispered, her face cuddling into his chest.

"Not yet." He took the twin globes of her derriere in a firm hold, bringing her up to him as he glided between her thighs. Her earlier moisture that he had so expertly brought forth aided his slide.

He nibbled along her collar while he teased and moved. Chloe caught the scent of roses, and jasmine, and her own personal scent mingled on him. The result was rich and evocative.

She uttered a brief declaration at the discovery.

"I know," he intoned in a husky voice. " 'Tis a perfect blend."

"John . . ." She took his face between her hands, kissing him deeply.

He stroked along her back with one hand while the other still cupped her to him. He seemed content to stay like this with her, rocking back and forth, holding her as he came to a measured boil.

A pair of swans glided across the pond under the moonlight. Their smooth passage added to the magic of the night. Seeing their passage, John stood Chloe before him, turning her in his arms so she could view the lovely scene.

"They're mates," he whispered behind her, his arms encircling her waist, bringing her flush against him.

"It's so beautiful, John." His warmth behind her was a comforting counterpoint to the cooler breeze.

"Yes," he said, but he was not looking at the swans; he was looking at her—his mate. He placed a gentle kiss on her shoulder, his powerful thigh wedging between her legs.

"Hold on to the edge of the balcony." He hinted in a hoarse undertone what he was about to do.

A puff of air escaped her lips; she hadn't known it could be done in such a way. "Like this?" she asked, her voice faint with surprise.

"Oh, yes, sweet." He smiled, enchanted with her winsome naivete.

The thick head of his manhood pressed against her feminine portal. Chloe sucked in her breath.

He pressed forward slightly. John could feel her clamping up on him; she was nervous with the new position, yet didn't want to tell him.

"Watch the swans, love. See the way they glide on the water." He pushed forward slightly, gliding into her a few inches.

Chloe swallowed. "They—they look so lovely."

"Yes, you are." Another inch.

Chloe gasped, her inner muscles tightening.

"Ease up, Chloe. Relax . . ." He captured her earlobe with his teeth to shift her focus.

"I-I'm—"

John tried a different tactic. "Do you see the splendor of this estate, Chloe? It belongs to us—every tree, every blade of grass, every flower. Together. It blends perfectly, like a man and woman . . ." Another inch.

She clutched the masculine arms around her waist. "John!"

"Like us, Chloe." His breath was hot at her ear; he nibbled the edge of her lobe. "You feel so, so good, kitten. So incredibly perfect."

Chloe could feel him trying to come inside her

yet more. The position was allowing him to enter her very deeply. He burrowed in another inch.

John was a very big man, and she was still tender from the newness of her experiences with lovemaking. She whimpered, a combination of confusion and desire.

"Don't fight it." He laved the indentation of her collarbone. "You'll enjoy this, sweet; you'll see . . . trust me?"

Chloe bit her lip, silently nodding her head. In this, as in all things, she trusted him. If he said he was going to bring her pleasure, then he would. She relaxed around him.

Her unconditional acceptance of him moved him greatly. He hugged her to him. "I'm going to glide all the way into you now—as far as I can go. We'll be like the swans, Chloe, gliding together. . . ."

He did as he said.

Slid into her as far as he could.

The fullness of him throbbing within her took her breath away. In fact, he was within her so tightly . . .

"John."

He moaned something low, his hand cupping her chin to turn her to him. Angling his head, he joined their mouths.

"Like the swans," he mouthed against her lips, moving now inside her, gliding back and forth in an easy rocking motion.

The white owl hooted into the night; the breeze drifted around them; the moonlight silvered them. They became one with the night—part of the very essence of the magic of the scenery around them.

Lord John made love to her.

His compelling slides within her took on strength and purpose as he increased his actions. Caught along with his wife in the spell of *Chacun à Son Goût*. In the spell of Chloe's charms.

Bringing her hips into the contour of his own, he pinned her to him in a taut hold, stroking firm and fast. He called out her name over and over. He remembered her taste and inhaled her essence all over again as he strained inside her. His cries matched hers as he strove to bring them higher and higher.

Chloe knew she would never forget this night. Ever.

Her head fell back, encountering the muscled wall of his chest. It was all she could do not to yell out her true feelings for him. Somehow, she managed to hold back. It was not time—nowhere near time. . . .

One of his hands released her hip to palm her breast, while the other maintained its firm hold on her. He brushed the tip with a skimming caress. The fine touch, so at counterpoint to his other motions below, made her ache with longing.

How could a woman want a man so much?

A sob of desire escaped her lips.

John answered her by placing hot, hungry kisses on the back of her neck. His hand left her breast to skim her nether curls. She knew what he was going to do. Her hand came over his wrist to stop him—it would be too much.

"No, please, don't." She gasped, breathless.

He ignored her request, sinking his fingers in the rich, red hair. Finding what he was looking for in a well of her liquid honey.

His forefinger stroked the hard little nub in circular motions as he mirrored the action inside her by rotating his hips.

Chloe screamed her release into the night wind.

With a guarded strength, he drove into her fiercely, his raw cry echoing hers as he too found completion.

Chloe sagged in his grip, almost fainting in his hold. The experience had overwhelmed her physically and emotionally. John gathered her in his arms, carrying her back into their room.

When he bent over her to place her in their bed, he was surprised to see tears on her face. He wiped one away. "What's this?" he asked, concerned, his voice still hoarse from his own experience.

"Beautiful," she whispered. "It was so beautiful."

His eyes became suspiciously damp. "Yes, sweet, it was."

John was at a loss for words himself, so he simply joined her in bed, covering them both with a thin coverlet. Making sure to wrap her securely in his arms.

It had been the most wondrous experience of his life.

And it worried him profoundly.

Chapter Nine
Surrounded by Cyns

A few days later, John happened to be crossing through the foyer when a great pounding commenced at the front door of the house. Eyebrow raised, he stood in the center of the entry, wondering what new trouble was about to fall on his doorstep. One thing could be said for *Chacun à Son Goût*—it was never dull.

The butler hastily walked to the door, apologizing to Lord Sexton the whole way, as if the noise on the doorstep were somehow his fault. He opened the door to seven shouting Frenchman, all speaking at once.

And a bedraggled bunch they were too.

The poor butler put his hands up to try to bring some order to the fracas, but the French were having none of it. Each one tried to talk over the other in an effort to get his opinion heard.

John calmly stepped forward. "Having a bit of a problem, Calloway?"

The staid butler cleared his throat. "Aye, my lord. Can't make heads or tails of what they're saying."

"Allow me." John faced the motley group, surprised to recognize the Cyndreac brothers on his doorstep.

"In English, lads." He grinned at them, oddly glad to see they still had their heads. For all their rowdiness, they were an engaging bunch.

"Lord Sexton," one of them spoke up in perfect, unaccented English above the yammering of the others. "We are seeking Countess de Fonbeaulard and her granddaughter—if this servant will only let us by!"

"And what is your business with them?"

"Do not be foolish! We seek asylum, of course! We have just escaped from the Place de Greve! We are great friends with the Fonbeaulards; now if you would let us pass . . ." He was younger and slightly shorter than John but still managed to look down his aristocratic French nose at the viscount. "We have had an ordeal—as you can see."

They did appear some the worse for wear. They were bedraggled, filthy, and probably starving as well. Despite their state, they were still remarkably elegant.

Apparently even the rigors of dungeon life weren't enough to dampen their joie de vivre.

He was going to let them in, of course. But he needed to make one thing clear to these wild pups before he did.

Leaning insolently against the door frame, he blocked the one who had spoken to him from sweeping past. "Let's get one thing clear between us, Count Cyndreac."

Seven count faces watched him haughtily.

"I am the master of this estate; it is my approval you need seek—for *everything*."

"You?" One of them sneered. "You are but a fixture, from what I hear!" He tried to elbow past John, but the viscount held his ground.

"Hmm. Sorry, lads, but this fixture is wed to the mistress of the estate, which means . . ." He let the idea sink in.

All fourteen of the golden eyes widened at once. *Message delivered.*

It was rather comical, the speed with which they began to ingratiate themselves to him.

Two of them slapped his back; one winked at him; another nodded approvingly; while still another declared him the finest choice for the countess.

"Who said anything about the countess?" he asked softly. "I am husband to Chloe."

"Not Chloe!" A great wail issued forth. Apparently this news did not sit as well with the brothers. "But *we* intended to marry her!"

John shook his head. "All seven of you?" he asked dryly.

"Do not be foolish! We decided on the way here that Adrien would marry her! Now what will we do?" They all threw their hands up in the air.

John couldn't help but smile. "I hadn't realized any of you fellows were on the marriage mart. All of the stories I've heard have indicated just the opposite."

"Well, yes, but this is different!" one answered.

"How so?"

"We need an estate!"

"Ours has been confiscated!"

"What is a count without an estate?" They all speared him a pointed look.

Up until very recently John had been a viscount without an estate.

"Believe me, lads, you'll survive," he intoned sardonically. "Come on inside—you look about ready to drop." He held the door open for them.

They gratefully entered.

The Cyndreacs were brash but likable; John bore them no ill-will, and they were close friends of his wife's family.

"*Merci,* Lord Sexton," the one who first spoke said. "We are grateful for your hospitality; it has been a difficult journey."

"How did you get here?" he asked quietly.

"It was the Black Rose. He saved us from the blade in the *nick* of time." The youth grinned cheekily at his pun, although John noted he was a tad white around the mouth. The experience had been no lighthearted romp for them. John admired the lad's bravery.

"And he brought you here?" John inquired curiously. This was a peculiar turn of events.

"To your very doorstep, Lord Sexton."

John rubbed his chin. "Hmm." First Zu-Zu, now the Cyndreacs. Very curious.

The butler led them up the stairs. "One thing else, Counts." They all turned on the stairs to look at him. They really did appear exhausted. John felt a trifle sorry for them.

"*Oui*?" They all said at once.

Whatever he had to say could wait. He smiled kindly at them. "Rest well; you're safe here."

They all smiled gratefully at him, hurrying after Calloway.

Good Lord, they were younger than he thought. Younger and bound to be trouble. They appeared to be from about sixteen to around twenty-one or thereabouts; although he couldn't tell who was what, they all looked so much alike.

Wonderful. Seven brothers who, by all accounts, had had no parental guidance in years and, as members of the—until recently—privileged class, were probably spoiled rotten. They certainly had a wild reputation. It almost rivaled his. Not quite, but then, not many did.

He grinned. The Seven Deadly Cyns. Here in his house.

The smile slowly died on his face. *In the same house as his beautiful Chloe?* The viscount's normally golden skin tone paled.

He would guillotine them himself if they didn't behave!

See if he didn't.

Percy ambushed John as he made his way down for dinner that evening. Already he was late.

Chloe had spent the afternoon helping the countess bottle some aromatic oils, a task she told him she especially enjoyed after the winter.

Since they had barely left their room the past few days, he had sent her on her way with a quick kiss, deciding to explore some of the Heart family legacy stored in the attic.

He had unearthed two very interesting personal diaries and they captured his attention the entire afternoon.

Briefly, he wondered what had become of the Sexton personal belongings. Perhaps he could begin tracking some of his own family's legacy and purchase it back? The idea intrigued him. He made a mental note to ask Chloe what she thought of the idea. Chloe was very good at ferreting out details; she would be of invaluable help in the project, if they decided to undertake it.

Admitting the fact that he had no head for figures, he acknowledged that she would probably be the one to do the research, cataloging, and purchasing as well.

Actually, she would have to take charge of the whole thing.

He blew out a gust of air. Maybe it was too much to ask of her. Well, if he let her know he would work right alongside her, perhaps she would consider it.

The Lord of Sex goes on an antique-hunting mission. He snickered. Who would believe this?

He was thinking about how enjoyable it might turn out to be—chasing down the pieces, traveling together to acquire them—when Percy waylaid him in the hallway.

It was the Spanish fly dilemma revisited.

Why did I take this hallway? John recoiled from the injustices of fate.

"Percy, will you cease! I am not interested in the noddy color of your breeches!"

The fop squeaked in horror, the sound reverberating through John's skull. "Breeches? I am not referring to breeches! I speak of a much more important accessory—the waistcoat!"

"Give me strength." Lord Sexton gnashed his teeth.

By the time they made it down to the dining room, everyone was already seated around the table, several voluble conversations going on at once.

Percy paused with him in the doorway to remark, "You see, John? You are like Don Giovanni—the ghosts of the French aristocracy dine at your table." Lips twitching, he gestured with his hand, indicating the impatient assemblage. They kept to town hours at *Chacun à Son Goût.*

"Very amusing, Percy. Let us hope they do not portend my demise." Winking, John took his seat at the head of the table.

Percy raised his lorgnette to examine the viscount. "There are all kinds of demise, my good fellow. Just see if there isn't." Grinning at his own private amusement, Percy took his own seat next to the Zambeau, who had managed to capture a place for herself at John's right.

John wryly glanced down the table, noting that the Cyndreacs were cleaned up, reclothed, and bushy tailed. Two of them sported black eyes that hadn't been there a few hours ago.

He recognized several articles of his own clothing, hanging in a poor fit on the younger men. Across the table from them, Deiter was wearing his gold waistcoat. He squinted at the far end, where his uncle was sporting a new shirt under a dark coat.

That's my ivory shirt!

No wonder his clothes kept disappearing. Something one of the Cyndreacs was saying caught his attention.

". . . we are Cyndreacs; we live for romance!"

Wonderful. That was what he needed to hear.

One could only endure. He sighed, lifting his soup spoon to his lips.

"Aren't they marvelous?" The Zambeau placed her hand on his thigh, smiling coquettishly as she confided, "They're a bit too young for my taste—I prefer the more accomplished."

John halted in the act of tasting his mulligatawny soup and blinked once. The woman's hand was traveling up his leg with the speed of a fast trotter. Slowly, he raised his eyes to glance across the table at—

The phrase *throwing daggers with one's eyes* took on new meaning. His wife lifted her wineglass and swallowed a measure of drink. Then she turned to the nearest Cyndreac and gave him a devastating smile.

John's nostrils flared. It wasn't as if he had invited this!

He turned to Zu-Zu. "Countess, I believe you have misplaced your hand."

"Have I?" she toyed with him.

She was a woman used to getting what she wanted. Viscount Sexton had no intentions of encouraging her. Nor would he allow Chloe to continue to flirt with that young pup.

"Do not trifle with me." He spoke harshly, under his breath. "Remove it."

The Zambeau pouted; then instantly brightened. "You are hungry, no? How inconsiderate of me—we will pick up again later."

"No, we will—" But she had already turned her attention to something Percy was saying. Desultorily, he went back to his soup.

At the other end of the table, Maurice curiously watched the exchange, his shrewd gaze going back and forth between Chloe and John. *Ho-ho.* He fixed his sights on the Cyndreacs, a slow smile spreading across his features. It was past time he took them under his wing.

"So . . . the Black Rose has once again appeared in the nick of time." Maurice took a sip of wine. "Was it close for you, Jean-Jacques?"

"Jean-Jacques?" John asked, confused.

"*Oui,* I am Jean-Jacques." Jean-Jacques, John soon learned, was the name of one of the Cyndreacs. Chloe gleefully informed him of the others.

"This is Jean-Paul, Jean-Louis, Jean-Claude, Jean-Jules, Jean-Pierre, and . . . Adrien."

John's lips twitched. "Adrien?" Where did that fit in?

"*Oui,*" the one at the end answered.

John noted it was the same brother who had spoken to him in the hall. The one the others seemed to listen to. Good lord, he was starting to tell them apart. "You are the oldest, then?"

"*Non,* I am the youngest."

John's jaw dropped. "But they listen to you."

"I have the best title." He beamed proudly. "Papa saved it for me."

"Besides that," Jean-Jules piped in, "he is the smartest of us. Papa said he finally got it right with Adrien."

Adrien grinned.

"What about the twins?" Chloe asked.

"*Twins?*" John echoed.

"Yes, Jean-Paul and Jean Claude are obviously twins, John."

How could she tell? They all looked alike to him. Same black curly hair, white teeth, and gold eyes. He shrugged.

"The twins were before me," Adrien answered philosophically.

John rolled his eyes, for once grateful he had never had to deal with siblings. Although this group seemed happy enough with each other—if you overlooked the two black eyes and the constant squabbling. The corners of his mouth curved upward.

Maurice returned to his earlier topic of the Black Rose. "Whoever he is, we owe him a great debt for saving our friends." He gestured to the table at large.

"Hear, Hear!" Many at the table concurred by clinking their wineglasses with their forks.

"To the Black Rose!" Percy suddenly stood as if overcome with benevolence for the unknown savior. He raised his glass in toast. "*Arma virumque cano*—I sing of arms and the man!"

Please don't. John winced, knowing what was coming. Sure enough, Percy started in on that dreadful poem.

"They search high and they search low . . ."

Chloe, Maurice, and the two countesses joined him. ". . . the proletariat wonder where he could go . . ."

The malady is spreading. John pinched the bridge of his nose.

Finally it ended with the appalling finale: ". . . that blasted, evasive Rose!"

John breathed again.

The Cyndreacs seemed to like it, all of the counts immediately begging Chloe to teach it to them. If they started reciting it, John decided he was tossing them out, guillotine or not.

"It was close for us." Jean-Jules spoke quietly. "Others were not so lucky."

"Anyone we knew?" Maurice asked.

"The Duc de Montaine and his daughter, Barone Dufond."

"You remember them, Chloe, do you not?" Jean-Claude asked. "He was always with his nose in the air and she with her buck teeth and cockeyes." He demonstrated by crossing his eyes and sticking out his top teeth.

"She cannot help the way she looks," Jean-Jules defended the lady, showing a sensitive streak in his nature.

"True." Adrien shrugged. "But she is forever whining, Jules. You must admit that."

"Well, she will not be whining soon." He threw down his napkin and left the room.

Everyone was surprised by his abrupt departure. Finally Adrien spoke. "It was hardest on

Jules; he is of a reflective nature and the injustices have sickened him. He was ill in the prison. . . ." His voice trailed off as if he too did not want to remember the horrors they had witnessed.

"Will he be all right?" Chloe was worried for the kind young man.

"Yes, Jean-Jules has enormous strength of character."

John viewed Adrien with a new respect. It was becoming clear to him why the Cyndreacs looked to him for direction. Despite his age he was a born leader.

"These stories are so distressing." Percy dabbed his eyes with his lace handkerchief. "To think—the seven of you fine young men thrown into prison simply because you—"

"Wait a minute." John sat straight up in his chair. "Seven of you! Countess Zambeau, didn't you say *six* were imprisoned, that one had escaped?"

Zu-Zu looked quite surprised. "Why, yes, I thought there were six."

John speared Adrien with a challenging look. "What have you to say, Comte Cyndreac; how is it one of you was not in prison yet is here now? Perhaps it is because one of you is the Black Rose, hmm?"

The Cyndreacs looked at each other.

Adrien clearly did not like this turn of events. "That is ridiculous, Lord Sexton! With all due respect, Zu-Zu, you are mistaken; we were all taken."

The Zambeau furrowed her brow. "Perhaps I was mistaken. I would recognize the man who saved me; it was not a Cyndreac."

John wasn't convinced.

"Don't blame you for trying, Sexton; everyone is dying to know his identity." Percy swallowed a piece of fowl. "They say he used to be a pirate. Fancy that, what? Robbing the aristocracy one day only to save their heads the next."

Everyone began commenting on that juicy tidbit. Until Deiter's moribund tone broke through the chatter.

"*In my village, a man died four times*."

Everyone stopped speaking to stare agog at the man who had uttered this bizarre snippet.

"The first time he died, we buried him in the churchyard." He pierced his captive audience with a morose glower. Schnapps helped by showing his tooth. "He came back."

Everyone gasped.

Except Chloe, who, John noted, had a gleam of anticipation in those violet eyes. The bloodthirsty little wench, he thought with a chuckle.

She loved nothing better than a lurid tale.

"The second time . . ." The dinner guests leaned forward. "The wolves . . ." He trailed off.

"The wolves," Jean-Louis prodded him. "What about the wolves?"

Deiter's chin dropped onto his chest; a loud snore followed.

"Ohhhh!" Everyone sat back in their seats, disappointed.

John stifled a chuckle. *They get bamboozled every time.*

"Well, I heard an amusing story the other day." Percy patted his mouth with his napkin. "You know the Earl of Louder, John?"

John opened his mouth to answer; however, in that briefest of pauses wherein one takes a breath, Percy continued on. Sir Cecil-Basil apparently lived by the maxim He who hesitates is interrupted.

"The fellow is rather an impossible hypochondriac. Can't tolerate anything that even hints at rumpling his perfectly ordered existence."

"Sounds somewhat familiar," John mumbled into his glass.

"They say he hasn't spoken a word for five years!"

"Why?" The countess hadn't heard this.

"Don't know; one can only assume he felt the

spoken word disrupted his orderly life, somehow bringing the threat of disease with it."

"How eccentric." Zu-Zu never considered any member of the aristocracy as out-and-out peculiar.

"Oh, there's more! Seems he was told that a certain authoress was coming to see him—believe it was Mariane Turnery—the one who wrote that romantic novel . . ."

"Oh, she's marvelous!" The countess smiled.

Percy made a moue with his mouth. "Couldn't go by the earl; he suddenly started screeching, 'Take me away, take me away!' "

Everyone at the table started laughing, including John.

Percy added drolly, "Seems that the horror of an infestation of *literary pestilence* was enough to snap the man out of his monomania."

The dining room roared with laughter.

The following afternoon, John sat in the study staring morosely at the ledgers before him.

He detested ledgers.

Why was he even bothering with them? Especially on a day like this? His sights went to the French doors behind his desk that led out into a garden. It was a beautiful day, sunny and warm.

What he really wanted to do was take Chloe out into that garden and . . .

There was little chance of that happening.

His nostrils flared. For some reason, Chloe was furious with him. She had even refused to make love with him, turning her back on him in bed last evening.

That had angered John.

He had wanted her so much that he had almost been tempted to inform her that as her husband it was his right, if he so desired it.

However, he came to his senses when he realized what he would sound like. John had never been close to pompous and he wasn't about to start now.

It was the Zambeau's fault, no doubt about it.

After the men had partaken of their port last evening and rejoined the ladies in the salon, Zu-Zu had shamelessly pursued him. The entire evening. No matter what he said to discourage the woman, it made no difference. She simply ignored his wishes and proceeded with her lavish fascination.

Chloe was sure John had somehow invited the attention, hinting that she would respond in like manner while subtly remarking that Adrien was the handsomest of the Cyndreacs, in her opinion, even if they were all stunning.

At that point John supposed he got a bit pompous. He informed her in no uncertain terms that she had better not be spending her time wondering who was the handsomest Cyndreac, for it surely would have no meaningful effect on her.

She had turned away from him in a huff, although at the time he could have sworn he caught the hint of a pleased smile on her face. He convinced himself it was a trick of the low lighting.

There was no reason for her to be pleased that he practically *ordered* her to stay away from the French counts.

In any case, she had gone to sleep, leaving him to stew in more ways than one.

Another new experience for him, thanks to Chloe.

Sexual frustration.

Whoever said abstinence was good for the soul? His fingers drummed the desktop. He didn't care for it much and he certainly didn't feel good!

When he woke this morning—still painfully aroused—he had reached for her, only to discover that she was already gone. "Picking violets," her note had said.

He sighed. This was an odd twist of events for him: the Lord of Sex with no sex. And no substantial relief without his wife.

He passed a hand over his face.

The thing was, he couldn't figure out how he got into this labyrinthine situation in the first place. But since he had, he didn't see why he should have to suffer.

Dejected, he opened up another ledger, staring blankly at the page. He noticed the majority of the entries were in the flowery script of the Countess de Fonbeaulard. As he scanned the columns he noted a section where she had put several question marks in the margins. This area was followed by a bold, brash style that John recognized as his uncle's.

He smiled, immediately figuring out what had occurred. There had been some discrepancies and Maurice had straightened out the problem for her.

The two of them had watched out for Chloe so well, taking care of the estate for her with meticulous care. The later entries, he saw, were done in a neat, precise imprint along with his uncle's. Maurice had been teaching Chloe how to keep the books.

He was like a grandfather to her. . . .

Which made it all the more amazing that he actually entrusted her welfare to John, a man he knew to be a notorious rake.

Why did everyone trust him so much?

Now they were actually looking to him for guidance! It baffled him completely.

Idly, he examined the ink entries.

She had the most winsome nose. It crinkled when she laughed. Sometimes he liked to tease her by kissing the tip—

What was he doing?

He needed to see to these ledgers! He focused on the small figures in dark blue ink. Almost violet, really.

Like her eyes . . .

He could drown in those eyes.

John slammed the book shut. Later. He would look at the books later.

He rested his chin in the palm of his hand. Perhaps he should write a letter to his solicitor, requesting any information the man might be able to find on the Sexton heirlooms.

Yes, that sounded like a good idea.

He opened the desk drawer, taking out paper, quill, and ink. A tiny lock of carroty hair, tied with a pink ribbon, rested in a corner of the drawer.

He removed it, smiling faintly. Chloe's baby hair.

His finger stroked the soft lock. He remembered when her hair had been this fine. A little girl he treasured.

Now a wife he cherished.

Where had that thought come from? A film of sweat broke out across his brow. He did not want to deal with entanglements in his life. Chloe was—

Outside the French doors, he heard the faint voices of the Cyndreacs, "*. . . un . . . deux . . . trois!*" followed by what sounded like a squeal of delight. He shook his head, going back to his thoughts.

She was—

"*. . . un . . . deux . . . trois!*" This time he heard a definite shriek and identified it as Lady Sexton's exclamation.

He bolted out of his chair and raced to the doors, throwing them wide.

There on the lawn in front of him, the Cyndreacs had his wife in the middle of a sheet and they were tossing her up in the air as if she were a new toy or a playful little trinket for their diversion.

He stormed out onto the lawn. "Put her down at once!" he roared.

They all gave him similar looks of stupefaction mixed with a dollop of fear. Fortunately they kept their hold on the sheeting, as Chloe was in the process of tumbling through the air.

She landed in the center with a *whump!*

"Did you not hear me?" His voice was very low and very threatening.

The seven brothers let go of the sheet and took off.

Chloe sat in the center, surrounded by violets, which were scattered over her, over the cloth, and on the ground. Her hands were planted firmly on her hips, a frown of disapproval gracing her lovely face.

She was not pleased.

"John, whatever is the matter with you?"

"Have you no sense? They were flinging you in the air!"

"So what?"

"So what? You—you could have . . . they shouldn't . . ." Not sure exactly what he wanted to say, but positive he needed to say it, John crossed his arms over his chest and scowled.

A huge grin spread across Chloe's face. "Come here, John." She patted the spot next to her.

He raised an eyebrow, reluctantly joining her on the sheet. "What?" he muttered.

Her dimples deepened. "Are you jealous?"

He snorted. "Don't be ridiculous."

"You seem jealous to me." She smoothed out the material beneath her hand in a laissez-faire attitude.

He placed his hands on her shoulders, commanding her full attention. "No more jealous than you were last evening over the countess."

Chloe looked him right in the eye. "Then you are very jealous."

A gust of air escaped his lips. She had surprised him again. "Chloe . . ." He hesitated; then his expression darkened. "Don't play with me—I don't like it. Not from you."

"I'm not playing with you, my lord." She moved closer to him so he could feel her heat.

He stared at her silently.

"I wouldn't play with you, John." She smoothed a lock of his hair back off his forehead. "Unless you needed it," she clarified.

This was more than he could handle. There had never been these kinds of games between them.

He grabbed her wrist, stopping her intimate action. His jade eyes sparked down at her. "Do not look for trouble, madam," he responded in a clipped tone, "for you shall surely find it."

Chloe flinched, taken aback by his brusquness. It was a side of John that not many saw. The determined strength of him, the shutter that closed over him when something scratched the surface of his feelings.

This was the first time she had attempted it and it was the first time he had ever shut her out. It hurt her deeply.

Tears filled her eyes and she pulled away from him.

John felt instant remorse, along with a peculiar tightening in his chest.

Placing his hands on her shoulders, he pulled her back to him. "I'm sorry, Chloe-cat; I didn't mean that the way it came out."

Although shocked at his apology, Chloe immediately realized the leap he had just taken. Sniffing, she peeked up at him. "How did you mean it?"

He opened his mouth but couldn't seem to find the right answer. "I'm not sure," he finally admitted.

Chloe viewed him curiously. John was starting to have the most wonderfully confused looks on his face. To her, it was a picture lovelier than the finest Fragonard!

Confusion was *excellent*.

She cupped his mutinous chin, placing a soft kiss on his mouth. "Let's forget it for now, John," she whispered. "Anyway, I think I should like to take a nap." She faked a yawn, sending him a burning look from under her lashes.

Lord Sexton brightened immediately.

"Napping" was an excellent topic for him.

And a safe one, too.

Chapter Ten
The Rose Reappears

Several days later, the Duc de Montaine; his daughter, Baronne Dufond; and several other expatriated French showed up at the door of *Chacun à Son Goût*.

All with the same story.

They had been saved from the guillotine by the Black Rose. John did not find it odd that they landed on his doorstep; he found it downright suspicious.

He also began to suspect that he was harboring the Black Rose in his household.

His conclusion was based on several factors. One, many of those who had been rescued were personal friends of the Fonbeaulards; two, once one saved these people, one needed to have a place to deposit them.

The location of *Chacun à Son Goût*, in Southern England between Dover and Portsmouth near Brighton, made the estate an excellent base of operations.

A man could easily cross the channel from here, landing in Calais if he crossed at Dover, or not landing at all, simply crossing the channel to Le Havre and sailing up the Seine to the heart of Paris. If he went strictly by water, then he would have to contend with the vagaries of wind currents. In some cases, the wind might aid him and he could choose such a route.

The land route, from Calais to Paris, was the most popularly traveled and would pose the risk of discovery. A better route would be from Brighton in England, crossing the channel to Boulogne, then from Boulogne on land to the city of Paris. The land travel would be quicker going, for one wouldn't have to fight against the river current en route to Paris.

Of course the more time he spent on land, specifically French soil, the greater risk of discovery. And then, the Black Rose would have to be sure to have fresh mounts along the way, not to mention someone he trusted aiding him in hostile country.

John was betting that the man crossed into Boulogne or thereabouts and sailed back with his liberated souls—for he would not chance being on French soil longer than necessary, especially with his aristocrats in tow.

Considering the fact that the Cyndreacs and the Zambeau had been rescued with some haste, it meant that the man knew how to ride like hell, fight like the devil, and sail like the wind.

The rumor Percy had told about the man being a pirate might not be far from the truth.

John tried to think back as to who was present on what occasions and who was absent. It was very difficult, since there were so many guests in the house and, at the time, he hadn't been paying attention. At least, not paying attention to that. As he recalled, most of that week had been spent almost exclusively with Chloe. The few times they did join the rest of the household, there had been plenty of time in between for someone to come and go.

Case in point, the new group that had arrived this morning.

Several of them had mentioned that they weren't brought directly to the house, but secreted for the night in an old shed on the outskirts of some village, the location of which they did not know. Then they were escorted to *Chacun à Son Goût*.

Since the man who saved them always appeared in disguise, they did not even know if it was the same man who brought them here from France.

John believed sometimes it was and sometimes it wasn't. He also believed whoever it was might, on occasion, return to the house a day *prior* to the arrivals to allay suspicion. It all depended on what kind of help he had; something John had no way of knowing.

The Black Rose, safely encamped in the house once again, would wait with the rest of them for new French visitors, showing the appropriate surprise when they showed up.

Now who could it be?

John went down a list of possible suspects in his mind.

The interesting thing was that Maurice, Percy, and Deiter had all been called away for the past few days on various excuses.

Maurice had gone to check out his estate, having received a message that a fire had broken out in one of the wings of his homes. He returned yesterday with the story that no fire had broken out and no one knew who had sent the message.

John would have liked to believe his uncle, but he knew for a fact that Maurice had been somewhat wild in his younger days, and he wouldn't put it past the Frenchman to see it as his obligation to rescue his fellow countrymen.

Deiter had not shown up for two days and when questioned had claimed someone had drugged him and he had slept for two days straight without anyone checking up on him—a fact he seemed extremely disgruntled over. He seriously asked John if no one thought it strange that he had slept all that time.

John couldn't very well say the truth, which was no, not really. Deiter was something of an enigma; however, John had a hard time picturing the grim Bavarian in such a dashing role.

Then there was Percy. The fop had decided to visit a friend of his in the next township for a few days, and Lord Sexton was not about to interfere with that fine decision. As far as him being the Black Rose, that was difficult to fathom under any circumstances, so he moved on to the next candidate.

Or candidates, as the case might be, that being the Cyndreacs. Or one of the Cyndreacs, to be precise.

This was John's best guess. But which one was it? They were very hard to keep track of, and since they looked so much alike, unless they were all together it was almost impossible to tell if one was missing.

They were young, brash, and foolishly brave. Impersonating different characters while taking on the citizen army would be exactly the thing that would appeal to a young count bent on adventure.

Come to think of it, it could be more than one of them . . . except that Zu-Zu had said she had seen them in prison and he believed her. He also believed that she saw *six* Cyndreacs, not seven. The seventh saved her from a beheading, then went back and liberated his brothers.

And he was still doing it.

Now, with so many in the house, it was almost impossible to keep track of who went where. Last night they had to move into the large banquet hall. Some came to dinner, some didn't.

It was a perfect foil.

John was determined to find out who it was, though. He resolved to keep an eye and ear out, and do some espionage of his own. He could be very good at subterfuge, if need be.

Even so, he knew there would be one person he would soon have to discuss this with. Chloe. It would not be long before she intuited something amiss. The carrottop had always been sharp.

So he was not overly surprised that night when they got into bed and Chloe asked him,

"Have you noticed an odd pattern happening with the—"

"Yes."

Her brow furrowed. "Who is it, do you suppose?"

"I don't know yet, but I will tell you this. . . ."

"What?"

He took her in his arms, snuggling her close to him. "It is not Baronne Dufond."

Chloe giggled. The widow had been annoying everyone with her impossible whiny demands since she arrived. Her father, the duc, was even worse. Only Jean-Jules seemed able to put up with her, often defending her, much to the bafflement of his brothers.

"Do you have any guesses?" she asked, rubbing her face against the warm skin of his chest. John always felt wonderful and smelled even better. Grandmere had once devised a scent just for him, and gave him soaps and cologne made with the woodsy fragrance every Christmas. He seemed to favor it, as he used it almost exclusively, albeit sparingly.

"Yes, I do." He stroked her hair absently. "I think it's one of the Cyns."

"The Cyndreacs?" She wrinkled her nose as she thought about it.

John bent down and kissed the tip.

"Why a Cyndreac?"

He told her his reasoning.

"Hmm . . . I don't think so, John. For one thing, they seem too young to accomplish such daring exploits."

"Some of them are older than you, and youth is often flamboyant."

She raised one of her brows. "Then what is your excuse?"

"That is not humorous, Chloe-phant."

"I hate that name."

He grinned. "I know."

"I still don't think it's one of the Cyndreacs." Her lower lip pouted as she thought the situation over.

"Why?" He captured that lower lip between his teeth and suckled on it.

Reluctantly, he released the delectable morsel so she could answer him. "Well, Percy did remark that the Black Rose was believed to be a pirate, and none of the Cyndreacs have ever taken up such a profession—so that rules them out."

"No, Percy said it was *rumored*. That doesn't mean the Black Rose actually was a pirate."

"I'm not convinced."

"Then who's your guess?" His hands stroked down her back, massaging as they went.

"I think it is someone we don't know . . .

someone not a guest in the house, who knows we are French aristocrats. He reasons that we would be sympathetic to his cause and certainly would never turn away a fellow countryman from our door. He might even be posing as one of the servants, for all we know."

"I disagree."

Chloe placed her palms on his chest to lever back from him. She gazed up at him. "Why?"

"Because"—John brought her in close again—"he knew who your friends were and he made it a point to save them."

"All right, then he is a house servant—that would explain his knowledge."

He shook his head. "It just doesn't seem right."

Chloe peeked up at him through her lashes. "Shall we wager?"

He raised one eyebrow. "To see who's right?"

She nodded, two mischievous dimples popping into her cheeks.

"Very well, madam. What do you propose to wager?" His voice drawled with wicked possibilities.

"I wager . . ." She stopped to think about it a moment. "That if I am proven correct, you will have to do whatever I say for one night."

John looked up at the ceiling, shaking his head in disbelief. He met her perplexed expression with a teasing smile and twinkling eyes. "Chloe, Chloe, Chloe, remember what I told you in the bath that time? You must choose a forfeit that one would not welcome wholeheartedly."

She pouted again, realizing her error.

He snickered. "However, I'll gladly accept your terms, sweet." He rubbed her nose with his own.

"Good." She beamed, already getting excited over the prospect of having John at her mercy for an entire night. "We need to come up with a plan as to how we can track him down."

"That shouldn't be too hard, actually."

Chloe gave him a questioning look.

"Now that we are aware that he's operating in and about *Chacun à Son Goût*," he explained, "all I have to do is monitor the front of the estate in the wee hours of night. Most of the 'deliveries' have been in the early morning hours. Something tells me, though, that any future ones will be in the middle of the night."

"Why do you think that?"

"He's too sharp to take unnecessary risks. He would have to assume that one of us would now be on to him. Night allows the cover the darkness to protect him."

"That makes sense. I never realized you were so smart, John." She tickled his ribs.

He quickly grabbed her hand. John was very ticklish there and she knew it.

"Since we just had an arrival, I think we won't see any action for several days. Starting tomorrow night, I'll be waiting for him."

"Let's say he does appear; then what?"

"Then I follow him."

Chloe paled a little. "You don't think he could be dangerous, do you? I mean, they do say he is a pirate, John, and I don't want you in danger."

"Thank you, my carrot," he said dryly, "but I can assure you that I am not worried."

John was said to be an expert shot and just as good with the blade. He had fought enough duels with irate husbands and jealous lovers to prove it. With his reputation he would have to be the best bloody swordsman in England.

She frowned at the annoying thought. Then she kicked his shin.

"*Ow!* What did you do that for?"

"I have my reasons."

"Do you care to share them?"

"No." She stuck her chin mutinously in the air.

No matter how much he thought he understood women, they always came up with something totally new and unfathomable to present to the sea of floundering males.

He exhaled deeply, deciding to let the matter

pass. There was no telling what arcane misdeed of his had set her off.

"I'll get Cook to pack us some food."

His brow furrowed. "What for?"

"In case we get hungry during the night."

"*We?* Who said anything about *we*? You are not going, Chloe."

"Yes, I am." Her finger trailed down the center of his torso.

He stopped her when she reached his navel. "No, you are not; it is too dangerous."

"You just said it wasn't."

"For *me*. You are not going anywhere near the Black Rose."

"Well, John, if it is too dangerous for me, then it is too dangerous for you, and I simply cannot allow you to do it."

John's jaw dropped. "*What?*"

"I'm sorry, but that's the way I feel." She patted the side of his face consolingly.

The rogue was speechless. No one had ever even hinted at telling him what he could and couldn't do, not even his uncle. "A wife does not tell a husband what to do!" he sputtered.

"This one does." She yawned, snuggling into his chest.

"What makes you think I would ever allow that, Chloe?" he said in a very low voice.

Chloe wasn't the least concerned. She licked his flat nipple. "So you are going to leave me here . . . with the Cyndreacs?" she asked sweetly.

Dead silence ensued. For several minutes.

"We take one horse, mine. And you'd better be prepared for a long vigil."

She smiled secretly. "I'll speak to Cook about that food."

He exhaled gustily. "It is not a bloody picnic, Chloe!"

"You'll be happy I thought of it; you'll see. I wonder if I should pack an extra blanket. . . ."

John threw his arms up in the air. "Chloe!"

"Very well, I'll forgo the blanket." Her face lit up with excitement. "This is really intriguing, John. Just think—we might be the ones to discover the Black Rose's identity."

But who will we tell? he wondered.

Chloe nibbled teasingly along his collarbone. "How long do you think it will take?"

"To discover who the Black Rose is?"

"No." She laved a spot under his chin. "For you to show me . . ."

He watched her with an altogether sensual expectation, his clear green eyes sparkling. "For me to show you . . . ?"

Her lips followed a trail down the center line

of his muscular chest, stopping to tease at his navel. Here she used the tip of her tongue to swirl around the perimeter, taking small, delicate licks. John shivered.

"For me to show you . . ." he prodded her, surprised yet pleased at her bold actions.

Her mouth dipped lower, laving the sensitive skin beneath his flat stomach. John was falling under the sensual spell she was weaving, which was just the way Chloe wanted him.

"For you to show me *everything* you know. How long do you suppose that will take?" She punctuated her question by taking his member in her hand and running her tongue across the tip in a quick, light swipe.

It took a moment for her words to sink in over the splendor of her action.

John sucked in his breath just before comprehension sank in. She was asking him how long it would be before she could assume her life as the premier female rake of England!

"It will take me a long time, Chloe," he uttered softly. Very softly.

Her fingers drummed along his shaft as she thought about his answer.

She bent her face, taking him in her mouth briefly before she stopped to ask him, "Do you know that much then, John?"

He placed his hands on her head, guiding her back to him. "Yes," he drawled in a low-pitched tone. "I know that much."

Her lips pressed against him. "And you don't mind if it should take a long while?" She brought him fully into her mouth and suckled on him.

John moaned aloud. "No, love, I don't mind," he rasped, his normally smooth voice of a sudden unusually husky.

Chloe smiled to herself. For a notorious rake, John was really doing well. She was quite proud of him. This Lord Sexton tasted very, very good, she decided; he tasted of rich possibilities.

He tasted of the man she loved.

John closed his eyes, letting the feel of her mouth sink deep into his senses. The only thing he seemed capable of thinking about was of that mouth on him. *Those lips . . .* Those incredible lips which haunted his every waking hour of late—tempting him beyond reason!

The fact that she was unpracticed in such a recreation only seemed to add to his enjoyment. He didn't think he had ever felt anything so splendid as what he was feeling now.

Not counting when he was inside her, of course.

Her industrious, active little tongue was driving him mad. She nibbled softly on him, causing his fingers to clench in her thick hair. He moaned anew.

Chloe watched him. His eyes were closed and he appeared quite overcome by the moment. Almost awed. Dark lashes rested against his high cheekbones in a spiky crescent.

With those breathtaking eyes closed, the rest of his face came into relief and she marveled as she always did at the pure, classical lines of his features. He was so incredibly handsome.

He was also a complex human being who had enormous depth of character.

"Chloe." He whispered her name as she massaged him, kissing him tenderly. The ends of her long hair swept over his thighs. A deep groan rolled from his throat.

Taking that as a cue, Chloe sat back, tossing her head forward to let her hair fall in a cascade over him, entangling him in the strands. She wondered what his reaction, if any, would be to such a—

He bit out something that sounded savage from between his clenched teeth and, surprising her, lifted her right up to sit atop him.

"John!"

He sank into her, his strong masculine hands firmly planted on her hips.

The thick fullness of him was exquisite!

Her lips parted and a small sigh escaped. She knew John heard her exclamation, for she felt him twitch inside.

His eyes opened a slit.

Lazy green orbs dilated with desire viewed her from underneath those sexy black lashes. He *rolled* his hips.

Chloe cried out in ecstasy.

"I have always believed in giving as good as I get, madam." His velvet voice was a husky rumble. "For that, you, my beautiful wife, are going to get very, very . . . good."

With that brief warning, his knees came up, forcing her down and forward on him. He entered her, very, very deeply.

"Mon Dieu!" Chloe gasped, levering her palms on his chest.

When Chloe began uttering French, John knew he was on the right path to driving her wild. He didn't give her a chance to adjust to the new sensation before he gave her another.

Knees bent, he maneuvered himself up to a sitting position, bracing himself against the pillows at his back. He brought her legs forward to either side of him before his powerful arms locked around her in a tight embrace.

"Mer—"

His mouth seized hers in a deep, fiery kiss, his tongue delving as he thrust into her.

Chloe moaned into that hot mouth. He rolled into her below.

Kissing her with strength and purpose, he pulled her to him tightly and stroked once more. The sensations he created within were so intense, Chloe clutched at his shoulders, her fingers pressing into the taut skin. She began whimpering.

John flexed inside her. Twice.

She cried out at the unbearable pleasure.

Chloe suddenly realized the danger she was in; John was too focused—what if he made her lose control? This had to stop! She pushed at his shoulders, afraid to allow him to continue.

She tried to break away but John wouldn't let her.

Instead, he locked her more firmly to him, his arms embracing her closer, and he rocked against her.

Her fingernails scored his back, her breath coming in short gasps. Chloe was not even aware she was scratching him.

"*Yesss . . .*" John purred sexily into her mouth. "Oh, yes . . ."

He ground into her, refusing to release either the captive hold he had on her mouth or his captive embrace.

She began yelling in French. "*John!*" She panted, "*C'est coup de maitre!*"

John's lips curved into a hidden smile as he continued to ravage her. Chloe had just told him in French that he was delivering a master stroke to her.

"Mmm-hmm," he murmured in amiable agreement, pressing deeper into her.

"Fin! Fin!" She pleaded with him to put a finish to the torture.

"I've only just started, love." He growled. Taking hold of her ankle, he lifted her leg over the crook of his arm.

Chloe was shocked. "Wh-what are you doing?"

"This." He thrust, angling into her. The friction of the tight movement sent her immediately into a release.

"Ohhh . . ."

Before her spasms had stopped he had rolled over with her across the bed from one side to the other. He stopped with her positioned directly under him.

Chloe looked up at him in a stupor, her hair hanging half over her damp face as if someone had put her through a grain mill.

John locked onto her wrists, pinning them down on either side of her.

He raised himself above her and stopped for a moment to stare down at her. Golden hair swung forward to tease at the peaks of her breasts.

Silently, Chloe watched him with bated breath.

Then John slowly plunged into her dewy warmth. His movements became languid and measured, as if he had all the time in the world to stroke her to heaven.

"Ohhh, John, ohh . . . please . . . please . . . !"

His clean, hot breath drifted across her lips. Tiny drops of moisture dampened his brow. He lowered his face to her so his lips almost but not quite met her mouth to whisper in a mere hint of sound, *"Tant mieux."*

Much better.

Capturing the rosy peak of her breast, he began to suckle on her as he continued his pulsing, flowing movements. The pace he set served only to inflame her further. He was leading her to follow this building dance.

The chain around his neck slid forward, its tiny carrot dangling across her breasts as he drew on her. When he lifted his head, he let the carrot slide across each pointed tip.

The gold metal was almost hot from his skin, and it seemed to scorch right through her. John's personal brand.

She jumped, moaning. Her hands twisted but he would not let go of his hold on her wrists.

When he began to imitate his earlier motions

of rolling his hips while deep inside her, Chloe actually said, "*Non . . . Non . . .*" as if she were being tortured. Which she was.

The edges of his sensual lips curved slightly as he went right on with what he intended. He rocked them both as he stroked and rolled. Oh, but he was killing her! *The little death.* Chloe bit her lip to keep from saying anything she absolutely did not want him to know.

"Look at me." His strong voice penetrated her senses. She opened her eyes to stare up at him. He looked wild and masculine and beautiful.

And he said but one word.

"*Now.*"

His mouth again seized hers. He began to move in her with powerful force, determination guiding his strokes. His hands released her wrists, sliding up her upturned palms to tangle with her fingers in a threaded grip.

Chloe mewled into his mouth, his relentless thrusting motions completely devastating her. It did not take long before she felt the powerful tremors rise up in her once more. The spasms shook her frame from head to foot as she found her release yet again.

With one last mighty push, John ground his hips in a circular motion to put exclamation on the sliding deed.

He actually shouted out his own satisfaction.

He lay heavily on top of her, trying to recover his breath.

"Voilà tout," he whispered huskily in French into her neck.

He was telling his wife that it was finished for now. Chloe never heard his final words; she had lost all sensibility with the outstanding pleasure her husband had afforded her.

John had "given" her very, very good.

Chapter Eleven
Ships that Pass In the Night

Once again carriages began lining the drive as the ton descended.

Always a popular spot for the beau monde due to its location near Brighton, the house generally drew more than its share of guests. With the Prince of Wales in residence at his farmhouse on the west side of Steyne, *Chacun à Son Goût* was often a convenient resting spot for the ton who wished to freshen up for a few hours before heading on to Brighton.

Fortunately, the house was situated far enough off the main roads so this wasn't an unbearable occurrence but rather an anticipated one. Guests arriving on a regular basis from

London kept the house lively in between periods of relaxation.

John always thought the estate had the perfect location. Only a five-hour carriage ride to London town, it afforded country living with all the amenities of town life within reasonable travel.

Apparently the Black Rose thought the estate perfectly situated as well.

In whatever extraordinary way gossip travels, it was soon discovered that many French aristocrats were showing up at the estate, miraculously saved from beheading by the infamous Black Rose.

Everyone was dying to hear the stories first hand. *Chacun à Son Gôut* became *the* place to be.

So they came.

They descended upon the estate and its new lord like locusts upon a field of grain. It wasn't long before the house was full to overflowing with guests once more, and Chloe lamented finding room to put the next group of the "saved" should such a group arrive.

Grandmere had taken herself back to the sanctuary of the garden conservatory, Maurice was hiding somewhere, Deiter had probably fallen asleep in some obscure corner with no one to wake him, and Percy was sometimes seen here and there flitting about, dropping jewels of innuendo and wit wherever he went.

The countess had threatened not to show her face again until *Chacun à Son Goût* was back to normal. This caused Lord John to laugh outright, remarking drolly that the house had *never* been normal.

With all the people in the house it was impossible for John and Chloe to keep track of the comings and goings of various people, most notably the Cyndreac brothers, one of which John still suspected of being the Black Rose.

The Cyndreacs were aware of his suspicion, seeming puzzled and proud of it at the same time. Apparently the young men reasoned they had to cut quite dashing figures to be suspected of being such a man.

This did not stop the notorious brothers from getting into trouble on the half hour, however.

Besides chasing all of the females in residence, the brothers had a knack for causing mayhem wherever they went. In the pantry, one of the undercooks had told Chloe two of the Cyns had come looking for a something to eat and somehow dislodged half the shelving on the walls. It had taken the kitchen staff the better part of an afternoon to clean up the mess. Chef LaFaint had removed himself from the upset, refusing to prepare the evening meal due to his nerves.

He wasn't the only one.

The upstairs maids refused to enter the Cyndreacs' rooms for fear they would be cornered by the frisky youths. John had been forced to speak to the boys about that, feeling very uncomfortable at having been put in the position.

The Lord of Sex giving a lecture to the young men on proper behavior seemed about as effective as having a highwayman chastise a pickpocket on the impropriety of thievery.

In the end, John simply threatened them with bodily harm. This the Cyndreacs understood, and so they switched their focus to the feminine guests, which was not much of an improvement, but at least they had clean linens for their rooms.

The groundskeepers reported that three of "them black-haired Frenchie devils" had a roustabout, knocking over several urns and one garden statue of an angel, which immediately cracked in two, its head rolling from its shoulders to land under the feet of the portly Marquise LaClempe.

The marquise, upon seeing a lolling head rolling by her feet, immediately fainted onto poor little Marquise LaClempe, who was now bedridden with a wrenched back.

Meanwhile, John's garments were disappearing from his wardrobe at a brisk clip.

"Aren't you glad you married me, John?" Chloe teased him. "Look at what you would have missed if you hadn't."

John laughed, hugging her. "I still would have been here; I just wouldn't have had to deal with it."

Chloe's face brightened. "I hadn't thought of it that way."

He tugged a lock of her hair. "Of course, we could simply disappear back to our chambers like the rest of the family and let the madness carry on by itself while we . . ."

Chloe sucked in a breath. "We can't, John."

"Why not?" he drawled suggestively.

"You know how carried away you get, Lord Sexton." She crossed her arms over her chest and tapped her foot playfully.

"Ah, yes, all that sighing and moaning and screaming *I* do." He flashed her a steaming look from under his lashes, his lips twitching in amusement.

"And what is that smile for?" Chloe wagged her finger at him.

"The smile is because I see Baronne Dufond making her way over here to complain about something and I am about to leave."

"Oh no! Not her! John, don't you dare leave

me to deal with—Come back here!" But John was already out the door and gone. "He'll pay for that later," she mumbled under her breath.

"Viscountess!" the nasal, whiny voice called out to her.

Chloe gritted her teeth, took a deep breath, and forced a smile on her face. "Yes, Baronne Dufond?"

The aggravating woman clung to the old fashions of the court of her king, Louis XVI. Her powdered hair was pulled up into a coiffure that was almost the same height she was. A model ship was perched precariously at the top, its tiny sails blowing in the light wind from the open doors.

"There is a problem with my room."

"I'm sorry to hear that; what is this problem you speak of?" Chloe peered at the ship at closer range, recognizing it as one Maurice had given John. Up until recently it was in his old room, on his writing desk. The model was a particular favorite of his. *Oh dear.*

She bit her lip. *Perhaps John won't recognize it.*

"The room is noisy in the morning!" the baronne complained, nose in the air. "I can hear the carriages arriving with the visitors and I cannot sleep!"

"I apologize for any inconvenience, but you see, because of all the guests, most of the rooms are taken. It would be very difficult to move you right now."

Baronne Dufond, whose father was a duke, stared down her nose at the viscountess with the haughty, pursed expression of acute displeasure mastered only by the crème de la crème of French nobility.

Chloe had been seeing the expression since the woman arrived. She was heartily sick of it.

Although the baronne wasn't exactly cock-eyed, as some of the Cyndreacs had indicated, her beady eyes did have the unfortunate tendency to drift toward her nose when she was displeased. Which seemed to be most of the time. Her protruding bite added immeasurably to the intense facade she had perfected so well.

Chloe didn't know what to say. How could she appease the woman? There was nowhere to move her. She was saved by a most unlikely candidate.

Jean-Jules came up behind them, having overheard most of the exchange. "You may have my room, Baronne. It overlooks the east woods and is quite pleasant."

A startling change came over the woman. Her face almost took on an amicable cast. She nodded in a pleased way, fluttering her fan. "*Merci*, Count Cyndreac. You are the gentleman."

Chloe was surprised by Jean-Jules's gesture but not shocked. He had been defending the lady since before she arrived. It was puzzling. "I'll inform Calloway that your rooms are to be switched." She smiled reassuringly at the woman.

"Thank you, Viscountess Sexton." The baronne turned to leave, gliding toward the open French doors. Chloe swore she saw the little ship weigh anchor as it swooped the waves of hairstyle.

Outside, John, spying a Cyndreac near his wife, decided to make his way back into the room. As he was entering the house, he passed by Baronne Dufond in the doorway, his sights drifting idly to the ship sailing by his nose. He frowned absently at the odd hairstyle, continuing on.

Two steps later, he stopped dead in his tracks.

Slowly he turned, arms akimbo, squinting at the decorative headdress. "My model!" he mouthed under his breath.

His emerald eyes kindled with indignation. John instantly changed course and followed the towering hair out the door. He was after that ship!

Chloe watched John storm after the woman.

Her hand came to her mouth to suppress her laughter. She had no doubts that the model would still be perched on the baronne's head at the evening meal. John was about to receive the haughty Dufond glare.

"The hairstyle is most original," Jean-Jules said to her left, a teasing smile flitting about his well-shaped lips.

Chloe grinned at him. "You seem to be her champion, Jules."

"Do I?"

Chloe shook her head. "May I ask you something?"

He raised an eyebrow, and in that moment she caught a glimpse of the man he would become in ten years.

"Do you have a *tendresse* for her, Jean-Jules?"

He shrugged noncommittally. "She was kind to me one night in the prison."

Chloe raised her brow.

"*Non*, not that way."

"What happened?"

"I was very ill; I had contracted a fever there. One night, the worst night . . ." His cheekbones flushed a dull bronze in his uncertainty whether to continue the personal tale.

"Yes?" Chloe prompted him.

He took a deep breath. "She held my head in

her lap and put her hand on my forehead. She told me I was too courageous to die like this in a filthy prison that stank of evil."

His gold eyes watched a bird hopping tree limbs. "That night the fever broke. I remember there was one moment of such profound joy that I was going to live. Then some soldiers came to escort the next group to the guillotine and it all fell into perspective. But she was kind to me that night."

Chloe watched the Count as he wrestled with his emotions. He was an impressionable young man, she thought, warmhearted and sensitive.

One night a condemned woman had found the decency within herself to be kind to a young man on the verge of death. She had given him a mother's touch.

It is the small acts of kindness that are remembered most, Chloe realized. Jean-Jules would forever overlook Baronne Dufond's annoying nature because in that one instant, she had risen to her best self and showed him her basic goodness.

"Thank you for sharing that with me; I shall always remember it."

Jean-Jules nodded briefly, somewhat embarrassed over the disclosure. He quickly excused himself, going in search of his brothers.

* * *

That evening at dinner Chloe noted that the model ship still hung gleefully from the Baronne Dufond's coif, while John sat at the head of the table, a disgruntled expression gracing his handsome face.

She was not overly surprised at the outcome. Poor John. He was just too good-natured. Half the guests were walking around displaying at least one item of his personal belongings.

Adrien Cyndreac, seated next to her, took the opportunity to move closer to ask about the fishing in a stream he had come across on the north side of the property.

There was so much noise in the banquet hall that she had to get very close to him to answer, speaking practically into his ear.

When she finished speaking, she glanced up, shocked to see two green eyes, narrowed and dangerous, boring into her from the other end of the table.

John clearly did not like the familiar rapport she had with all the Cyndreacs. *Good.*

Just to annoy him, Chloe smiled brightly at him from her end of the table, giving him a little wave of her fingers.

He contemplated her in an utterly stone-faced manner.

Chloe immediately turned to her left to engage the person sitting next to her in conversation.

Unfortunately, it was another Cyn.

Jean-Paul, seated to her other side, began regaling her with an amusing anecdote regarding a baker and a gypsy. The story captured her attention, and when Jean-Paul finally got to the end, only to have the punch line delivered by Adrien, she had no choice but to laugh outright at his exasperation with his younger brother. They were so engaging—

A hot chill raced down her spine. Chloe peeked John's way.

A small muscle ticked in her husband's jaw.

Bien! Chloe took a slow sip of her wine, supremely happy with the rogue's progress. Such a fixated expression surely meant he had some jealous feelings for her. Jealous feelings were often a cornerstone to other feelings.

She decided to encourage the Cyns a little by being terribly amused by them. John obviously felt something tender toward her.

At the other end of the table, John was debating on whether to get up and "tenderly" wring her dainty neck.

What did she mean, encouraging those wild pups like that? Didn't she realize what she was doing? They were already after her like bees to a blossom, flitting around her day and night. All seven of them. He had to watch her every minute to be sure one of them didn't toss her over his shoulder and carry her off.

He was going to have to have another talk with his little *wife*. Apparently she hadn't understood how serious he was about the conditions of the agreement.

Picking up his goblet, he took a sip of his wine, narrowly observing her over the rim; he simmered.

Chloe felt that molten exchange right across the room.

Her hand went to her throat and she coughed, gagging slightly on her wine. Perhaps she had been overdoing it a wee bit? John appeared somewhat . . . furious.

Well, she supposed she had been shamelessly flirting.

Now what should she do? She needed to appease him quickly, for that night they intended to begin their vigil for the Black Rose.

He wouldn't be a very good traveling companion if he was still frothing with anger at her.

Chloe got an idea.

Standing up, she excused herself momentarily from her seat and made her way to John's end of the table. When she came over to where he was sitting, the viscount pretended he hadn't been watching her every move by taking another slow sip of wine.

Very good, John. As if I don't know that you haven't taken your attention off of me for one moment!

She placed her hand on his shoulder, leaning over to whisper, "I'm terribly sorry about your model, John. Perhaps I can find you another just like it?"

John's temper soared another notch. *As if the loss of the small ship is the entire source of my mood!*

He was not fooled by her token gesture for a minute. Putting his cup down, he turned to view her over his shoulder. "That's very kind of you, Lady Sexton," he intoned flatly.

Chloe reasoned the better part of valor was in the exit. She pivoted to return to her seat, hoping he would cool off on his own. A strong hand clasped her wrist.

He tugged her back to him, practically onto his lap.

"John! Everyone is looking at us!" Chloe braced her hand on his shoulder.

"Do you think I care?" He watched her from beneath heavy lids.

"John, stop this! It is embarrassing; what do you think—"

His other hand came up to cup the back of her head, pulling her to him. He kissed her soundly on the lips.

It was not a loving kiss.

But it *was* a kiss of ownership. And it was directed at the Cyndreacs.

Upon seeing their host and hostess so romantically engaged, the diners at the table banged on the cloth and clinked their glasses in good-natured joviality.

John released her abruptly. Turning back to his meal, he all but ignored her standing there, dumbfounded at his behavior.

Adrien Cyndreac caught Maurice Chavaneau's attention at the next table, winking at him before lifting his glass in a toast to declare to one and all, "The thing speaks for itself!"

John grimaced while everyone saluted him.

Serves you right, Lord Sexton, Chloe thought sourly. Staging a show like that simply to . . .

Chloe sucked in a breath. John had staked a claim on her! A possessive claim.

Stunned, she looked over at the rogue, but he wouldn't meet her eye, instead choosing to engage the Zambeau in an intimate discussion. Chloe was not happy about that; however, considering what he had just done, she was inclined to overlook it.

John had never been possessive over a woman

in his life. Why had he done it? Was it simply to stake a territorial claim in the manner of the male beast or was there something else behind it? Their agreement was still in effect, so why did John feel . . . threatened. *Did he?*

She examined his profile, not even daring to hope.

A rake who felt threatened was . . . a . . . a . . . husband!

The Zambeau winked at Lord John, sliding her fan down his arm.

Well, half a husband. Apparently still half a rogue too. Chloe pouted. John was tugging at the tether.

A sudden horrible feeling assailed her. She could yet lose everything.

A light sweat broke across her brow. Feeling suddenly ill, she excused herself from the table and made her way back to her chamber.

Undressing quickly, she got into bed, sliding naked between the cool sheets. She wanted to be alone in the darkened room with just one candle—her thinking candle.

There was no need to feel this way yet. John was doing remarkably well and . . .

A wave of depression overcame her.

Placing the cause of it on her recent lack of sleep—John had been keeping her up until the small hours of morning making love to her—she decided to take a nap and see how she felt when she woke up. If she was still worried about him, she was going to be forced to thump him over the head again.

She sighed mournfully.

Even if it was in his best interest, she doubted Lord Sexton would welcome the remedy.

She was dozing lightly when she felt the bed dip. "John?" she murmured sleepily.

"It had better be." He took her in his arms. "What's the matter? You're not ill, are you?" There was concern in his voice.

"No, just . . ."

He smoothed back a strand of her hair from her face. "Just what, Chloe?" His lips pressed against her brow.

"I . . ." She gazed up at him.

"What," he whispered. "Tell me."

She couldn't.

"I-I just want to nap, John."

He seemed disappointed with what she had chosen to say. "Of course, Chloe. Whatever you wish." He still held her, though.

"I'm very tired, John."

"Then sleep, sweet; I'll wake you later, when it is time to leave."

Nodding, she burrowed her face into his

warm chest. The familiar woodsy scent, so comforting to her, caused her to feel teary eyed for some reason.

What if he never realized . . . No! *Don't think it, Chloe.*

John felt the dampness from her eyes against his chest. Puzzled, he gazed down at the woman in his arms and wondered what had upset her so.

He was the one who had been annoyed over her behavior with the Cyns! Did she really want them that much? Too bad. He wasn't going to allow it! And he was going to have to start making that clear to her.

There would be no others.

She was his.

Period.

Chloe did feel better once she woke up.

Her general good spirits restored by the revitalizing nap, she was raring to go after the Black Rose while still having enough energy to cosh her husband on the head.

In fact, it was Chloe who woke *him* by tugging at the sheet until he finally rolled off the bed in a tangle of linens.

He hit the floor like a stone.

"*Ow!* Dammit, Chloe!" He rubbed his head, thinking if he took one more knock on it, he would be a candidate for the village idiot.

"Get up, John; we need to be going if we have any hope of catching him."

"It's not as if he's down there waiting for us, Chloe," he grumbled.

"We do have to lie in wait for him; chances are he won't even appear this—*What in God's name are you wearing?*"

"Do you like it?" Chloe pivoted for him, showing her backside covered in black leather breeches. The material stretched taut over her rounded derriere.

"Where did you find that?" he asked softly through clenched teeth.

"The Cyns helped me; they—"

"You told the Cyns." He spoke in a flat even tone. "The ones who are the prime suspects."

"Oh, not about that." She waved her hand impatiently. "I just told them I needed some breeches."

John closed his eyes and shook his head.

Chloe bit her lip. "They all offered me theirs, but they were much too large and . . ."

John's eyes popped open. "You tried on their breeches?"

"Well . . ."

That muscle in his jaw started working.

"Just one," she added placatingly. "Since they

were too big, the Cyns found these . . . somewhere."

In the attic, to be precise.

"I think they belonged to Great-Uncle Harry. Hellgate Harry. They called him that because he had the most dreadful temper! I think it was because he was so short; all that disatisfaction didn't have much room to—"

John pinched the bridge of his nose. "Chloe."

"What?" She put her hands on her hips and frowned.

"Just make sure you bring a cloak with you."

"Because of a chill?"

"No. To cover that ridiculous getup!"

"Oh, really. Well, the Cyns thought it was very charming."

He gave her an incendiary look. Untangling himself from the sheets, he rose off the floor stark naked and backed her against the wall.

Placing his palms on either side of her head, he purposely leaned into her. Several strands of his tousled golden hair fell across his forehead as he stared down at her through glinting green slits.

"Stay away from them when you're by yourself, madam," he said in a tellingly low tone. "Do I make myself clear?"

It was all she could do not to grin. "Yes, John."

Placing her arms around his neck, she stood on tiptoe and brushed his mouth with hers.

He closed one eye and cocked the brow of the other. The effect was rather roguish. "I'm serious, Chloe."

"I understand; it's not in line with what we agreed."

"It has nothing—" But Chloe had already ducked under his arm.

She began tossing clothes at him, urging him to hurry. "I have a feeling he's going to make an appearance tonight."

John's nostrils flared. He didn't think he had quite gotten through to the carrottop, but at least she wouldn't find herself alone with the playful counts.

"Mmm," was all he said as he stepped into his breeches and fastened them about his lean hips.

"I just think you should ask someone, that's all."

"I said I would find it."

John had been saying that for the past several hours. They were atop his stallion, traveling through the misty night, headed heaven knew where—for John certainly didn't, no matter what he claimed to the contrary.

Earlier, they had settled in a comfortable spot

to observe the entrance to the estate.

It wasn't long before John got bored and his hands started wandering. All over Chloe. A convenient hayloft almost caused them to miss seeing him. The Black Rose.

True to his name, he appeared out of the mist dressed entirely in black, riding a powerful black horse. Behind him, he led a group of ragged French in a rickety cart.

He brought them just to the entrance of the gates of the drive, then disengaged himself to disappear in a flash down the wooded lane.

Chloe had gasped. "Did you see—"

John was already up and moving.

With admirable reflexes, he tossed her onto the front of his horse and took off in pursuit, careful to stay behind, out of sight of the dark rider.

They had trailed the Black Rose for two hours, losing him inside a small hamlet they had entered. The man had entered a run-down tavern there and had never come out.

Or at least it appeared that way.

John instructed Chloe to stay hidden by the horse while he went inside to see if he could find out anything. Leaving her his pistol, he told her to fire it in the air if there was an emergency.

He came out soon enough, concerned about leaving Chloe alone for any length of time. His wife was nibbling contentedly on a piece of chicken. He shook his head disbelievingly.

"The tavernkeeper remembered him; he said that the man had asked some information about Randolph, a small village to the west. He must have left somehow and we missed him."

John placed Chloe on his horse and remounted behind her. "He's probably heading to Randolph right now."

"Do you know the way there?" she asked him, handing him a chicken leg. He hesitated a second before taking the offering and eagerly biting into it.

Chloe smiled to herself. She should have brought that extra blanket too.

"I'll find it." he replied, directing the stallion around onto the side road heading west.

That had been several hours ago. In fact, Chloe was sure they had passed this lake before. Twice.

"Are we lost?" she asked plaintively.

"No."

"Are you sure? I think we went by this lake before and—"

"We are not lost."

"But John—"

"Chloe."

She exhaled nosily. She knew they were lost!

Why didn't he admit it? *Men.* Something came into view up ahead. A small roadside inn.

"Look, an inn! Why don't you go in and ask them the direction to—"

"We are not lost!"

"You've been saying that for hours. I don't understand why you just don't ask someone how to get there! We've been traveling in circles forever!"

John clenched his teeth. "Madam, I will find it."

Chloe's shoulders sagged. Men could be so cussedly stubborn!

Another hour went by and dawn was starting to break. The same inn came into view.

Chloe made a sound of disgust.

John was suspiciously silent.

"We might as well forget it; the man is probably in Wales by now," she added flippantly.

"We'll try another night." He headed them back home. He hoped it *was* the way back home.

By the time they reached the front steps, cold and tired from the night's journey through damp woods and misty vales, Chloe refused to speak to him.

Of all people, Percy was there on the front steps to greet them.

"Been out for an early morning ride, what?" He smiled gaily at them.

"Didn't know you were the early morning type, Sexton; leave it to a lovely bride to change a man for the better!" He fluttered his lace-trimmed sleeve in the air. "*Nulla dies sine linea*—Not a day without something done!"

John inhaled deeply, staring stonily at the fop. In Latin. *Percius, I am readius to strangleus.*

"Actually, John and I decided to view the entire countryside from Brighton to Portsmouth. Several times," Chloe volunteered sarcastically, while jumping down from the horse. She did not wait for John to help her. "It seems Lord Sexton is an *expert* on the landscape."

With that, she trounced into the house, leaving the men standing there.

"Zounds!" Percy watched her enter the foyer. "Don't look good for you, my man. Perhaps I could give you a few pointers?" he added helpfully.

John looked at him incredulously. The night wasn't bad enough; now Percy was offering to instruct him on how to deal with a woman!

"Come back into reality, Lord Cecil-Basil," he murmured dryly before heading toward the door.

"Quite." Percy blinked, his beringed hand scratching the side of his powdered head.

He smiled ever so slightly.

Chapter Twelve

Of Dark Armoires and Dark Horses . . .

Chloe stormed in the house and up the center stairway, right past Deiter and Schnapps, who were coming down for breakfast.

The dour German watched her march by him with a pensive look.

A few seconds later, John came in and, with a firm tread, started to follow the path his wife took up the stairs.

Deiter stopped him as he came abreast of him.

"A word with you, John," he decreed in his usual clipped way.

"Can it wait, Deiter? I need to—"

"We will walk out to the pavilion. Schnapps

needs some air." With that pronouncement, he marched down the stairs, thoroughly expecting Lord Sexton to be following.

Muttering under his breath, John trailed after him. He couldn't even guess what this was about.

Deiter strutted across the lawn in short, choppy steps, heading to the edge of the wooded glen.

John was not in the mood for this; he was tired and wanted nothing more than a hot bath and a hot bed—the latter a compliment to his wife's superb ability to generate heat under the covers. In all ways.

The truth was, he was getting rather spoiled by her warm, velvety presence curled up to him when they slept. The other night, when she had left the bed briefly, he had noticed that he couldn't sleep until she came back.

She was probably in bed right now.

The image of Chloe sleepy and warm in the middle of the bed, waiting for him, was enough to make John increasingly impatient. "Deiter, if you would please just tell me what—"

"Sha!" He looked at him sternly. "Schnapps needs the silence."

"For what?" John was annoyed and perplexed.

"To do his business." Schnapps gave John a

wounded look. Deiter placed the small dog gently on the ground.

John rolled his eyes. "For God's sake! I want to—"

"Sha!"

John's nostrils flared. Silently.

Schnapps tiptoed across the edge of the lawn as if he were made of glass and much too delicate for such a mundane task.

John rubbed his eyes. The way Chloe had stomped off it was unlikely she was actually waiting in bed for him anyway.

Finally Schnapps finished, running back to the security of his master's arms.

The allusion to John's wanting to run into his wife's arms in bed was not lost on Lord Sexton. *Good God, I'm thinking like a dog! An attitudinal dog, at that.*

Deiter casually petted the small head of his pet. "Do you know how to please a woman?"

At first John wasn't sure whether Deiter was talking to him or the dog. When the Bavarian pierced him with his unwavering glare, John realized it must be him.

Did he know how to please a woman! Where had the man been for the past thirteen years? *Ah, yes, sleeping.*

"Somewhat," he answered sardonically. He

didn't even want to speculate where this was leading.

"They are such delicate creatures. They must always be romanced."

"Mmm." John was noncommittal. The vision of Deiter romancing was too much to take on an empty stomach.

"I have noticed that you wish your wife to pay more attention to you."

John tripped. "What?"

Deiter ignored his incredulous face, plowing on. "You must cater to her whims, ya?"

Oh, this was rich. Deiter was giving him advice on women! *First Percy, now this. Must be some kind of infamous holiday today.*

Deiter frowned at the scoffing sound. "Once there was a man in my village. . . ."

Not another village story! John groaned.

"He pleased many women, but could not please *one* woman."

John squinted at him.

"We tied him to the barn for two years."

"Is that all, Deiter?"

"Ya. Remember, John—woo her!"

Lord Sexton was already heading back to the house. Wooing was not what he had in mind.

John Sexton had never been referred to as "Lord of Wooing."

* * *

Chloe pulled together the sides of her dressing gown, peering into the wardrobe for something to wear.

The outfit she had worn during their ride was draped haphazardly over a chair. She wouldn't be needing it for several days. *Damn and blast!*

Since the Black Rose had left his latest "deposit" on their doorstep last evening, it was reasonable to assume the man would not be active again for a while.

She pursed her lips. If John hadn't been so stubborn and had asked someone how to get to Randolph, they might have already confronted him!

The irritating thought angered her all over again.

She stepped inside the wardrobe and closed the door.

This called for some very unladylike venting.

John entered their rooms, surprised not to see Chloe.

At first.

Until he caught the faint sound of French steam coming from the wardrobe.

He recognized his name liberally laced within the rapid-fire invectives.

Hmm. Maybe he should try the Sexton brand of wooing.

Chloe heard the wardrobe door open.

She stopped ranting long enough to notice a thin stream of light on the ceiling. Since she was burrowed back into the far corner of the enormous piece of furniture, she couldn't see anything beyond the clothes in front of her.

The light narrowed and disappeared; she heard the distinct sound of the door closing again, returning her to the pitch black solitude she wanted.

Must have been one of the maids, she reasoned, shrugging.

Remembering Lord John's obstinacy in all ways, Chloe picked up where she left off, calling him an impossible high-handed rogue—among other things—in French.

The wardrobe shook slightly. A rustle of muslin petticoats followed.

Something was headed her way. Chloe swallowed nervously. Someone was inside there with her!

A firm hand clasped her ankle. A sound came out of Chloe that resembled a high-pitched squeak. The mysterious hand tugged at her, pulling her toward it. She began to slide down from her sitting position against the back wall of the armoire.

All too soon she was lying flat on her back on the bottom of the wardrobe.

In the darkness the masculine hand came over her lightly to graze the silk robe that covered her breasts. The peaks immediately stood up in automatic response, despite her trepidation.

Then she felt the knot on the sash of her robe being undone. It fell open, exposing the length of her to the cool air.

The warm hand glided across her skin, the pads of its fingers a silken stroke. It caressed the sides of her breast, skimming the tender underside.

A single finger stroked down the center line of her chest to her belly, stopping to dip capriciously into her navel. There it circled the perimeter, the edge of the nail gently abrading in a most stimulating manner.

The satin fingertips dipped lower.

They tangled in the curls at her mound, raking in short, light passes. The erotic movements were highly sensitizing.

Chloe moaned softly.

Fingers moved deeper between her legs. They stroked down inside to trail the soft inner flesh of her thigh to her knee and back up to the hidden apex.

A second hand joined the first to skim around her hip, then to lie flat and hot against her derriere.

Chloe could hear her own breathing in the confines of the wardrobe. Shallow, rapid puffs.

A hot mouth captured her nipple. She cried out, an exclamation of pure pleasure.

The mouth drew on her. Damp, insistent, practiced.

Chloe sank her hands in silky hair, running her fingers through long strands as she freed them from the thin ribbon tied at the nape of his strong neck.

He came over her then.

Satin lips moved up her chest, laving as they went, to fasten on the curve of her throat and suckle. Chloe undulated beneath him as his full weight pinned her down.

The hand wedged between them manipulated the buttons on his breeches. The hand cradling her bottom drew her flush against him.

Taut up against his manhood.

He was burning hot velvet. Long and thick and hard.

Chloe's breath caught.

The pulsating member skimmed along her moistened cleft, a short back-and-forth prelude before he suddenly slid full inside her.

In a rush of passion, she called out his name.

"How did you know it was me?" he drawled as he licked the swirl of her ear.

Chloe nipped his shoulder. "More to the point, Lord of Sex, how did you know it was *me*?" she teased him.

He stilled for a second, deep inside her. John knew exactly what she was insinuating. That she was no different from the rest to him. How wrong she was.

His breath heated the skin at her neck as he rasped in a sizzling, hoarse voice, "Chloe . . . if I could do nothing more than *feel* you like this"—he flexed deep inside her—"I'd know."

A small sigh escaped her as he pulsated within.

"If I could do nothing but *hear* you sigh like that," he continued, pressing in on her to rotate his hips, "I'd know."

"John," she whispered shakily.

"If I could do nothing more than *inhale* your scent"—he breathed in her flowery fragrance, his voice becoming huskier—"I'd know."

Chloe hugged him tight to her, wrapping her legs around his cloth-covered hips.

"And if I could do nothing but *taste* you, Chloe-cat"—his burning, open mouth slid down her throat and played about her collarbone before capturing her parted lips in a steaming seige—"I'd know, I'd know, I'd know," he chanted in a rough purr while stroking vigorously within her.

The dark, musty wardrobe became a sultry haven of passion.

John's expert movements, hot breaths, sensual words, impassioned caresses, served only to fire her desire for him higher and higher.

He took her in the dark. In the bottom of an armoire. While she begged for more.

Chloe Sexton forgot all about being put out with John Sexton.

She supposed that was why they were called rogues.

The upstairs maid walked into the master bedroom with several freshly laundered items of the viscountess's thrown over her arm. She opened her ladyship's armoire and stopped a moment, frowning at the pair of black men's top boots, which were sticking out upside down from under a pile of frilly lace underthings.

"Wonder how they got in her ladyship's closet?" the maid grumbled to herself. "Must've been that new girl—she's always makin a mess o' things."

The maid had bent down to retrieve them when they suddenly moved.

"Jesus, Joseph, and Mary!" She let out a bloodcurdling shriek.

The viscount's tousled golden head popped through the clothing.

He was not overly surprised to see it was the same maid who had caught him running naked down the hallway that first night. This was his usual luck.

"Mercy me!" She put her hand on her heart. "What-whatever are ya doin' in there, my lord?"

"I, ah, I was just . . ." For once John was at a loss for words.

"I lost a button, Fiona; the viscount was helping me find it," came a muffled voice from inside the armoire.

The maid recognized the voice as belonging to her mistress. "A button, my lady? Well, step aside, my lord. I'll be happy to find it fer ya; there's no need fer ya to—"

"No!" they both said at the same time.

The maid stepped back. "Are ya sure? 'Tis no trouble and—"

"We're sure." John smiled rather sickly at the woman. "Thank you anyway." He cleared his throat.

These titled folks are a mighty peculiar lot, the maid reasoned, not for the first time.

"Just put those clothes on the bed and you may leave, Fiona," Lord Sexton's deep voice directed.

Fiona did as instructed, closing the door to the room behind her with a dull thud.

Chloe giggled. "And you said no one would find us in here."

"I should've taken into account what household I was in." He grinned, "Button, my lady wife?"

Chloe chuckled.

"Must be this one here." His two bent fingers captured the tip of her nose and tugged playfully. "Or perhaps these buttons?" he flicked the tips of her breasts with his fingers; the small nubs went pebble-hard.

Chloe giggled.

"Maybe it's this one." His finger tickled her belly button.

"No, I don't think so, my lord." Chloe grinned, wagging a finger at him.

"Then it must be . . ." He reached down between her legs to find a special, hidden button. He wiggled his finger teasingly.

"John!"

A masculine hand came out of the armoire, groped for the knob, and slammed the door shut again.

"John!"

"I'm simply helping you, madam, with your . . . buttons."

He did indeed.

* * *

Late in the day everyone decided to attend a horse race being held at a well-known track outside of Brighton. At first John had been reluctant to go, but Chloe finally cajoled him into it.

It was a large party that descended upon the country gathering.

Many gentry from surrounding estates and towns, as well as Prinny's house guests from Steyne, were in attendance.

The Prince of Wales, although once an avid race enthusiast, would not be in attendance. He had withdrawn himself from racing in a pique back in ninety-one over a notorious scandal involving one of his horses, Escape, and a jockey named Chifney.

Escape, having lost a race on the day before, miraculously won the next day when the odds had been raised. Stories of race-fixing flew about the ton. In this instance, Prinny did seem blameless, but the jockey club had ruled against his jockey, Chifney, demanding that Prinny no longer utilize his services.

Reluctantly the prince agreed; however, he had not actively participated in racing since. Although he did continue to wager on the sport.

The first race of the day was a three-year-old filly.

John baited Chloe. "Why don't you enter Nettie? All you have to do is put a dish of food at the finish and she's sure to win."

Chloe elbowed him smartly in the ribs.

He grinned, revealing two deep dimples. "She wouldn't even have to be jockeyed."

"John, that's not funny. Nettie happens to be a very sweet horse."

"Not as sweet as you, carrottop." He pulled her around, placing a kiss on her forehead.

Chloe blushed at this public display of affection. "John, everyone is looking at us!" She tried to wriggle away from him.

"Everyone? Here I thought they were watching the race," he teased.

"Heard you got yourself hitched, Sexton," a pompous-sounding voice spoke from behind them. "Couldn't hardly believe it."

They both looked over. Lord Snellsdon was standing there, surrounded by his usual group of cronies.

John had never much cared for Lord Snellsdon. The man was a mean-spirited braggart who took pleasure in berating others not as fortunate as the favored son of an earl.

He surrounded himself with an obnoxious circle of men who shared his nasty disposition. Lord Crandall, Lord Howardsby, Lord Lakeston . . . They had no regard for anyone save themselves.

Many a time John had seem them purposely run people into the streets by walking four abreast on the sidewalk; sometimes these poor unfortunates got hurt.

Of course, they had all been to Eton together.

John had not attended Eton. At the time, the young viscount was living a hand-to-mouth existence, trying to survive in the rural countryside of England. When he found him, Maurice—never a supporter of the cruelty of the English public school—had elected to acquire tutors for his nephew.

John's independent nature and carefree spirit would not have made him a good candidate for Eton.

Besides that, the marquis believed the boy had suffered enough in his youth; he would not subject him to the deprivations to be found in that "noble" establishment.

In later years, John had always applauded his uncle's decision. From what he had heard about the place, he would never send a member of his family there. Strength of character, he believed, was fostered in other ways.

The proof of his theory was these offensive, hateful men standing before him, who most likely started their ways thrown together in the deplorable hellhole known as Eton. Because

John had not been one of their group, they always went out of their way to put him in his place. Or at least they tried. With Lord Sexton's carefree, amused attitude, such behavior never seemed to strike its mark. Insults appeared to roll off the viscount's broad back.

His success with women irritated them further, their envy often prodding them into trying to goad him more.

Naturally, all of this was thinly cloaked within the civility of English manners.

Chloe fumed silently. She knew exactly what these scapegraces were about. The compassion she felt for her husband rose to the surface. John was too good a person to be subjected to this. She slipped her hand into his.

He squeezed it briefly before answering Lord Snellsdon. "Yes, pity you couldn't make the wedding, Snellsdon; half the ton was there."

Good for you, John. Chloe mentally patted her husband's back as his mark hit. Lord Snellsdon had missed the most talked-about event of the season.

Snellsdon bristled. "Happened in a hurry, what? Shocked everyone, I must say." He stared pointedly at Chloe's middle.

That barb did hit. Not to him, but John wouldn't allow anyone to insult Chloe. His green eyes kindled. He made to step forward, but Chloe held him back.

She smiled prettily at the group. "It might have seemed that way to everyone else, but John and I had always planned to wed. He was only waiting for me to grow up; weren't you, John?"

He looked down at her, a contemplative shadow cloaking his eyes. "Yes," he said quietly. "That is exactly right."

"Ah, it is so romantic!" Adrien Cyndreac came up to them, slapping John on the back. "Hard to believe he is not French!" The count speared the motley group, expecting them to answer at once. Especially since he outranked everyone present.

They all immediately assented, agreeing that it was most romantic, indeed.

Adrien winked covertly at Chloe. She smiled back at him.

Lord Snellsdon was not so easily put off, however. "Got much blunt on the big race, Sexton?"

Except in jest, John never wagered. Never. The entire ton knew that. It was often remarked that it was quite strange that the viscount could be such a profligate in one area, while declining to waste himself in the other.

Only Chloe knew the truth.

After what his father had done to him and his mother, John could never bring himself to engage in the poisonous pastime. He would never risk anything of meaning in his life to the turn of a card.

His convictions were even stronger now that others were depending on him to safeguard the estate.

"I don't gamble." His response was clipped and cold.

"Don't got the stomach for it, eh," Lord Snellsdon ribbed him. These men put great store in a man's willingness to dare all on a baize table. John had always been amused by the ridiculous assertion. One thing he had always been secure in was his masculinity.

The Lord of Sex looked down at the shorter man through veiled eyes. "I do not need to validate my manhood in such a way."

The insult was barely concealed. Lord Snellsdon turned bright red. Everyone knew he had never been lucky with women. "If you'll excuse us, Lord Sexton; I see the Marquis of Langton and I must speak with him."

John nodded curtly and the group moved off.

"Is that why you didn't want to come, John? If so, I'm sorry I talked you into it." Chloe's face mirrored her regret.

John smiled, kissing the tip of her nose. "No, sweet. That has nothing to do with it. I do not approve of the way they treat the horses."

Her nose wrinkled. "What do you mean?"

"They are subjected to severe sweats and purges. Their stables are overheated and they are never allowed to enjoy fresh air except when they run. I sometimes wonder how they manage to walk onto the course."

Chloe blanched. "I hadn't known that."

"I don't subscribe to such a regimen."

"Nor I," a heavily accented voice said next to them.

Chloe and John were surprised to see an Arab man. He was covered head to foot in flowing robes, a burnoose shading the top of his face partially from view.

Beside him stood the most magnificent horse they had ever seen. The animal was pure black, with exquisite lines.

An appreciative smile crossed John's face. "What a beautiful horse!"

As if the horse understood him, it made a snuffling sound, leaning in to nuzzle John.

He grinned, scratching the smooth fur above its nose. "Hello, fellow."

"He is something of a show-off, I'm afraid," the Arab man said fondly of the animal. "But he has the heart to run."

"What kind of horse is it?" Chloe asked, adding her hand to the animal's fine coat to stroke it. She had never seen a horse like it.

"It is an Arabian horse, of course!" The man grinned at his own humor.

John chuckled. "Never saw a black one."

"There are very few."

"Why is that?" The horse nibbled at Chloe's hair; she brushed his mouth away.

"He thinks it's a carrot," John said teasingly to her.

Chloe made a face at him.

"The blacks have all but been destroyed," the Arab explained.

"But why?" Chloe gasped. "They are so beautiful."

"They are too easy to spot on the desert. Against the white sand, they stand out. It makes a man too much of a target."

"What a ridiculous reason for killing a horse!" Chloe was incensed, her innate sense of fair play outraged at such a practice.

"I agree. That is why I saved him. I am Sheik Ali al Hussan and this is Shiraz." He reached over to pat the horse. "Today he races. You will see, my lady, a horse who runs with heart."

"He's magnificent." John admired the stallion's lines.

"I saw the horse you rode in on—the gray stallion. A beautiful horse as well."

John nodded, thanking him for the compliment.

"Perhaps you would like to race?" the Arab said hopefully. When John hesitated, the man added slyly, "The others won't be much competition for Shiraz—it will be as if we race together—despite the others. Just the two of us in a real match."

Chloe could see that John was considering it. "I don't wager," he said.

A flash of white teeth showed beneath the burnoose. "Who needs to wager? The race will be our prize. A true competition."

John smiled, nodding slowly. There was a flash of wicked anticipation in the rogue's eyes.

"I will see you on the course then." The man bowed shortly to Chloe before leading the proud stallion off.

"Do you think you can take him?" she whispered to her husband. John was an excellent rider. *In all ways*.

He chuckled. "That horse? Not a chance."

Her mouth dropped. "Then why did you agree to race?"

"Well, I can try, Chloe." He winked at her, excusing himself to get ready for the race.

Chloe bit her lip as she watched him leave. Men were such odd . . .

Baronne Dufond walked by, the ship crowning her hairstyle, sailing the breeze.

A mischievous light came into Chloe's violet eyes. John might not wager, but she certainly did. Especially on special occasions.

Like a husband racing.

Chloe stood by Deiter and Schnapps on the side of the road as the crowd drew close in anticipation of watching the race.

She could see John and Sheik al Hussan jockeying for position at the start line as they tried to control their horses. Shiraz reached over and nipped the horse next to him, then seemed to grin at the outrageous deed. He was raring to go.

Chloe shook her head, smiling. He was a captivating horse. But he wasn't going to win. Chloe had put her money on John.

The race began with a *bang!* and the riders were off, galloping down the road in front of them, their horses sending bits of turf flying out from beneath their hooves.

Adrien, Deiter, and Chloe cheered as they flew past, yelling out encouragement to John over the noise of the wildly animated crowd, hooting for their favorites.

The course was a long one—three miles over the rolling terrain, ending down the straightaway in front of them.

Chloe stood on tiptoe to watch their progress. When they went out of sight, officials would convey what was happening via a series of specially positioned observers who were stationed along the route.

All three of them waited with bated breath for the first report.

When it came, they were somewhat disappointed. Both John and the sheik were somewhere in the middle of the pack.

"He bides his time," Deiter explained. "Once in my village, a man raced—"

"Not now, Deiter!" Adrien pointed to the raised stand. "Another report is coming in!"

"Lord Sexton has just taken the lead. . . ." A huge cheer rose up from the throng. They were not the only ones who favored John. Besides being known as an excellent rider, he was well liked. In addition to that, over a third of the people here were guests in his home. It was always good manners to cheer one's host.

Chloe jumped up and down, clapping her hands.

A third report came in. *"Viscount Sexton has*

been overtaken by the black!" The crowd gasped.

"Oh no!" Chloe pulled at Adrien's shirt. "Do you think he can overtake him?"

"I don't know—let's listen!"

John leaned low over his saddle, squinting at the horse in front of him. From this angle, behind the rider, something seemed vaguely familiar about that horse.

The sheik was about two lengths ahead of him now. The rest of the pack was far behind, having been left in the dust by the two of them just as al Hussan had predicted.

A high hedge appeared in front of Shiraz. Instead of going around as the course recommended, he took the dangerous jump without breaking stride.

John followed right behind him.

A low laugh reached him on the wind. "Excellent, Viscount! You offer me a true race!"

John didn't answer; he just leaned lower over his stallion's neck to gather speed.

There was something familiar about that damned horse . . .

The riders took the final turn in the course, thundering down the straightaway.

"There he is! There he is!" Chloe almost

yanked Adrien's shirt off his shoulder in her excitement. John had gained on the black—he was about a length behind now. Would he be able to overtake him by the finish?

The crowd grew frenzied as the race drew to a finish. Pushing forward on the sidelines, they jostled together as the excitement of the race washed over them. Everyone was cramped together.

Deiter was suddenly bumped by a heavyset man, his elbow going smartly into the German's side. Schnapps was flung from the Bavarian's arms—right into the middle of the course.

Chloe screamed, covering her eyes. *Not Schnapps!*

Deiter tried to lunge into the road to save his beloved pet, but Adrien held him back. "You'll be trampled," he yelled above the crowd.

John, still trying to overtake Shiraz, gazed down the course, horrified to see Schnapps frozen in terror in the middle the road. What was he doing there? The little dog hardly ever left Deiter's arms. When he glanced over and saw Count Cyndreac holding Deiter back, he realized what had happened.

John took a deep breath. He would have to try to save the animal.

It was dangerous; he was on the far side of the

road from the dog and it meant he would have to veer across the line of oncoming riders. No one would be able to stop on time if he didn't make it on the first pass.

Furthermore, he wasn't sure his horse could make that rapid a turn at the speed he was going.

Gritting his teeth, he was about to swerve over when the black suddenly pivoted in an incredible transition.

It was a sight he would never forget for the sheer artistry of movement.

The man and beast moved as one. Sheik al Hussan swooped down and, in a single fluid motion, whisked Schnapps into his arms, out of harm's way.

The galloping horse turned and pranced over to the sidelines as John thundered past on his horse to take the race.

Not waiting to hear his accolades, John turned around and rode over to where his wife was. The sheik was just handing the dog down to Deiter, who accepted the small animal with tears in his eyes.

"That was a noble act, Sheik al Hussan." John thanked the man. "Accept my gratitude on behalf of my household."

The man shrugged as if it were simply a small

deed. "One can see he is like a member of the family." He smiled at John. "Congratulations on your win."

" 'Twas you who should have won."

The man shrugged again.

"We're heading back to my home now; would you care to join us at the estate?" His lips twitched as he surveyed the crowd—most of whom were his guests. "We seem to have an extensive house party going on."

The man shook his head. "Thank you, but I must be off—prior engagement, you understand. Perhaps some other time."

"Most definitely," John said sincerely.

"Yes," Chloe added. "Thank you so much for saving him—we all adore him so; he has the best personality."

John gave her a side-long look. He supposed that was true, if one counted the showing of a tooth as a personality trait.

"You are a kind man, Sheik al Hussan." Chloe smiled gratefully at him.

"I don't know about that, Viscountess."

"Well, first you save Shiraz and then you save Schnapps; I'd say that qualifies."

A flash of white showed beneath the shadow of his headdress as he grinned. "Well . . . you might say I have a knack for *saving* things." Saluting them with a flourish, he kicked the sides of his mount, disappearing into the crowds.

It wasn't until he was gone that John realized he had spoken the last in perfect unaccented English. *Saving things?*

Suddenly John knew exactly where he had seen that horse.

He grabbed Chloe by the arm, taking her aside.

"That was the Black Rose!" he exclaimed.

Chloe snorted. "It couldn't be. He's a sheik."

John took a deep breath. "No. What he is, is an expert in disguise."

Chloe paled. "Do you think he was warning us?"

"Not at all." The corners of his mouth curved. "I think he was playing with us."

Later that evening, Sir Percy asked John how he had enjoyed the races.

John viewed him curiously. "You didn't attend?"

Percy threw his hands up in the air. "Goodness no! I can't stand all that dust flying about. Makes my lace wilt."

"Does it really?" John said softly. For there was a film of the substance covering the bottom edge of the man's left boot.

Chapter Thirteen
The Gate Begins to Open

"But I have tried everything! The man is liaison-proof!"

"Are you sure, Zu-Zu? Everything?" The two women were sitting in the conservatory, sipping tea.

"*Oui!* I have cornered him in the dark corridors; I have practically invited him to my rooms; I have even placed my hands upon him in an unmistakable manner—he ignores everything!"

The Countess de Fonbeaulard pursed her lips in thought. "You are an expert, Zu-Zu. If he rebuffs your advances . . ."

"I tell you, he does not look at other women! The thing speaks for itself, Simone. Why do you not let it be?"

The countess returned her cup to its saucer with a distinct click. "You mistake my meaning, my friend. That is not the reason behind this! I do not wish to drive them apart—*au contraire;* I want to put them together!"

Zu-Zu waved her hand in a dismissing motion. "They are already together. What more could you ask for?"

"A great deal more," she said quietly.

The Zambeau patted her friend's knee. "I understand, but these things sometimes must take their own course. Perhaps it is best to leave such matters be." She shrugged fatalistically, the French euphemism for the complexities of *amour*.

"Nonsense! I am her grandmother; it is my duty to interfere."

The two women looked at each other and laughed.

"You do realize that Chloe is barely speaking to me. What must she think of me?"

The countess waved aside her concerns. "She will get over it; Chloe never holds a grudge. In that regard she is like her grandmere." She looked at the Zambeau pointedly.

Zu-Zu pouted. "You have never truly forgiven me for that one time with Maurice."

"I do not wish to discuss *that* subject."

"Oh, but let us finally get it out in the open, my dear Simone. What can it matter after all these years?"

As usual, whenever this topic came up between them, the countess's temper began to rise. Zu-Zu could always tell because her friend's movements became choppy, her speech brisk.

"I have told you I will not discuss it!"

"Yes, we will." Zu-Zu put down her cup. "Why have you not married Maurice? Do you not love him?"

"Of course I love him! That has nothing to do with it!"

"Is it because of what you think happened between us all those years ago?"

"*Non.*" The countess took a deep breath. "I have forgiven him for that."

"How very noble of you, Simone; especially since there was nothing to forgive him for!"

The countess looked at her incredulously. "Do you expect me to believe that? Zu-Zu, you slept with everyone! Why not Maurice? He was at your chateau that night."

Zu-Zu slammed her palm down on the table; tea sloshed over the sides of the cups onto the lace tablecloth. "I did not sleep with everyone!"

The countess made a scoffing sound.

"All right . . . I slept with almost everyone—but not with Maurice."

"If what you say is true, then why not?"

"I wanted to, make no mistake—he was and is a very handsome, charming man. He would not."

This was surprising. In his younger years, Maurice had a reputation as a *bon vivant,* a gourmand of fine women. "But why?"

"He loved you, Simone." Zu-Zu sighed deeply. "He has always loved you."

The countess was struck dumb. Maurice, faithful? Back then?

Zu-Zu sat back in her seat. "I never could really understand it."

"You mean he never . . ."

"Absolutely not."

The countess was silent as she digested this bit of information.

"So if it wasn't because of that night, then why haven't you married him, Simone?"

"Oh, well, it keeps a man on his toes, does it not? They so enjoy the chase; I think it is more enticing to them to be kept waiting."

"For *twenty* years?"

"I do not wish to discuss this." The countess sulked.

"Very well." Zu-Zu sighed. "As far as John is concerned, I still think you should give it up. He is simply not interested, darling, and Chloe doesn't seem to want to play the possessive wife."

The countess thought it over. Perhaps she should let nature take its course.

"Simone?"

"Yes?" she answered distractedly.

The Zambeau fanned herself in an altogether laconic manner, the edges of her lips twitching. "Do you think Jean-Jacques is too young for me?"

Her friend gazed at her incredulously. "*Zu-Zu!*"

Relaxing in his usual place in the delightful conservatory, Maurice Chavaneau was beginning to think the choice spot was the mecca of hidden motives at *Chacun à Son Goût*.

He smiled obscurely.

"How on earth did you get it from her?"

Chloe had just handed John the model ship. They were relaxing in their private suite before dinner. She smiled smugly.

"I made a little wager with her concerning the outcome of the race."

A small smile played about John's sensual lips. "You wagered on me, Chloe-cricket? Even after you saw the black?"

"Of course!"

He shook his head, laughing. "It was a good thing Schnapps was in the road, then . . . or was that planned to throw the sheik off his stride?" His raised his eyebrow.

Chloe laughed. "I hadn't thought of it, to tell you the truth; but I was determined to pry the model off of her head. She was very reluctant to offer up the prize."

John pulled her onto his lap. "And how did you get her to do it?" He nuzzled her cheek.

"That was easy. You know that ugly little horse you have on your old bureau? The metal one with the yellow paste eyes? Well, she said she thought the piece would look stunning in her hair, especially during a race. I agreed, naturally."

He stilled of a sudden. "You didn't wager that, did you?" he asked faintly.

"Yes." She turned on his lap, noting his curious silence. "What is it? You weren't fond of it, were you?"

"It was my mother's," he said quietly.

Chloe felt instant remorse. "Oh, John, I had no idea!"

"Those are not paste eyes, sweet; they're yellow diamonds."

Chloe stared at him, stunned. "You had that horse all those years you were trying to survive

. . . when you were starving? And it was real! Why didn't you sell it? At least you would have had something to live on."

"I was just a boy; I was afraid if I showed it to someone they would steal it from me or else cheat me out of it." He hesitated. "That's not the true reason I kept it."

"Why then?"

"It was all I had left of . . . of who I was. Long ago, my father had given it to my mother and it was the one thing she would not give up. She held it clutched tight to her when she died, still calling his name." A small line appeared in his brow. "Even after what he had done to us, she still . . . she forgave him." He took a deep breath. "I never understood it."

Chloe cupped his cheek, her eyes filling up. He had never understood it, yet he had still kept the small horse. It was no mystery to Chloe.

John had kept the figurine *because he loved his mother*.

"I'm so sorry, John; I had no idea. Well, it's a good thing you won the race." She tried to smile at him.

His focus returned to her. "I would never have given it up in either case. Even if I had to offer her a hundred times the value of the piece."

Chloe felt even worse. "I'm so sorry," she whispered. "I only wanted to get your ship back."

John suddenly realized how upset she was.

He leaned down and kissed the tip of her nose. "I know that—don't worry about it, Chloe. It was a very nice gesture on your part and I thank you for it."

Chloe's palms captured his handsome face, bringing it to her for another kiss. "I'll just be more careful in future with what I wager."

"That is very wise," he murmured, capturing her mouth.

It wasn't until a few hours later that Chloe realized that he had saved the horse *the same way he had saved her carrot*.

A few nights later, John and Chloe decided to resume their vigil for the Black Rose.

Enough time had gone by since the last rescue; the man would have rested up and been ready to face the new French army with yet another bold plan of liberating the condemned.

They had taken their places by the side of the house, concealed and ready to wait the night, when John noticed that Chloe had forgotten her cloak.

"Go and get it, Chloe; the nights are still chilly."

"It's not too bad," she stated, not wanting to

miss a moment of the excitement, should any occur.

"It is very damp and we just might be here all night. There's no telling if he'll show tonight. I don't want you catching a chill. Now go."

Chloe put her hands on her hips. "You can't just order me about!"

He looked over at her and raised an eyebrow.

"Really, John, you are becoming insufferable."

He grinned, a flash of white teeth in the night. "Thank you, madam."

"What if I miss something?"

He snorted in exasperation. "What are you going to miss in five minutes? The play of moonlight on the drive?"

"Very funny, my lord. You do promise if something happens, you'll wait for me?"

"Yes, I will wait for you. Now go up and get it."

Reluctantly, Chloe left, entering the house through a side door. Taking a back stairway, she quickly raced to her room, retrieving the garment.

Throwing it about her shoulders, she decided it would be faster if she took the west wing, for there was a servant stairway that led very close to the spot from where they were watching the drive.

She quickly skipped down the darkened hallway heading to the west wing.

Thankfully, due to the late hour, it was very quiet; most of the guests were already sleeping. While the cloak covered her unconventional outfit, she didn't want to be forced to explain her presence at such an hour alone in this corridor. Lord knew what kind of rumors that would inspire. First they would wonder why she wasn't with her new husband; then they would wonder who she was going to visit.

The chances of running into someone were quite slim, so she was very surprised when a door suddenly opened and a man stepped into the hall, gently closing the door behind him.

The top button of his breeches was undone and the front of his white silk shirt hung open, revealing a tan, muscular chest. Long, jet-black hair draped to his shoulders in a silken slide. He was devastatingly handsome.

Who was he?

Surely she would have remembered someone who looked like him among the guests?

It was obvious that he was just returning to his room from an assignation. Chloe glanced at the door he had exited, trying to recall who was in that particular room.

Ah, yes, the lovely widow, Lady Courtney. No

wonder the man had been so engaged.

As she came abreast of him, he straightened from closing the door, obviously just as surprised as she was to see someone in the hall.

His eyes were robin's egg blue.

Even in the darkened hallway, they glittered palely in contrast to his jet hair. Staring at those eyes, Chloe almost walked into him. Odd, but they looked familiar somehow.

"Excuse me." Chloe spoke first. "I didn't see you standing there."

"Think nothing of it, madam," a deep, smooth voice responded.

Now that she was abreast of him, she could see him quite clearly, and he was a stunning male. Sinful almost.

She briefly wondered who he had come with, then shrugged as she resumed her way down the hall. John was waiting for her and she didn't want to miss seeing the Black Rose!

The man passed by her and continued strolling down the hallway.

A sexy, slow smile inched across his enigmatic face.

She had not even recognized him. . . .

A low chuckle rumbled in his chest.

It was a tired husband and wife that trudged back up the stairs later that night.

They had waited almost the entire night and the Black Rose had not shown himself.

Around four-thirty, John had called a halt to the vigil, saying he didn't think he would be coming. It was too close to dawn and the man would not risk discovery in daylight.

Chloe was disappointed he hadn't appeared, but glad to be seeing the right side of her bed. She could barely keep her eyes open, and the dampness of evening had seeped right into her bones. John had been right about the cloak; she was glad she had retrieved it.

They both undressed rather quickly, scurrying under the warm covers to cuddle together in the predawn hours.

Chloe fell asleep almost instantly. John, despite being as tired as his wife, could not seem to drop off.

He rolled over on his pillow for the umpteenth time. Finally turning on his side, he watched Chloe as she slept next to him.

In the dim, predawn light, he could just make out her sweet features.

She was lying on her side, facing him. One of her hands was resting next to her face, palm up, fingers curled, in an innocent, childlike picture of repose.

He smiled faintly to himself. He had seen her

sleeping like this for almost her entire life. It struck him then that he had known Chloe that long. Almost half of his life and nearly all of hers. He knew her moods, her likes, her dislikes, her sense of humor, her outlook, her opinions, her sense of justice, and since their marriage, he knew much more. He knew her intimately as a man knows a woman. Her passions. Her abandon. Her touch. Her feel. The taste of her. The scent of her. How she quivered inside when he entered her . . .

He sights fell to her lips. Those full, soft lips that he so—

What was going on inside her?

He watched her silently.

She was holding something back from him.

John wasn't sure when the idea had first entered his head, but since it had, he couldn't seem to get rid of it. It had been bothering him—a nagging, below-the-surface irritation that wouldn't go away.

In fact, it was getting louder and louder.

Gently, so as not to wake her, he brushed his mouth across those sweet, lush lips. Lips that knew how to deliver heaven.

Then he eased out of bed, careful not to disturb her sleep.

Donning his green robe, he padded barefoot

across the room. Silently, he opened the French doors to the balcony and walked outside.

The sun was just coming up on the eastern horizon. Its rays spread across the orchards and gardens of *Chacun à Son Goût*, bathing the surrounding treetops and the forests beyond in soft gold light. Everything was so still and peaceful.

Waiting to awaken.

A shiver went down his spine.

He felt so much a part of everything around him that he wondered if he too . . .

He shook off the odd perception, watching a small rabbit hop across the lawn, its reddish ears twitching.

A Chloe-rabbit.

He smiled tenderly, his thoughts turning inward once more.

They had come out on this balcony that one night. He had set her on this ledge and made love to her. The moonlight had bathed her in silver just as the golden sunlight bathed him now.

And he had realized how much he wanted this life, this estate, this—

Contemplatively, he ran his finger along the edge of the stone wall where she had sat looking down at him, watching him in that Chloe-cat way of hers. He imagined he could still feel her heat infusing the cold stone even now.

What was she holding back from him?

He didn't know, but whatever it was, Lord John Sexton decided he wanted it.

"I am disappointed in you."

Seven handsome Cyndreac heads bowed in shame.

"But we have tried everything, Marquis Chavaneau!" As usual, Adrien spoke for the group. "Nothing seems to be working."

"*Oui*!" Jean-Jacques stepped in, coming to their collective defense. "She is not interested in an escapade with us."

Maurice threw his arms up in the air, looking at the ceiling for divine help. "Of course she is not interested! The idea was to make John *think* she is interested! And you call yourselves Frenchmen!"

The seven curly heads dropped down again.

"What else can we do?" Jean-Claude asked the older and wiser man. It was rumored that the marquis was quite knowledgeable in the ways of *amour*.

Maurice sighed. "You must make John jealous! Arrange for him to catch you with his wife in a compromising situation!"

"That would not be right to Chloe," Jean-Jules

said solemnly. "What if he blames her?"

The marquis began shaking his head and muttering in French under his breath. "The youth of today know nothing! What would your father think of you, hmm? Not to be able to make one Englishman jealous over his woman!"

The seven heads sank lower.

"Perhaps we could take her into the maze?" Jean-Claude ventured.

"Yes! And then we could remove our shirts as if—"

"*Mon Dieu!* All of you? He'll take out a pistol and murder the lot of you on the spot!"

The Cyndreacs turned deathly pale. They all swallowed at once.

It was all Maurice could do not to laugh out loud. The frisky pups were about to get their tails clipped and they didn't even know it.

Maurice shook his head back and forth, sorrowfully. "*Non, non,* I see now it will not work—best we forget this idea for now."

They sat straight up in their chairs. "But we wish to help you!"

"Yes, you were great friends with our papa."

"The countess has always been very kind to us."

"We will think of a way to entice Chloe—"

Maurice put up his hands to stop the sincere

outpouring. "I see there is much you need to learn, my boys, on the mysterious subject of romance."

"We live for romance!" they all shouted.

"Good. That is good. A Frenchman should live for romance. However . . . there are some nuances you need to learn. Ordinarily your father would have taught you; unfortunately that cannot happen." Maurice let that thought sink in.

Adrien rubbed his ear. "What you say is true; we could use some guidance."

Maurice nodded.

"Marquis, in light of the relationship our families have always enjoyed . . . would you be willing to teach us?"

"*Moi?*" Maurice asked, feigning surprise.

"*Oui,* you are very knowledgeable, and Papa always trusted you."

"Hmm." Maurice pretended he was thinking it over. The brothers leaned closer to him, eagerly awaiting his answer, their faces alight with hope.

"Yes, I believe I will."

Identical grins lit up their faces.

"With some conditions, of course," Maurice added shrewdly.

"Conditions? What conditions, Marquis?" Jean-Paul gave him a worried look.

"Tonight, the countess is staging an elaborate 'end of party' ball in the hopes that the ton will get the message that the house party is over and move on. I will be leaving sometime at the end of the ball to return to my estate in Somerset."

Adrien was puzzled. "Does the countess know this?"

"Not yet," Maurice replied mysteriously. "That is not your concern, however. If you wish my guidance then you must be willing to listen to me as you would have your father—for I will accept no less."

They were all silent at that pronouncement.

"You may enjoy the ball, naturally, but you will follow me to Somerset directly after. There you will be instructed in proper deportment for men such as yourselves."

That did not sit so well with the young counts. They were used to their freedom. Indeed, they had run with it.

"How do you ever expect to catch a worthy bride if you continue this way? What have you to offer?"

They hadn't thought of that.

"We—we have no estate; everything has been taken from us," Adrien said sadly.

"I will take you under my wing—but only under those conditions." He was telling them that the Chavaneau name would be behind them *if* they agreed to place themselves under his watchful eye.

The brothers hesitated under the weight of the terrible decision.

Maurice took out his pocket watch and opened it, implying he was much too busy to wait very long. "Do you agree?"

The Cyndreacs looked from one to the other.

"Would we have to give up fighting among ourselves?"

"Yes."

They sighed.

"Your papa would want you to do this," Maurice said softly.

"Very well," Adrien answered for them. "We will agree."

"I have the word of all Cyndreacs?"

"Yes," they answered dully, not at all sure about this.

"*Bien.* Now you will go and get ready for the ball, and I expect you to behave yourselves tonight."

"*Oui*, Marquis Chavaneau," they responded in unison.

"Well, what are you waiting for? Go!" He shooed them out.

Chairs scraped the floor as they pushed themselves off and rushed to the door to leave.

Maurice smiled, shaking his head. They were engaging, but they needed guidance. Now for his countess . . .

He began to hum his favorite song about a mouse that swallowed a cat.

Chapter Fourteen
Dancing with the Truth

"You look beautiful, Chloe."

The ball was well under way and every one of their guests, both English and French, was enjoying himself at the largesse of the Sextons.

John swung his wife around the ballroom floor in an English country dance.

His unconventional wife had chosen to appear at the ball in emerald green instead of the omnipresent white most women seemed to favor these days. The deep tone was a perfect foil for her red hair and complexion. She looked exquisite.

In John's opinion, Chloe was a true beauty—within and without. Unconsciously, he hugged her closer to him as they twirled around the dance floor.

"Thank you, John. You look very handsome tonight." She smiled graciously up at him. "But I think you always look handsome."

So did most of the women there, for they hadn't once taken their eyes off her stunning husband.

John was dressed in buff-colored breeches with a black waistcoat, jacket, and boots to match. The white silk shirt he wore stood out in stark contrast to the simple yet effective color scheme. His gilded, shoulder-length hair hung loose about his shoulders, gleaming under the light of hundreds of candles.

John noted the way Chloe was observing him. Like he was a box of her favorite truffles. He chuckled. In some regards, she was not adept at hiding what she was thinking. In others . . .

The nagging thought resurfaced again. What was she holding back from him?

He intended to get to the bottom of that. *Tonight.*

"I'd like to take you upstairs right now," he murmured, half to himself.

Chloe was scandalized. They were the hosts; they couldn't leave. "John, we can't!"

"Hmm?" He gave her a confused look, not realizing he had spoken out loud.

Chloe grinned. Well, what could she expect from the Lord of Sex? It seemed to be a subject never far from his mind. Or other places, she thought with a snort as he adeptly led her into the dance.

The octagonal ballroom at *Chacun à Son Goût* was eighty feet in length and was lit by no less than six magnificent chandeliers. Due to its size and grandeur, the room wasn't used very often. Tonight, however, was a special occasion.

John eyed the full-to-overflowing room with resignation. So far no one was taking the hint. Not one person had arranged for his carriage the next day. Apparently everyone was having too good a time to leave.

John's nostrils flared in annoyance. "How do I get rid of them, Chloe?"

She laughed gaily at the frustrated expression on his face. For a man who, until recently, lived the carefree life of a rake, he was certainly having his share of situations to deal with.

Chloe pretended to give the matter a great deal of thought. "That is a difficult dilemma, my lord."

John quirked an eyebrow at her. "Surely you can think of something, Chloe-cat. As I recall, you were always good at schemes."

Chloe started. What did he mean by that? She

peeked up at him from under her lashes.

She let out a sigh of relief. He seemed to be speaking in general terms.

"Well . . ." she wrinkled her nose. "You could always hint at the outbreak of fever at the neighboring estate."

John gave her a concerned look. "Is there?"

"No, but you could *hint* there is." Two mischievous dimples scored her cheeks.

"Chloe, you are devious." An appreciative smile etched his handsome face; he winked down at her. "I admire that."

She flashed him a gamine grin. "Watch how fast they clear out, my lord."

John chuckled. "I believe I shall begin spreading the rumor after supper. The staff has gone to a great deal of trouble preparing everything—no sense in letting their efforts go for naught."

"Oh, I agree, my lord. I confess I have been looking forward to tonight, and why should we spoil our evening?" She smiled conspiratorially at him.

"My evening could never be spoiled as long as I have you in my arms." He smiled disarmingly back at her.

Chloe's heart sped up. Despite his reputation as a notorious rake, Viscount Sexton never said anything unless he meant it. He had never been an idle flatterer. Chloe had always believed it was part of John's attraction to the women of the ton, who were so used to hearing false flattery that they welcomed his straightforward demeanor. They always knew what he wanted. Sex.

And that was all.

So his tender words had special meaning for Chloe. "That was a very nice thing to say, John." Her violet eyes shone up at him.

"I suppose I must be a glutton for punishment," he added teasingly, kissing the tip of her nose.

Her mouth formed an *O*. "That's not humorous!"

"No?" He smiled secretly.

Chloe frowned at him, debating whether to step on his toe. The thick boots he wore probably wouldn't let much pain in. She sighed.

"May I cut in?" Sir Percy smiled at the couple, holding out his hand for Chloe.

Reluctantly, John handed her over to Sir Cecil-Basil.

As Chloe took the fop's hand, the edge of her finger scraped against one of the many rings he wore.

"My apologies, Lady Sexton."

"It was my fault, Percy, I—Look! The ring

opens." Chloe took his hand between her own to have a closer look at the intricate ring.

The ornate domed top was cleverly hinged. The inside revealed an elaborate design. The ring appeared to double as a seal of some kind.

John, standing next to them, bent over curiously to have a look as well.

Percy stiffened slightly.

" 'Tis beautiful," Chloe remarked. "What is this here? It appears to be a flower of some kind, draped in a dark cloth."

"It is a pimpernel, my lady—the cartouche of my family."

John stilled. *A pimpernel* . . . Part of the primrose family. Dark cloth . . . *The Black Rose!*

Stunned, he gazed up from the ring, meeting Percy's light blue eyes dead on.

They stared at each other in silence.

Percy looked away first, closing the ring with a snap.

"Oh, damn and blast, John!" Chloe captured his attention. "It's that obnoxious Lord Snellsdon!" Her lower lip pouted in disgust. "What is he doing here?"

"I have no idea," John murmured, distracted for the time being from his momentous discovery.

Lord Snellsdon approached them. A man who

had accompanied him to the ball walked alongside him.

"I don't believe it," Chloe said in a hiss. "Of all the gall! To bring that man into my house!"

John didn't recognize the guest with Snellsdon, but Percy apparently did, for he stiffened at his side.

Lord Snellsdon greeted his hosts. "Good evening, Lord and Lady Sexton; Sir Cecil-Basil. Lovely party . . . Allow me to introduce a friend of mine; this is Citizen Malleaux."

"I know Citizen Malleaux," Chloe rejoined coldly.

John had never seen his wife behave so rudely. He didn't know the man, but by the look of him it wasn't hard to figure out his wife's reaction. There was something about him that was downright chilling. John nodded curtly to him. "Malleaux."

"A pleasure, your lordship," the man responded in a sibilant tone.

"Sink me! 'Tis an ambassador!" Percy made a great show of bowing before whispering very loudly so half the room heard him, "Mustn't wear that drab brown—too plebeian, my man."

The surrounding guests who had overheard his remark snickered at Malleaux's expense.

Malleaux bristled at the expert set-down. Fortunately, someone waved at Snellsdon and the two men moved off into the crowd.

Chloe fumed. "Grandmere will be furious."

"Who is he?" John asked quietly.

"He is the henchman of Robespierre," Percy informed him. "They say he is personally responsible for sending thousands to the guillotine. He is a butcher in the guise of a diplomat."

John's eyes met Sir Cecil-Basil's. "I see."

"How dare he show his face here!" Chloe's fists clenched. Half of their guests had narrowly escaped this man's form of justice.

Percy took out his scented handkerchief, fluttering it in the air as if to disperse the man's noxious effluvium. "Let's hope no one takes it into their heads to execute *him* tonight. John certainly doesn't want to be forced to deal with an international incident. Besides, 'twould ruin the supper collation if his head rolled into the pudding, what?"

Percy's attempt at humor helped to lighten Chloe's mood. She laughed softly. "You are one of a kind, Percy."

"I daresay." He held out his hand to her for their dance.

John took the opportunity to signal to the orchestra to strike up a minuet. The dance, with its short steps, was his way of paying homage to the French refugees who sought asylum in his home. The aristocracy had vowed to keep the dance alive.

Chloe flashed her husband an expression of gratitude, her eyes shining.

As the two of them entered the dance, John scanned the hall for Malleaux. He spotted him over by the punch bowl. His beady eyes were scouring every guest in the house.

By the fierce glower of distaste on the man's face, it was safe to assume he was not happy with the choice of music. The minuet was an affront to the new regime.

Thoughtfully, John glanced at his wife, dancing with Sir Percy.

The criminal he was harboring in his home.

The ex-pirate and God knew what else.

The man who was the Black Rose.

It was a tense table at the supper banquet.

Somehow Lord Snellsdon and his guest had managed to secure seats for themselves at the head table.

Chloe suspected the odious Malleaux of sneaking into the hall and switching place cards. She also suspected he had a very compelling reason for attending their party that evening.

The new French regime was being made a fool of by the Black Rose.

Malleaux undoubtedly was dispatched to find and capture the criminal of the people's government. The fact that many of the rescued had ended up at *Chacun à Son Goût* would naturally lead the man here in his investigation.

John tried to lighten the mood by engaging in pleasant conversation with the Cyndreacs, all of whom were scowling on their side of the table, throwing murderous glances at Malleaux. John did not know that the man had been responsible for stealing their heritage.

It was rumored that Malleaux now lived at the Cyndreac estate, having appropriated it for the state. Many believed he had signed the boys' death warrants simply because he coveted the choice location of their home.

All of the brothers wanted to throttle the man with their bare hands. Every now and then one of the Cyndreacs would almost bound out of his chair to do the deed. A stern look from Maurice Chavaneau was the only thing that kept them in their chairs.

"Have you heard that Lord Iversly is having a sheepshearing next week? I am terribly excited about it. Just think, all those lovely little balls of wool." Percy gave a heartfelt sigh. "There must be a place in heaven for sheep."

John almost choked on his drink. "Why?" He

didn't even know why he bothered to ask, except for the fact that the inquiry had slipped out before he could stop himself.

"Oh! Think of all the garments to be created from the dear little buggers. When one thinks about it, they are the cornerstone of fashion."

John rolled his eyes and tried not to burst out laughing. Now that he knew . . .

"Aren't you going, John?"

"I think not," he replied drolly.

"Yes, well, no need to, what? One can see his lordship has already been clipped."

Percy's comment caused a round of laughter at the table.

"What do you mean by that?" John scowled.

Percy simply sipped his wine, a smile playing about his lips.

John turned to Chloe. "What does he mean by that?"

Chloe shrugged, her focus shifting nonchalantly to the wall.

"I shall be attending," Snellsdon offered, though no one had asked.

"What about you, Malleaux?" Percy fluttered his handkerchief in the air as he had done previously and winked at Chloe.

"To some, there are more important things to attend to than sheepshearing." He sneered at the fop.

"Really?" Percy stared at him agog. "Like what?"

"I would not expect one such as *you* to understand, Sir Cecil-Basil, but the Black Rose is what interests me."

Well, now we have it out in the open, John thought.

"He interests everyone!" Percy waved his beringed hand. Flaunted it, almost. Right under Malleaux's hooked nose. "Such a dashing fellow."

John coughed.

"I've written a poem about him—would you like to hear it?"

"Not really." Malleaux swallowed a hunk of pork pie.

"Oh." Percy made a moue with his mouth.

John's lips twitched. *He is good.*

"So what interests you about the Black Rose, Malleaux?" Maurice asked somberly.

"I seek him, of course—to bring him to justice."

"Whose justice?" The Countess de Fonbeaulard was seething that this man was at their table.

"The justice of France, madam," he answered, refusing to use her title.

Maurice stared the man down. "He keeps you up at night, hmm?"

Malleaux reddened. "I will find him and he will die; it is not a difficult equation. Such men usually make mistakes at some point. When he does, I will be there."

"Do you have any suspects?" Chloe wanted to know, so she might be able to warn the man.

"Yes, I do." He took an irritatingly slow sip of wine. "A few suspects." He turned and pierced the Cyndreacs with intense scrutiny.

They all returned bland faces to him.

"Seven brothers . . . yet six were taken. Now we have seven again. An amusing conundrum. No one seems to know which brother was not taken."

The Cyndreacs remained silent. Malleaux turned to the marquis. "And you, monsieur—a little old to be playing hero, but perhaps you see a need to liberate your friends from their just punishment."

"Their just punishment?" Maurice sneered. "For what? The crime of being born into families that trace their lineage back centuries?"

Malleaux ignored Maurice's distaste for him and his regime.

"He might be English," he continued, "which matters naught if he is caught on French soil, or somehow finds himself there."

The implied threat was there. Malleaux would

kidnap such a man if he had to, simply to render what he considered justice.

"An Englishman?" Chloe wondered about that herself.

"Yes. Take our host, for instance." He focused his malevolence on John.

The green eyes of Lord Sexton coolly returned his look.

"The viscount has a reputation for being daring; he has been known to laugh in the face of convention; and he has repeatedly flaunted authoritarian mores. He is an excellent rider, an accomplished swordsman and, by all accounts, a crack shot. His escapades with the gentler sex are known even in France."

John raised his eyebrows. "Thank you," he murmured. The table laughed.

Unperturbed, Malleaux continued, "His wife is half-French; his uncle is French. One might draw a conclusion from that."

"And what would that conclusion be?" John helped himself to a slice of beef.

"That you feel a responsibility to them. Your background is well known, Lord Sexton."

John sliced into his meat. "Surely not all of it." His eyes flashed with humor and a glint of steel as well.

"Where have you been those times when the

rescues took place?" Malleaux asked straight out.

The diners gasped at his rudeness.

"Not that I am bound to answer you, Malleaux, but I was with my wife."

"Surely not every time?"

"We are newly wed; yes, every time."

Chloe blushed. *He didn't have to be that honest!*

"Nonetheless, I believe the Black Rose is sitting at this table."

So do I, John agreed silently. *Why not let the bastard think it's me?*

John despised men like Malleaux. He stared at him tauntingly, daring him to make a move against him. "Perhaps he is."

"Perhaps he despises the new order you have found," Adrien Cyndreac spoke out, bravely shifting the focus from Lord John to himself.

"Perhaps he recognizes you for what you are," Jean-Jules added to further shift his suspicions.

"Perhaps he detests oppression," Deiter enjoined, surprising everyone. The men of *Chacun à Son Goût* were banding together against this threat.

"Perhaps he enjoys the minuet," Maurice supplied provokingly as he proudly added his name to the list of suspects at the table.

Percy took out his snuff for a flamboyant snort. "Perhaps he simply detests English cuisine and must do something to preserve a decently prepared meal."

The entire table roared with laughter.

Malleaux endured the mockery, a smarmy grin on his weaselish face.

Despite the brash joviality at the table, John sensed a viper waiting for the right time to strike lurking beneath Malleaux's thinly veiled civility.

"Are you feeling all right, Maurice? Calloway told me you had returned to your rooms." The Countess de Fonbeaulard stood in the doorway to the marquis's room.

"I am perfectly fine, Simone." He opened the top drawer of a bureau and began removing the contents.

The countess watched him in confusion.

Maurice walked over to his bed and tossed the items inside a small portmanteau.

"What are you doing?" she whispered.

"What does it look like I'm doing?" Maurice closed the lid with a snap.

Before the countess could respond, Calloway appeared at the door with some servants.

"These here and those over there." Maurice pointed out the cases he wanted taken down.

The men dutifully bent to the task; they closed the door behind them on their way out.

"You are going to your estate?" she asked, perplexed.

"Yes."

The countess let out a sigh of relief. "You have received a message of some kind? You should have told me; I—"

"There was no message. I am going to my estate," he intoned.

"What do you mean?"

"I think I was perfectly clear."

The countess paled. "You—you are leaving me, Maurice?"

He hesitated, hating to have to put that look on her face, yet set in his choice of action. "That depends."

"On what?"

"On whether or not you come with me."

Mistaking his meaning, she immediately brightened.

Until he added, "As my wife."

"What are you talking about? You know that—"

Maurice interrupted her. He was through listening. "My coach is waiting for me. The Cyndreacs will be following me out to Somerset in the morning. They will be residing at my estate.

I know you are fond of them, as I am. If you come with me, I have arranged for a marriage ceremony en route."

The countess pulled herself up straight. What had gotten into him? He had no right! "When you return, we will discuss this." She waved her hand, trying to dismiss the objectionable subject.

The marquis stood firm. "I will not be returning unless you are beside me as my wife."

"Maurice, you are being unreasonable!"

"Am I?" He took out his pocket watch and checked the time. "I will wait five minutes for you, Simone. Five minutes." Snapping the lid shut, he strode purposefully to the door.

The countess was stunned. Surely he didn't mean this? She knew him; he would think it over and—

Maurice stopped at the door. "I won't be coming back, Simone," he said quietly before he shut the door behind him.

It took a few moments for the silence of the room to penetrate her fog.

Maurice had walked out! Left her. A dull ache started in her chest. She glanced at the clock. Four minutes.

He was bluffing! He would be back . . . he always came back. Three minutes.

Who did he think he was? Telling her that—Two minutes.

The Countess de Fonbeaulard picked up her skirts and, for the first time in her adult life, *ran* down the hall to the center stairs.

She literally raced through the front door of the house.

At the bottom of the stairs the marquis's personal coach emblazoned with his family crest prepared to depart.

As the countess reached the bottom step, the door to the vehicle was flung wide and an outstretched hand yanked her inside.

"This is ridiculous, Maurice! I have no clothes with me—"

"I will get you what you need *Marchioness*." Strong arms embraced her.

"But—"

His mouth silenced her.

Merde! He should have done this years ago, he realized as the coach rolled down the drive.

"Might I have a word with you, John? Out on the terrace?"

John nodded, excusing himself from the group of men he was conversing with on the sidelines of the dance floor. He followed Percy outside onto a deserted terrace.

The two men, shielded by plants and an overhanging tree, leaned on the ledge and looked out at the night. Clouds dotted the sky, weaving in and out of a crescent moon.

John waited for Percy to speak his mind.

"Malleaux seems to think he will find the Black Rose here. What do you think, Sexton?"

"I think the Rose has exposed himself to great danger and his chances of being discovered grow greater every day."

Percy was silent for a few minutes. "Perhaps he likes this type of danger."

John exhaled. "Most likely he does, but I don't trust Malleaux. Even if the Black Rose should *happen* to be an Englishman, he might very well wake up to find himself in a French prison. About to lose his head."

"Some risks are worth taking."

John nodded. "Yes, they are. Nonetheless, the Black Rose has done more than his share of risk-taking. It might be time for him to stop testing his luck and be happy for what he has accomplished."

Percy said nothing.

"Perhaps he should remember those he has saved."

"One might wonder if the man thinks more of those he didn't," Percy murmured reflectively.

John raised a brow. There were levels here he knew nothing about. "He is only one man."

Percy smiled obscurely showing a hint of white teeth. "They say he is many men, what with his disguises and all."

"So I've heard." John turned to face him. "Such a man who dons these disguises might even seek a friendship with someone like my-self—knowing I would not turn him in to the authorities. He might use that friendship for his own ends."

"In what way?" Percy spoke very low.

"He could use my home as a point of operation; he could come and go here as he pleased under the cover of his disguise; he could have many types of dealings no one would know about or suspect. There's no end to the amount of mischief he could be engaged in."

Percy's lips turned upward in a poignant half smile. "You forgot one thing."

"What's that?"

"He might genuinely value your friendship, John."

John was taken aback; he looked out over the gardens. "It is dangerous for the Black Rose here; Malleaux will not give up until he has his head."

Percy seemed to listen to John's warning; he

adjusted the lace cuff on his sleeve. "I'm afraid I shall have to leave, John."

John smiled slightly. The fop was back once more. "When shall we see you again, Percy?"

"I'm not sure—when one is in fashion, one is forever in demand!" His lace-trimmed sleeve punctuated the air.

"Then take care of yourself, *my friend.*" He warmly clasped Percy's shoulder.

"And you, John," Percy said softly. "Although I somehow think you have found where you want to be."

John nodded, surprised to feel deep sadness at Percy's leaving. He supposed he had gotten used to him always hanging about. Even as a fop, the man had been . . . well, likable. He turned to leave.

Percy called out to him, "Do you know what you get when Heart is wed to Sexton, my good man?"

John shook his head no.

"Why, everyone knows heart and sex together form a perfect match! 'Tis called romance!"

John snorted. Grinning, he turned and walked back into the house.

"And what you get is very, very lucky. *Ave atque vale,* my friend. Hail and farewell." He saluted the direction of the door John had entered and agilely leaped over the stone wall to disappear into the night.

The ball was winding down.

Most of the guests had already departed, either returning to their rooms or their coaches for the journey home. John's rumor was already starting to work.

Chloe and John circled the dance floor one last time, the final dance of the evening. A Scotch reel.

When the lively dance ended, he pulled Chloe along with him out of the ballroom, as the amused onlookers waved a last good night.

Instead of taking the stairs as she expected, he tugged her along to the other side of the mansion.

"Where are we going?" She tried to dig her heels in but she was no match for his determination. Especially in silk slippers.

"You'll see."

This end of the house was still and quiet. Almost deserted.

The tap of his top boots along the parquet flooring was the only sound to be heard as he pulled her resolutely along.

He took her down a long side gallery, through a secret panel she hadn't known about, and through another gallery, not stopping until a specific door stood in front of them.

Standing to the side and in front of her, John unlocked the door, letting it drift slowly open.

"Welcome to paradise, my lady." He gestured to the space beyond with an outstretched hand.

Flowering plants of differing hues and sizes greeted her in a wave of color and scent. Chloe closed her eyes, inhaling the lovely combination of fragrances.

"It's another door to the conservatory!"

"Yes. I hadn't known about it until Maurice showed it to me today. He said something about finding it instructional; I wasn't quite sure what he meant." John drew her inside, closing the door behind them.

At once they were enclosed in a tropical world of exotic plants and lush foliage.

"It's so lovely!"

"Yes, you are, Chloe," he agreed in a low, sultry whisper.

Chloe glanced at him out of the corner of her eye. She'd recognize the roguish tone in her sleep. Indeed, she had *heard* it in her sleep on many an occasion. John was getting sportive.

She crossed her arms over her chest. "And just why did you bring me here, my lord?"

A slow, sensual smile was the rake's answer.

Chapter Fifteen

Immortelle

"Here?" she uttered, astonished. Only John would think of something like this.

"Yes, here," he whispered.

Chloe viewed the room that was bursting with a profusion of blooms. Flowers and herbs carpeted the stone floor, seeming to climb up the very walls in places. Some pots even hung suspended from the ceiling, their vines trailing down.

There were pink roses filling the air with their scent; pots of fragrant French lavender, with its gray, fringed leaves and tiny, bluish-purple buds; fragrant jasmine hung in overflowing baskets from above, its delicate blossoms the color of moonlight. It was said the intoxicating fragrance held magical properties at night. Breathing deeply of the glorious aroma, Chloe could well believe it.

Her gaze took in true myrtle as well, the large, brilliant white blooms emitting a spicy scent that fired the senses.

Interspersed in pots were Grandmere's herbs: rosemary, thyme, French basil—there were too many for her to name, although she was learning to distinguish them all.

John drew her down to the floor.

They were surrounded by a sea of flowers bathed in moonlight.

A white stone fountain—its cherub pouring out a continuous ewer of trickling water—gurgled in the corner. They were in the center of a night garden, a magical kingdom of lush serenity.

They knelt facing each other.

Silently John began to undo the buttons on the back of her dress. Chloe reached over to slip his jacket off his shoulders.

He gathered her dress in his hands and lifted it over her head. She undid his waistcoat, then his shirt, sliding them off.

He kissed her then, his muscular arms coming around her to pull her tight to his naked chest. The thin cotton of her chemise acted as the scantiest barrier to touch, adding to, rather than detracting from, the sensation. Her hands smoothed over his shoulders, feeling the contained strength under the warm, golden skin of his masculine structure.

The touch of his mouth brought with it tiny shivers cresting throughout her body.

John released her from his embrace, sitting back on his haunches once more. He drew her chemise over her head, removing it along with the rest of the items she wore.

Wordlessly, he ran his fingers through her hair, removing the pins that held it in place, so that it tumbled freely down her back.

She knelt in front of him, naked in a night of flowers. Waiting for him. Moonlight shining through the tall windows shimmered around her.

John had never seen anything more lovely; he drew in a sharp breath.

Fingers skimmed the band of his breeches, her nimble hands dipping under the placket to release the buttons.

The feel of her fingers lightly brushing him there as she went about her task seemed to him one of the most erotic experiences he had ever had. A simple thing like that and it moved him so much. . . .

When she finished with the buttons, her hands slipped inside the material at his sides and slid down his backside, until she was gently cupping his buttocks in her palms.

Closing his eyes at the tactile sensation, John dipped his head and captured her mouth in a savory, burning kiss.

She returned his kiss, slipping the breeches off his hips entirely so that she could rub against him—skin to skin.

A rough, gravelly sound of approval vibrated from him to her.

He released her to tug off his boots quickly and remove his breeches. Taking their clothes, he scattered them across the stone floor, making a unique pallet out of the combined materials. Then he carefully laid her down on the bed he had made.

"Are you comfortable?" he asked tenderly.

"Yes." She smiled softly up at him.

"Good—we might be here awhile." He winked roguishly at her.

A dimple popped into her cheek. "If I know you, my lord—and I do—I would say a great while."

"You underestimate me," he drawled.

Chloe's eyes widened.

Spotting one of Grandmere's worktables by

the window, John got up and went over to it. He picked up several of the small, dark bottles she had left, examining the contents of each of them by pulling the stoppers and sniffing.

"This one, I think," he declared, carrying it with him back to her.

At that moment the first rays of dawn broke the horizon, streaming through the east windows, capturing him in a wash of golden light as he stood naked among the exotic hothouse blooms.

It was such an erotic, sensual picture that Chloe knew she would retain the memory of it forever. Her private portrait of the Viscount Sexton.

He knelt down beside her.

Chloe frowned. "What are you going to do with the oil, John?"

"You'll see," he replied mysteriously as he cradled the small bottle between his palms to heat the contents.

The broad palm of his hand rested against the center of her chest, effectively keeping her in a supine position.

Taking the dropper out, he held it above her and released the warm oil drop by drop.

Chloe immediately recognized the woodsy scent as John's personal fragrance. She was pondering why he had chosen that particular one when the flat of his hand—the one on her chest—began a circular motion, rubbing the oil into her skin.

"Oh, that feels lovely."

He acknowledged her compliment with a tiny curve of his lips.

Chloe swallowed. He was up to something. . . .

Before he continued, his fingertips brushed the red curls between her legs, spreading her nether lips. Bending over, he gently placed a soft kiss there.

Chloe trembled in reaction to the passionate gesture.

"Forgive me." His green eyes glittered in the early light. "I got carried away."

The rogue didn't look like he wanted forgiveness. For anything.

Just the points of his fingers skated over her skin, soothing her with a light stroke. Over her collarbone, across the sensitized peaks of her breasts, skipping lightly over the plane of her torso, swirling around her hipbones, down the sides of her thighs and her calves, to the responsive arch of her foot.

Wherever he touched, a wash of warm, woodsy oil soaked into her skin.

Putting down the dropper, John took her foot

in his hands and began to knead the muscles and tendons with a rare skill.

His two thumbs pressed in and stroked up the center line of her foot, igniting key pleasure points along the sole of her foot. Cupping her heel, he rotated it into the palm of his hand, loosening every tight muscle in her body.

Chloe melted like butter in the sun.

When he was through with one foot, he placed it flat against his warm chest for safekeeping while he proceeded to attend the other one.

"I can't tell you how good that feels, especially after dancing all night."

He simply smiled again, saying nothing.

Chloe bit her lip; he was definitely up to something.

Soon his capable hands began stroking their way up the entire length of her body, massaging, kneading as they went, until she was so relaxed, she wondered if she could force herself to move.

When John reached her shoulders, he neatly turned her over. He brushed her hair off her back with the edge of his hand.

Picking up the dropper again, he dripped oil down her back, over her buttocks, across the backs of her knees. . . .

Then the flats of his hands were on her—massaging in deep, firm strokes—shoulders to back.

She felt the oil slide down the underside of her breasts; his hands followed the track, slipping underneath her from behind.

Chloe held her breath but he didn't stay long—just long enough to heighten her sensitivity by rotating her hardened nipples in the palm of his hands.

More oil . . . more caressing.

She was so languorous from his ministrations that it took her a few moments to realize he was rubbing the oil in with more than his hands!

John had brought his body over hers. The entire length of his body slid the oil against her as he pressed down on her at intermittent points. She was covered by his oil and him.

Heated lips brushed down the curve of her spine to the small of her back. She jumped when a hot tongue lightly grazed her buttocks.

"J-John," she choked out.

"Mmm?" Male teeth nipped her right buttock.

Chloe scooted away from him and turned over onto her back.

He chuckled low. "However do you expect to be a female rake, sweet, when you get so embarrassed at certain things?"

Chloe's face flamed. "Never mind that! I-I . . . it's none of your business!"

He arched a brow. "No?"

Chloe did not like the look on his face. She swallowed. "N-no."

He just smiled again.

Chloe watched him curiously.

He broke off the stem of a yellow flower from a nearby plant. "What do you call this flower?"

"It is called immortelle, or the everlasting flower—some call it sun gold. I believe Grandmere uses it in your fragrance mix."

"Everlasting flower," he murmured, leaning over her to brush the ball-shaped blossoms over her lips. Bracing himself with one arm on the floor, he gathered her to him with the other. His mouth very gently took hers.

"So that's what the sun tastes like on your lips," he whispered.

Chloe shivered at his words. He dipped his head again, taking another taste of her.

John scattered the small blossoms on the pallet he had made for them. "An everlasting bed for you, my lady wife."

He lowered her to the pallet once more, turning her on her side to lie nestled into him. His strong arms encircled her waist from behind, pulling her taut to him. Burning hot male skin adjoined hers from neck to shoulder.

Silken lips began laving the rounded edge of her shoulder. One hand massaged her breast while the other dipped between her legs.

Chloe nuzzled back into him. John was in an odd mood this eve, but if it was causing this bout of amorous behavior, Chloe reasoned that it couldn't be a bad thing. Normally her husband was extraordinarily sensual; tonight he seemed to be making new inroads on his own record.

He laved and suckled the curve of her shoulder. "Chloe?"

"Yes, John?" She moaned.

"Are you keeping something from me?" Before she could answer, he entered her swiftly from behind. A smooth, sure stroke.

Chloe froze at his question and gasped at his action. This was dangerous. "No, of course not," she managed to squeak.

He ran his hot mouth up the side of her throat. "Are you sure?"

"Yes . . . yes, I'm sure." She moaned. Her hands grabbed tightly onto the muscular arms encircling her.

Assuredly, John slid into her twice more, then withdrew. Unexpectedly, his hands at her shoulders rolled her over onto her back.

Chloe looked up at him questioningly as he rose over her.

"Because if I was to keep something from you, you'd know, wouldn't you, Chloe-cat?" His powerful thigh separated her legs as he found a spot for himself in between.

She swallowed. His eyes told the whole story. Intense, darkened, focused. John had a specific mission.

Chloe knew she was in trouble.

"Wouldn't you?" he prompted while licking busily at the rosy bud of her breast.

"I-I suppose so."

"I know so." He slid into her with a long, deep thrust.

They both groaned.

Chloe closed her eyes as he filled her, the sensation of having John inside her always overwhelming.

"Look at me, Chloe."

Her eyes fluttered open, dilated and passion dazed. *For him.* For a moment, John couldn't breathe as their gazes met.

His voice was very husky when he said, "Kiss me, my lady . . . kiss me." He dipped his head to her, his honey hair falling forward to brush her shoulders.

"Oh, John," Chloe responded tremulously.

"Don't hold anything back from me, sweet; give yourself to me."

Chloe shook in response; she definitely was in trouble here. "I am, John; I am."

He moved languorously inside her. "No. You're not."

"John, please—"

"Surrender into me, Chloe; don't be afraid. I'll carry us both." He tenderly rocked back and forth inside her.

Surrender?

Sometimes it went along with *conquer and seduce.* Terms of what a rake does . . . Chloe tried to marshal the strength of purpose she needed to maintain with him. "I . . . I—"

"This is something I can't take from you, Chloe; you must give it."

What is he referring to exactly? A tiny line furrowed her brow. "Is this part of what you said you would show me—something I need to know about men and women together?"

He sighed heavily. "No. This is something I want. From you."

Now she was really worried. "I don't know what it is you mean," she said evasively.

John pressed into her tightly and rotated his hips.

Chloe embraced him to her, moaning his name. The heat from their bodies released the scent of immortelle strewn about their bower.

"You do know what I mean," he negated her response in a raspy voice.

"No, I—"

He penetrated her a little bit more, then pulled her hips up onto him, giving him that extra depth she adored.

"Oh, dear God, please . . . !" Fused to him and pinned under him, Chloe knew she was close to losing her control. With him inside her like this, so close, so a part of her, her defensive walls were starting to crumble around her.

John sensed her indecision. He felt the tremors rack her body as she fought off completion and surrender.

So he spoke against her lips, kissing her, moving swiftly in her. "Yes, sweet, yes . . . don't hold back . . . don't ever hold back. . . ."

Everything happened at once then.

Chloe lost control. Completely. She became a wild thing under him, clutching him, biting him, calling out his name in a sobbing cry.

Moved as much as she, John roused to new heights. Something seemed to stir up in him, a kindling spark of passion that fanned higher and higher.

"Yes, yes, yes," he breathed. "Oh, God, just like that . . ."

For the first time in his life while making love, John lost track of where he was, who he was. Chloe became his entire universe. He couldn't think; he could only react. Lord Sexton took her as he himself was taken.

Their desire transcended mere passion.

It had never happened to him before. John knew not what he was saying, nor what he was asking. He was totally consumed by the raging emotion the two of them had created together.

He coaxed, he purred, he moaned, and he *begged*.

And so, when he ground into her to hoarsely cry out, overwhelmed, "Give me a child, Chloe. . . ." the last wall she clung to shattered and she released what she had held back from him all these years.

"Je t'aime! Je t'aime! I love you! I have always loved you, John! Always . . ." She clung to him, pouring out her love in a never-ending litany of completion.

Apparently, it was not what John expected to hear, for with her disclosure his sanity returned.

He went stock-still for an instant before his physical needs overcame him and he found release, a powerful and hot satisfaction from deep within.

He was ominously silent as he lay upon her, his face still burrowed into the curve of her neck.

Chloe did not move or speak. Always, when

John finished making love to her, he would kiss and hold her and laugh with her. Often he would begin anew, telling her she had a rare gift for inspiring a man.

This time he did none of those things.

Chloe swallowed down the trepidation rising in her throat. Now that the heat of passion had passed, she realized exactly what she had revealed to him.

What have I done? It was too soon—much too soon.

Silently, John disengaged from her. Standing, he pulled on his breeches and his shirt.

Chloe looked at him questioningly, but he would not meet her eyes. He picked his boots up off the floor and walked over to the paned glass door leading outside. He hesitated for a moment before he opened the door and walked into the dawn.

Leaning back on her elbows, Chloe stared at the empty doorway, stunned that he had left.

It was over. She had lost.

A sob escaped her throat. It was all over.

She threw herself down on the remains of the pallet he had made, the pallet they had heated with their own fire. It was cool now.

Only a hint of scented oil remained as testament to the desire they had just shared.

The enormity of what had occurred struck like a physical blow. She had lost her special love. She had lost John.

Anguished, she cried her heart out.

John walked into the maze, following the twists and turns even in the dim light. When he reached the center, he sank down onto the stone bench.

It was the same bench he had been sitting on when she had proposed to him.

In a daze, he leaned back against the trunk of the tree, seeking the solid support of the wood.

It had all been a ruse.

She had never intended to seek out other men. She had never even been with another man!

He closed his eyes and wondered what he had ever done in his life to deserve this. For the truth could no longer be denied.

He loved Chloe with every fiber of his being.

He always had and he always would.

Taking a deep breath, he opened the door to the memories he had tried to suppress his entire life. . . .

His father. The resentment he felt whenever he thought of him. The pain he had seen his mother endure—the pain he had endured.

The prior viscount had one terrible weakness,

which had destroyed his family. John had always thought the worst thing his father had done was not in the losing of his estate itself, but in the leaving of them. His self-inflicted death was something John had never been able to come to terms with. Not when it left his wife and young son so alone in the world. He could never forgive him for that. Not after seeing what it had done to his mother.

John exhaled heavily.

His mother.

She had loved so deeply. A kind, affectionate woman. The same depth of love she gave to her husband, she gave to her son. She had tried so hard to take care of him afterward.

Moisture filled John's eyes as, along with the memories, he confronted what he had never wanted to face in himself.

Everyone had always assumed he was exactly like his father. They surmised that instead of the baize table, it was women that lured the present viscount.

How wrong they were.

He had always been *just like his mother.*

She used to say to him, "John, you're my son for sure," before she wiped away his tears over some emotional hurt he had suffered. When his hound died; when the neighbor's boy had broken his leg and gangrene had set in and they had to remove it; when he found a bird with a broken wing and his father killed it to put it out of its pain . . . He cared so passionately about the life around him.

His mother's son.

He never wanted to end up the same way she had. Broken, alone, dying in a crofter's hut. Still calling the name of the person she loved. . . .

Her death had a profound effect on him. For years after, he had nightmares about it.

John had resolved at a young age never to care that deeply again about anyone or anything in his life.

In an effort to run from his true nature, he had slept with so many women . . . Meaningless tussles where passion was spent and that was all.

How blind could he have been?

Well, he wasn't going to run anymore.

John slipped his boots on and made his way back to the house.

She was in their sitting room.

The emerald dress she had worn to the ball hung on her now, wrinkled and gaping open in the back where she hadn't bothered with the buttons. She was leaning against the mantelpiece, one arm bracing her as if she needed something to hold her up.

When she heard him walk into the room, she looked over her outstretched arm at him.

He could see that she had been crying.

Their eyes met for an endless moment, uncertainty and fear in hers, pain in his.

Then he simply opened his arms wide.

With a cry from the depths of her soul, Chloe ran to him, throwing herself in his embrace.

"John, John." She sobbed, wrapping her arms around his neck.

He held her tightly to him. "I'd die without you, Chloe."

Trembling, Chloe wept, her tears moistening his throat as she burrowed into the warm place and wouldn't come out.

"Shh." He stroked her hair, soothing her. "Don't, love; there's nothing to cry about."

John didn't heed his own words, for his eyes were suspiciously stinging him. How had this slip of a girl brought him to his knees?

"However did you manage it?" he whispered to her.

Sniffing, Chloe stared up at him, love and wariness on her sweet face.

His heart melted all over again. "Hmm?" He kissed the tip of her nose.

"I . . ." She bit her lip. "I seduced you, John."

His eyes widened. "You seduced *me*?"

She nodded vigorously.

He cocked an arrogant eyebrow. "The Lord of Sex?"

"Yes." She smiled tremulously.

"Well, then . . ." He grinned, revealing two deep dimples. "I guess the thing speaks for itself."

Their joyous laughter mingled with everlasting possibilities as the dawn, golden and pure, spread its flowering light across the estate.

And John realized that love was not the dark emptiness of a lonely night.

It is the morning ray that awakens.

"Like moonspun magic...one of the best historical romances I have read in a decade!"
—Cassie Edwards

They are natural enemies—traitor's daughter and zealous patriot—yet the moment he sees Cassandra Merlin at her father's graveside, Riordan knows he will never be free of her. She is the key to stopping a heinous plot against the king's life, yet he senses she has her own secret reasons for aiding his cause. Her reputation is in shreds, yet he finds himself believing she is a woman wronged. Her mission is to seduce another man, yet he burns to take her luscious body for himself. She is a ravishing temptress, a woman of mystery, yet he has no choice but to gamble his heart on fortune's lady.

_4153-7 $5.99 US/$6.99 CAN

Dorchester Publishing Co., Inc.
65 Commerce Road
Stamford, CT 06902

Please add $1.75 for shipping and handling for the first book and $.50 for each book thereafter. NY, NYC, PA and CT residents, please add appropriate sales tax. No cash, stamps, or C.O.D.s. All orders shipped within 6 weeks via postal service book rate. Canadian orders require $2.00 extra postage and must be paid in U.S. dollars through a U.S. banking facility.

Name____
Address______________________________________
City ____________________________ State______ Zip______
I have enclosed $______in payment for the checked book(s).
Payment <u>must</u> accompany all orders. ☐ Please send a free catalog.

ATTENTION
ROMANCE
CUSTOMERS!
SPECIAL
TOLL-FREE NUMBER
1-800-481-9191
Call Monday through Friday
12 noon to 10 p.m.
Eastern Time
Get a free catalogue,
join the Romance Book Club,
and order books using your
Visa, MasterCard,
or Discover®.
Leisure
Books
Love
Spell